ABADDON
And The
Space Between Eternities

ABADDON
And The
Space Between Eternities

DANIEL R. DOW

Library of Congress Control Number:		2013916811
ISBN:	Hardcover	978-1-4931-0131-3
	Softcover	978-1-4931-0130-6
	Ebook	978-1-4931-0132-0

This book was printed in the United States of America.

Rev. date: 10/11/2013

To order additional copies of this book, contact:
Xlibris LLC
1-888-795-4274
www.Xlibris.com
Orders@Xlibris.com
138980

CONTENTS

Dedication

I dedicate this book to my brothers and sisters in prison everywhere who struggle to find the space and the means by which to develop and preserve their human potential.

DISCLAIMER

The prison violence described in this book is, for the most part, my interpretation of actual events. Names, places, dates, and some of the fact pattern of the events themselves have all been changed—and/or disguised—in order to protect the innocent and the guilty; this book is a fictional account of reality as I have experienced it.

ACKNOWLEDGMENTS

Through the magic of modern media, I've been exposed to the teaching of Pastor Rob Bell and Pastor Charles Price. Some of what I've written reflect their positive influence.

Though I cannot speak for either individual, I doubt that these men are in full theological agreement with each other. Further, I suspect that both will be somewhat critical of this book's content. Nevertheless, I'm deeply indebted and grateful to have experienced their insight.

SPECIAL THANKS

Margaret Ludwig-Dow
Who insisted that I undertake the task of writing this book and freely
shared her wisdom.
and
Sharleen Rutledge
For her encouragement, patience, assistance, and moral support.
and
Randy Graham
For helping me deal with the weight on my shoulders.

ABADDON

Within the Christian tradition, the word *Abaddon* is used interchangeably for the name of the devil of the bottomless pit of hell and the name of the bottomless pit of hell itself. In this book, Abaddon has been further used as the name of a fictional prison; however, in so doing, the original meaning is not discarded—on the contrary, it is a cornerstone of the narrative.

ABADDON

THE PRISON

Abaddon was unusually large for a medium-security penitentiary. It was an old-style prison that housed eight hundred inmates in the general population; there were two hundred in each of the four main blocks, and the count rose to roughly a thousand if one included the additional two hundred or so that were divided between protective custody, segregation, and the health-care unit.

Life within the large facility was also unusual in that prisoners were permitted to choose which part of the institution they wanted to reside. The result of this privilege was that they tended to self-classify, self-regulate, self-segregate, and display a high degree of cliquishness. The warden believed that, by allowing this freedom, he was helping to alleviate the stress of overcrowding and that the result would be a more manageable prison population. He was wrong.

The prisoner-determined demographics were predictable. First and foremost, they gathered together—though not exclusively—along racial and ethnic lines. The blacks were primarily housed in the East Block, Latinos in the North Block, Caucasians in the South Block, and Asians in the West Block. Everyone else was scattered randomly, according to their personal preferences and a wide variety of social pressures.

Within each block, there existed the usual jailhouse power structures, which sometimes extended beyond the prison walls—the gangs and the organized crime rings. In addition, each block had its own assortment of cultural entertainment and social distractions; these included male prostitutes, pimps, bookies, gamblers, drug dealers, and various forms of violence. In short, the warden had allowed his prison to devolve to the point where prisoners were able to organize themselves and do pretty much as they pleased.

This is not to say that prisoners were free, nor is it to say that they felt free. On the contrary, the vast majority felt completely overwhelmed and suffocated by Abaddon. The lack of personal space—physical, emotional, psychological, and spiritual—meant that all were constantly exposed to enormous pressures which simultaneously diminished them as individuals and compelled them to help perpetuate the ongoing nightmare. To a large extent, it was this intricate process of prisoners becoming both the product and the producer of the ongoing nightmare that enabled Abaddon to become something other than the sum total of its constituent parts.

Abaddon had long since taken on a life of its own. Its four blocks were fertile ground for the giant, self-sustaining, self-perpetuating Spirit Tree of Evil that the institution had come to be—a Spirit Tree of Evil that produces and consumes its own fruit while growing and threading its roots into the hearts and minds of all who reside and work therein.

CHAPTER 1

SLY

Sly winced as he heard his name paged: "Sylvester Alexander to V&C!" He always winced when he heard his name announced in such a manner; the speaker system was way too loud, and he hated the name Sylvester. Nevertheless, he felt pleased to be called to the Visits and Correspondence area of the prison. He'd been waiting for a very long time to hear from his court-appointed lawyer as to the final disposition of his appeal, and he supposed that the self-serving, money-grubbing bastard had finally arrived to give him the news—most likely bad news! Be that as it may, he remained buoyed by the thought that his seemingly endless legal battle was about to come to an end; whatever the verdict, Sly just wanted it to be over! He hurried to the central control to get the pass that would allow him to proceed to V&C.

The officer at the central control recognized Sly, but he ignored his approach. Sly waited patiently for a full minute before the officer acknowledged his presence. "What do you want, Sly?"

"I was just paged to V&C," he answered in an even tone of voice.

The officer reached for the phone. "Let me check on that!"

Sly suspected that the officer had actually heard the page and that he simply enjoyed playing something of a power-and-control game. Such behavior was not at all uncommon among the officers at Abaddon. However, during Sly's twenty-plus years of experience as a prisoner, he'd learned to keep his mouth shut and not react to subtle provocation. He chewed on his lip and held back his annoyance while the officer made the call. An additional minute later, his self-control was rewarded when the officer handed him the pass.

The hallway floor to V&C was smooth, polished, and bright; and it felt good under Sly's feet. It was not at all like the rough cement floor in the main section of the prison. The V&C area had been built some thirty years after the prison itself; it was so much cleaner and brighter. Even the atmosphere seemed to be lighter, lacking the soul-crushing weight that often made it seem hard to breathe throughout the rest of the institution. The polished tiles appeared as though a path to an alternate reality; he smiled as he imagined the possibility of such a path. "God, that would be so fuckin' wonderful!" Energized by the thought, Sly breathed deeply of the lighter atmosphere, and his mood improved with each passing step.

The guard at the front entrance to V&C wordlessly examined Sly's pass, then he gave him a quick pat down. Confident that all was in order, he spoke into the radio receiver, which was attached to the left shoulder pad of his uniform. "This is 111 to 113, I've got one at your door."

"Roger that," a female voice from within V&C replied, "send him in." There followed a metallic click; the electronic lock that released the door was triggered from within V&C. Sly promptly stepped through the door and onto the softly carpeted area on the other side.

The V&C officer seemed much more friendly than the others. She gave Sly a halfhearted smile and pointed to the relatively private table in the corner. "Have a seat, Mr. Alexander. Your lawyer will be with you in a moment."

Sitting in wait at the table, Sly surveyed the layout of the area. Not having regular visits, he rarely spent time in V&C. The change of scenery was pleasing, and he began to relax in mind and body. As he relaxed, his eyes fell upon a young prisoner who was visiting with his wife and daughter near the play area on the far side of the large room. Sly had seen the young prisoner several times in the main prison yard; he was a new arrival. He hadn't made much of an impression—just another face in the crowd, but watching him now, Sly was strangely affected by the joy that he saw in the young man's eyes.

Sly continued to watch in fascination while both parents played happily with the small child. The display of mutual affection between father, mother, and daughter caused him to longingly remember a woman that he used to know and a daughter that he would never know. The pain came quickly, and it caught him off guard. Sly felt the tears well up in his eyes, but as quickly as the pain arrived, he recognized the danger and adeptly switched off the underlying emotion. It wouldn't do at all for him to be seen crying; such a display of weakness would make him a laughingstock within the prison. He felt grateful that he'd caught himself in time. He smiled, confident that his mask had remained intact; but he was mistaken.

Sly didn't know everyone at Abaddon, but just about everyone at Abaddon knew him. The young prisoner did, and Sly couldn't possibly have imagined his surprise as he observed Sly's brief display of emotion. "Unbelievable!" he silently exclaimed. Then he extended the thought, "That mean old bastard actually has a soul. Who would have guessed?" However, the young man had little time for such thoughts. Visits were few and far between, and they were so very precious. He immediately turned his attention back to his wife and daughter.

Sly saw movement on his left; he looked up in time to see his lawyer approaching with an outstretched hand, and he stood to greet the man. They shook hands while the lawyer spoke in a carefully modulated voice designed to conceal his true feelings. "Hello, Sly, good to see you again." The two men seated themselves at the table; the lawyer continued talking, "I wish I had good news for you, but I don't. I may as well make this as quick and painless as possible. Your life sentence was upheld by the court of appeals. There's nothing more I can do. I'm sorry!"

This brief statement of fact came as no surprise at all to Sly. He'd been expecting it, and he wasn't at all fooled by the lawyer's attempt to conceal his feelings. He smiled wryly as he reasoned that one good lie deserved another. "You don't have to apologize. It's not your fault. And to be honest with you, at this stage, I don't think it makes much difference. I'm over fifty. I've served more than twenty years in prison. What would I do out there, anyway?" Neither Sly's voice nor the expression on his face betrayed the deep sadness that he felt in his heart.

The good barrister was somewhat taken aback by Sly's demeanor. Curious, he feigned concern. "Are you sure that you're okay? I know you must be hurt—"

He was abruptly cut off with a curt and seemingly inane reply, which actually revealed Sly's suspicion that his lawyer viewed him as being somehow less than human. "Don't be silly, animals can't feel pain." Then he quickly stood up and held out his hand. "Thank you for your efforts. I don't imagine that we'll meet again. I wish you the best." With those final words, he returned to his cell and never again thought about the lawyer.

However, as he exited the visiting area, the lawyer briefly thought about Sly. "That's one cold son of a bitch! I'm glad that I didn't work any harder than I had to on his case. Animals like that belong in prison, and I hope he never gets out." He promptly refocused his mind on a recently acquired wealthy client, who, for that reason alone, clearly deserved his undivided attention; and he never again thought about Sylvester Alexander.

CHAPTER 2

STEVE AND AL

His monthly visit was over. As he returned to his cell, Steve reflected on his good fortune to have been placed at Abaddon rather than a maximum-security facility. At least here there were open visits, and he relished the opportunity to be in direct physical contact with his wife and daughter—the two of them were, in fact, all that really mattered in his life.

Yes, the *Pit*, as so many prisoners referred to it, was definitely preferable to maximum security. Still, it was with great sadness and no small degree of trepidation that Steve walked out of V&C and headed back to his cell, his cellmate, and the prison subculture. With each passing step down the well-lit hallway, his thoughts gradually shifted from the joy of his visit to the dark realities of the main prison. Prison life could be brutal, even in medium security; and as one of the newer inmates at Abaddon, in addition to everything else, he could reasonably expect to be double-bunked for at least a year.

Being double-bunked was one of the many aspects of Abaddon that Steve didn't like—in fact, he hated it! However, he consoled himself with the thought that at least he had a cellmate that he could get along with; Allan McFarlan—little Al—was someone that he was very fond of. He further cheered himself with a reminder that there would be another visit with his wife and daughter next month. All in all, things could be much worse for a new *fish*! What he didn't know as he walked back down that strangely clean and well-lit corridor leading toward the main building was that things were, indeed, about to get much worse.

The main building of the prison had been constructed in the early 1940s. The many years of use had contributed much to the dark, dirty conditions and the heavy atmosphere. Security personnel and security protocols set the parameters of this experience; the behavior of the prisoners themselves completed it. Steve entered the main area. His nostrils immediately began to involuntarily flare as he breathed the vile but familiar odor of oiled hinges, rust, mold, dirt, mildew, and cheap disinfectant. His ears were assaulted by the general din of announcements over the loudspeaker system and the clanging of metal doors. The net effect was that all of his senses were almost completely overwhelmed by the noise and the behavior of so many prisoners, all performing their individual shtick for staff and each other, in the hope that no one would perceive just how frightened they really were and with the unhappy consequence of making life much worse for themselves than it would otherwise be. Steve wanted no part of their misguided theatrics. He hurried across the main floor to the West Block, up the stairs to the third level and down the tier to cell 15.

Steve's cell was typical of what would be found within any of the old-style prisons anywhere in North America—bars in front and three walls. The contents consisted of a double bunk against the side wall, a sink against the back wall, a toilet in the corner, and a two-drawer desk with a stool attached against the other wall. It was all packed onto an eight-by-twelve-square-foot floor space. Several years ago, so-called progressive reformers had seen to it that prisoners would be allowed to purchase their own personal babysitter—a television. The result was that there were television stands now attached to the wall at the foot of each bed, with a single cable outlet installed a few feet away. The entire space was lit from the ceiling with a long light that, at the scheduled times, would be brightened or dimmed, but which would never completely go out.

Steve entered the cell to find his cellmate of the last six months, Al, on the top bunk, lying on his side and facing the wall. Al immediately turned over to look at Steve. In doing so, he revealed a blackened eye and a large bruise on the left side of his face. Surprised and not knowing what to say, Steve waited for Al to be the first to speak.

Al looked down and smiled weakly. "How was the visit?"

Steve again ignored the obvious and politely spoke the honest truth. "Fantastic! I'm blown away by how much Taba has grown in the last month. It's hard to believe that she's not even quite three years old . . . even harder to believe that she'll be nearly six by the time that I get out of this pit! I can't imagine how much she'll have changed by then.

As for Shelly . . . well, she looked delicious! I could've eaten her alive." He smiled and chuckled a little to himself at his personal joke, while he privately extended his thoughts to all that he would have liked to have done with his wife. Unwilling to share such thoughts with Al, he simply added, "How about you? Is everything okay with you? Did anything new or interesting happen while I was out?" He spoke these last words with a meaningful look directly at Al's blackened eye and face, which was presently beginning to badly swell.

"Well, to tell you the truth, there is something that came our way while you were gone. You're not gonna like it . . . you better sit down and roll yourself a smoke."

Al tossed Steve a pouch of tobacco and rolling papers; Steve clumsily caught both. Then he sat sideways on the stool, half facing Al, steadied one of his slightly trembling elbows on the table top, and began to roll himself a cigarette. Task complete, he lit it, carefully tossed the match into the toilet, and took a long drag. Exhaling in satisfaction, he rose from his seat, turned to squarely face Al, and broke the silence. "Okay, let's hear it. What's up?"

"It's the assholes in the South Block. They came by while you were out."

"What the fuck did *they* want?"

Al sighed heavily, the embarrassment evident on his face; his voice seemed to betray genuine fear. "They've heard that you've got open visits, and they've decided that you're gonna pack for 'em."

There followed a moment of silence, which hung heavy in the air. Steve spoke first. "You said trouble came *our* way. Where do *you* fit in?"

"I'm your cellmate, buddy. They say it's up to me to convince you to play. They did this little bit of artwork on my face in order to make their point. They know we're friends. They believe that you're less likely to run to the man if you know that I'll be left behind, and they do mean business. If this goes bad, I go down with you—they say they'll kill me . . . they probably will!"

Steve had been prepared for bad news, but not quite this bad. His emotions spilled over. "Fuck! *Fuck! Fuck! Fuck!*" This was *real* trouble. Al looked as though he was about to say something more; Steve immediately held up his hand and shook his head. "Don't say anything right now, just . . . just let me think."

Steve was only twenty-five, and this was his first time in prison. He imagined that his youth and relative inexperience were at least part of the reason that he'd been targeted by the South Block crowd. However, he was also streetwise—no one had ever accused him of being a fool. He knew very well that, when it came to drugs, these guys were deadly serious. He tossed the last of his cigarette into the toilet, turned back to the desk, rolled himself a second one, lit it, and walked over to the bottom bunk where he settled in silence to consider his options.

His options were limited; and none of them, it seemed, were without serious consequences. Option 1, he could simply refuse to do what the South Block crew demanded, which could get he and Al killed. Option 2, he could do as the South Block crew demanded, which, sooner or later, would undoubtedly result in detection, the loss of his visits, institutional and criminal charges, a transfer to maximum security, and likely more time added to his sentence. Option 3, he could become the aggressor, but he knew very well that he wasn't near tough enough to stand up to the entire crew on his own; the end result of such bravado would surely be the same as option 1—it would likely get them both killed! Finally, there was option 4: become a snitch and request protection. That would mean being segregated for the duration of his sentence and being forced to live with the worst type of prisoners. There was also the possibility that the authorities might transfer him for his own safety, which could result in the loss of his visits.

Then there was a further possibility that he wouldn't even get the protection he requested, which would again put his life in serious danger. However, worse than anything was the risk that the South Block crew posed to his family, by way of their street connections. "What am I gonna do if they go after Shelly and Taba?" he wondered. The very thought left him feeling sick to his stomach. "No fucking way!" he murmured softly to himself.

Steve clenched his teeth in frustration; there seemed to be no option that would not pose serious danger to his family, Al, or to himself.

Steve knew that he needed help; he just didn't know where to find it. Throughout the remainder of the evening, he didn't speak, go to dinner, or even bother to turn on his television set. Al remained quiet, and Steve gratefully accepted his cellmate's courtesy while he simply rested on his bunk, smoked cigarettes, and played out each option over and over again in his mind until exhaustion finally began to overtake him. Then in that split second before slipping beneath a comforting blanket of sleep, his mind suddenly and inexplicably returned to wakefulness with a strange thought, "What about Sly? What about that old bugger? I know I saw something in his eyes. What was it? What *did* I see? Is *he* someone that I can turn to for help?" On the surface it seemed to be a bit of an absurd idea—after all, he didn't even know the guy. However, the idea persisted. "It wouldn't hurt to ask," he speculated while closing his eyes a second time. "The worst that can happen is that he says no."

CHAPTER 3

DECEPTION

As usual, Steve was the first to awake in the morning. He quickly and quietly made his bunk, urinated, brushed his teeth, and prepared himself to head to the dining room for breakfast. He would eat slowly, giving Al the time and the privacy that he needed to rise and tend to his own needs. If Steve timed it right, he'd arrive back at the cell just as Al was leaving; then Steve would have the privacy that he desired to complete his morning routine. Both men understood and appreciated the fact that, while double-bunked, such mutual cooperation was essential to their respective well-being; and Steve usually timed it correctly. He and Al were comfortable with each other; that is to say, as comfortable as possible, given the circumstances.

Steve was about to step out of the cell when he heard a sleepy voice from the top bunk. "Hey, buddy, are you okay? Did you sleep all right? Have you decided what you're gonna to do about our problem with those guys in the South Block?"

Steve surprised Al with a smile. "Yes to all three questions, my friend. I'll tell you all about it when I get back from breakfast." Without further comment, he flashed Al a second smile, turned, stepped out the door and onto the tier, and briskly walked down the hall.

Al rose and began his day. He finished brushing his teeth, placed his toothbrush back into its rack, and paused to view himself in the mirror above the sink. He liked what he saw—except for the black eye and the bruised cheek, which he now gently fingered. That had been a mistake! As fast as he'd suggested that Ike clock him once, the guy had come over the top with a left hook that had nearly collapsed Al's cheekbone, a blow which had left the young man sagging against the wall. In retrospect, Al realized that he might have been wise to think of some other way to make their story more convincing, but that was yesterday. Today he simply accepted the fact that he'd heal soon enough; he even allowed himself to chuckle a little over his own foolishness.

Bruise and black eye aside, Al felt thrilled by the image looking back at him in the mirror—twenty-three years old, blue eyes, shoulder-length blond hair, and slim features that were ever-so-slightly effeminate. It all came together in a 145-pound, five-foot-eight frame, with an effect that some men and nearly all women found quite attractive. Al never tired of seeing himself; he was about as narcissistic as a man could be. In fact, the only thing that Al was sure that he loved more than viewing his own appearance was methamphetamine, crystal meth, *ice*! However, there was no comparison between his two loves; when push came to shove, he wasn't the least bit hesitant to use his good looks in order to acquire drugs— methamphetamine was by far the most important thing in his life!

Al hadn't found it at all difficult to keep his meth addiction secret from Steve, and Steve had no idea as to Al's true interests. Al had carefully, patiently, and successfully established a deep emotional bond with Steve. The result was that Steve presently viewed Al as a really nice kid—a young man who was just a bit too good looking and way too vulnerable for a place like this. He felt protective of Al in the way that an older brother often feels toward a sibling, a fact that now enabled Al to feel confident that he was in a good position to take full advantage of Steve. Al felt certain that Steve would be an easy mark; he'd said as much to Ike when he'd laid out the plan.

Steve returned to the cell; without prompting, he began to reveal his late-night inspiration to his anxious cellmate. "Okay, guy, here's what I think. This is gonna sound a bit crazy . . . just bear with me." He paused and began to pace back and forth. "First of all, let me tell you, I saw Sly in V&C yesterday . . . I think he was visiting a lawyer—you know who I'm talking about, right?"

Al nodded. "Everyone knows who Sly is!"

"Of course. Okay then. Anyway, he was watching us—Taba, Shelly, and me, and he had the strangest look on his face!"

"Don't tell me you've turned gay," Al quipped in an attempt to conceal his sudden and deep concern over the mention of Sly's name.

Steve rolled with the joke. "No, fool, nothing like that. I'm just saying that I saw something . . . I can't be quite sure what it was, but I think we connected somehow, just for a moment. Call me crazy, if you want, but I think he might be willing to help us. Equally important, I'm pretty sure that he really can . . . that is, if he chooses to. What do you think?"

"You're right, I believe you're crazy. And I believe that Sly's crazy too—crazy as a loon! As far as I know, he's never gone out of his way to do anything for anyone . . . ever! Asking for his assistance sounds a bit risky, but I also agree that he certainly could help, if he wanted to." Al added the last comment as an afterthought, simply because he didn't want to give himself away by appearing too negative—he was, after all, supposed to be as desperate as Steve.

Al's attempt at subtle dissuasion failed. The idea had firmly rooted itself in Steve's mind; he expressed his intention to approach Sly. "I don't think that we've got anything to lose. I'm gonna start looking for an opportunity to have a talk with that old man and—"

"All right, brother," Al interrupted, "we're in this together. You know me. I'm always with you one hundred percent, no matter what happens."

Steve brightened. "I know you are, pal. And you're right, we'll work it out. Now get out of here so that I can do what I need to do before I have to drag my ass off to work. I'll see you tonight . . . With luck, I'll have some good news."

Al slipped into his jacket and stepped onto the tier. He tried to think fast as he walked slowly down the hall. This unexpected turn of events had shaken his confidence in the plan. Worse, this was something that Ike needed to immediately know about. Al knew that it wasn't going to go down well with the big guy, and he sure as hell wasn't feeling anxious to tell him! Still, it had to be done. With a pounding heart and a stomach full of butterflies, Al set of in the direction of the South Block.

Steve quickly readied himself for work. He rolled himself a smoke, lit it, and headed off to the canvas shop to do his part in the construction of government mailbags. He was feeling a little bit hopeful, almost optimistic, that the day would go well. He had no way of knowing—he would never know—that the day would turn out a whole lot better for him than it would for Al.

CHAPTER 4

IKE

The general social status of any prisoner on any tier in Abaddon could usually be determined by how far down the tier he lived. The cells closest to the main area were the noisiest, and they afforded the least amount of privacy. Conversely, the cells grew relatively and progressively more quiet and private, the further down the tier a prisoner resided. Ike was single bunked in the last cell on the top tier; it was one of many indicators that identified him as being the Big Dog on the block.

The Big Dog was known to be a callous, calculating, cruel Caucasian. His followers feared his mercurial mood swings. One hard look from his otherworldly green eyes, planted deep and narrow in his shaven head, was usually enough to send ripples of fear through anyone; and he was already in bad mood.

Though Ike would never admit it, he was also something of a bomber pilot. He liked his barbiturates. Oh sure, he'd indulge in pretty much any drug that came his way, but he liked the downers best of all! He would never admit to being a bomber pilot because he was one of those all-too-common prisoners who preferred to deny many things about himself in order to feel superior to others. He'd often said, "I'm no fuckin' junkie! I can quit anything, anytime I want. I'm my own man!" Though this was not exactly, in and of itself, an unusual attitude, what made Ike different was that he took his denial to a much higher level than did most other prisoners. To call him a junkie was to literally put your life at risk.

The reason for Ike's astonishingly violent defense of this and his other delusions was simple—Ike had more to hide than anyone else. His entire identity was constructed of lies. If certain truths were to emerge, his world would collapse like a house of cards. For instance, he dared not even contemplate what might happen if his skinhead subordinates ever found out that, as a child, his nickname had been Ike the Kike. And that was only one of many issues he chose not to think about. It was easier to simply refuse to tolerate any and all challenges to his authority and his lies. Though no one knew the reason why, all were aware that the least provocation would most likely result in a vicious physical assault.

A fight with Ike was something that most prisoners avoided at all cost. He was a well balanced and rock hard, six foot three and two hundred and twenty-seven pounds. A lifer at age nineteen, by age thirty-two he'd already been practicing his prison skills for thirteen years—lifting weights, pounding on the heavy bag, and kicking ass. Ike was proud of the fact that he was no-polish, soft-knuckled leader of organized crime and that he'd worked his way up the prison hierarchy the hard way—one fight at a time. He honestly felt that he'd earned the right to set himself above the other prisoners, and as a typical bully that nearly everyone acquiesced to, he was too stupid to realize and understand the difference between fear and respect. The fact that so many prisoners were willing to do his bidding allowed Ike to view himself as royalty, but everyone else just viewed him as dangerous. He was a man whose worst fear in life was that someone might recognize him for the coward that, deep down, he knew himself to be. Consequently, he was a very empty, emotionally isolated, and lonely man. Drugs and violence were the only things that he knew of that seemed to hold the pain of his emptiness and loneliness at bay; and at this precise moment in time, he didn't have any drugs. Violence was inevitable!

Ike paced his cell like a caged animal; he felt desperate for an outlet to relieve the strange combination of stress, boredom, and frustration. He was stressed because he hadn't been able to get high for two days, bored because he had nothing to do while he waited for his drug mule to arrive, and frustrated because the mule was late. Ike glanced at his watch; it read 8:47 a.m. The mule—a prison guard they'd bribed—should have dropped the package off when the cell doors first opened; Ike had no idea as to why he hadn't done so.

He stopped pacing and slammed the heel of his hand hard against the wall in anger. "Fuckin' stupid *pig!*" he cursed out loud. "Why do I even deal with these assholes? We've gotta get somethin' more goin' on in this fuckin' place!"

Ike's desire to expand his network caused him to think about Al. He recalled the plan that they'd discussed the previous day, and he laughed when he remembered smashing his fist into Al's face in order to lend credibility to their story. "I really hope that cellmate of his takes the bait," he fervently and silently wished, "we've got to get another mule packin'." The prospect of future access to larger quantities of drugs caused Ike to relax a little; he resumed pacing.

A minute later, he stopped in front of his desk; this time in order to roll himself a smoke. Al surfaced in his mind a second time, and he felt an unusual urge begin to push its way into his conscious awareness. "One of these days I'm gonna get to know that kid a little better," he promised himself.

Ike took the time to make a cup of coffee before lighting his cigarette. Coffee in hand, he flopped down on his bunk, lit up, and reached for his newest porno magazine. "This should help to pass the time until the pig shows up," he mumbled while balancing the coffee cup on the edge of the bed in order to free up his hand so that he could leaf through the pages.

He was surprised to discover that the pictures of naked women failed to take his thoughts off Al; and he was further surprised when his mind began to fill with questions. "What am I gonna do if he fucks this up? What if his cellmate refuses to work for us? How am I gonna handle Steve, given that Al's used my name?" Then came the biggest question of all: "What am I gonna do about all the money Al owes me?"

Ike took some time to reflect on the last question. "I guess I could pimp him out, like before—the fuckin' kid's definitely money in the bank when it comes to that. The guy had 'em lined every night!

"On the other hand, there ought to be some sort of punishment for failin' to properly reel Steve in."

Al's debt to Ike quickly became a secondary issue. The more Ike thought about it, the more he felt inclined to punish Al should he fail to successfully execute their plan, and the more Ike thought about punishing Al, the more sexually excited he became—he began to fantasize about the things that he'd like to do to the young man.

CHAPTER 5

ASSAULT

Al wasted no time; he headed straight over to the South Block to see Ike. He was worried about what the big man would do when he found out that their plan might be falling apart and that the drugs he'd promised, if Ike would back Al by allowing him to use his name and reputation as leverage, might not materialize. Al glanced down at his watch. He saw that it was eight fifty-one. He needed to be in his high school equivalency class by nine o'clock if he wanted to get paid his prison wages for the day. Al realized that he'd have to hurry! He scooted down the stairs of the West Block, across the floor of the main area, past the central control, and up the stairs of the South Block to the fourth floor where Ike lived. It was a long and frightening walk down the tier.

Al found Ike propped up on his bunk, his back against a pillow, sipping coffee, flipping through a magazine, and smoking his third cigarette of the day. He looked up as Al approached. It was always Ike's habit to greet people with some sort of personal put down. This morning he referenced Al's affinity for crystal meth and challenged his masculinity with a single phrase. "What's up, ice queen?"

There was something more behind the phrase than Al realized. Ike was on the verge of admitting that he was sexually attracted to Al. Not that he was gay—*hell no*! With his usual flare for denial, Ike would be the first to tell anyone that he was no fuckin' faggot! Pitchin' was not the same as catchin'. And when it came to the jailhouse girls, Ike did all the pitchin'. Nevertheless, he did feel that it wouldn't hurt to toss out a subtle invitation and see if he couldn't brighten his day by getting Al to play a little early morning ball, so to speak.

Al was too stressed with his own thoughts to perceive the phrase as a sexual invitation, and he ignored the put down. "We've got a problem, Ike," he responded in a weak and hesitant voice.

Al's weak response added to Ike's miserable disposition in two ways. First, he disliked having his invitations ignored. Second, he was quite certain that, whatever the issue at hand, the problem wasn't *his*, and it was a point that he was in a hurry to make. "Just *what* kind of problem do *we* have?" he angrily demanded.

"It's my cellmate, Steve."

"What about him?"

"He's got it into his head that Sly might somehow be willing to help him deal with his problems, if you know what I mean?"

The name produced an instant emotional and physiological reaction. Ike's blood pressure rose, his anger intensified, and he experienced a burning sensation in the pit of his stomach. He'd had dealings with Sly in the past. Things hadn't worked out quite the way he'd wanted them to. The memory produced feelings of inadequacy, which now combined with fear to further sicken him as, once again, he was confronted with a truth that he would never admit to anyone—Sly was one old man that he'd rather not contend with.

Dim-witted Ike had to pause a minute to digest the information and wrestle with his emotions. Like a man dialing a complicated combination lock, he slowly and carefully turned the information over in his brain until the tumblers began to fall into place; then he directed his anger, fear, and feelings of inadequacy at Al.

The hard look on Ike's face cause Al to feel uneasy; his uneasiness turned to genuine fear when Ike stood up, walked over to the door of his cell, and looked down the tier.

Satisfied that there was sufficient privacy, Ike turned to Al and towered over him in a threatening manner. Al stood there, eyes darting from side to side, desperately seeking an avenue of escape; there wasn't one. Ike spoke in a low, primordial, and menacing voice that triggered terror deep within the young man. "Why are you talkin' to me about Sly? Do you actually think that I give a fuck about that old cocksucker? What makes you think that this changes anything, *bitch*? Huh?

"This is between you and me. *You* came to *me*, remember? You owed me money. You had a plan, and I allowed you to use my name. You promised me a new drug mule for my mule train. I've done my part. Now it's up to you to do your part! You don't come up here and punk me off with some fucking bullshit line about how *we* have a problem. *We* don't have a problem. *You're the one with a fuckin' problem!*"

The attack came without warning; Al had no time to speak, to think, or to react. Ike used the heel of his hand to strike hard at the center of the much smaller man's chest. It was a vicious blow that slammed Al hard against the wall, leaving him gasping for air. Al raised his hands in an attempt to ward off a second blow, but Ike grabbed his left wrist and forearm, expertly spun him around to face the wall and easily pinned him there with a simple one-handed arm lock. Ike leaned his head forward and hissed into Al's ear, "I own you, bitch!" Then he reached around with his free right hand and loosened Al's pants.

This was no sadomasochistic role-play. It was a typical, brutal, jailhouse rape. When it was over, Ike dealt Al an emotional coup de grace. "That's your warning, punk—either I get what I want, or I hand your ass over to the rest of my crowd. And when they're finished with you, if you're lucky, they'll run you into protective custody with the rapists and the stool pigeons. Otherwise they'll bury you in the fucking yard! You got it? Are you listening?"

"Ya, Ike, I got it," Al whispered, and it came as no surprise to him at all that, on top of everything else, Ike now failed see himself as a rapist.

"Good! Now put your pants on and fuck off," he commanded.

Ike felt very satisfied to have temporarily replaced his emotional pain with the dark energy of his violent act. He exuded confidence while lazily rolling yet another cigarette. Oh sure, there was still the problem of Sly, but Ike didn't believe that the old man would really feel lucky enough to go up against him a second time. Moreover, it wasn't at all Sly's style to stick his nose into this kind of thing. If he did, well, Ike promised himself that he wouldn't make the same mistake twice—this time he'd kill that fucker, for sure! All in all, Ike was now feeling powerful and in complete control; it was exactly the kind of energy that Abaddon inspired and incubated.

Al wordlessly avoided eye contact with Ike. He quickly dressed himself. Then, placing one foot carefully in front of the other, he walked slowly and deliberately out of the cell and down the tier. He did his best to act as though nothing had happened; the last thing that Al needed was to have others know about what he'd just been through and to have them start to think that maybe they could get away with doing the same thing.

He stopped at the end of the tier, took a prerolled cigarette out of his pocket, lit it with a match, and turned back in the direction of his cell. "Fuck school for today!" he snarled. "I need some time alone!"

Al rested on his bunk within the relative safety of his cell; he began to think about the heretofore unthinkable. Ike didn't know it; but he'd achieved the near impossible. There was now something in Al's life that was more important to the young man than crystal meth—Al craved revenge! The humiliated young man wasn't certain where, when, or how; he simply knew that he'd find a way to make Ike pay for the assault.

While Al lay there, consumed by hatred, committed to vengeance, alone in cell fifteen, on the third level of the West Block, the evil Spirit Tree of Abaddon grew yet another leaf.

CHAPTER 6

SEGREGATION

The guards made their rounds every three hours, twenty-four hours a day, seven days a week, at three o'clock, six o'clock, nine o'clock, and twelve o'clock. Those prisoners who were without a job, as well as those who were not at their work location by 9:00 a.m., were expected to lock up until noon. Those with a job but not at their work location were also expected to lock up; however, they were required to explain their continued presence on the tier. Illness was not an excuse unless substantiated by way of a sick chit from a work supervisor; thus, it was absolutely routine for the officer inspecting the third level of the West Block to stop in front of cell 15 and inquire of Al, "Why aren't you at work? Where's your sick chit?"

"I don't work, I go to school," Al snapped back rudely.

"Well then," the guard asked patiently, "why aren't you at school?"

Al lashed out in displaced rage, "Because I don't fuckin' wanna be, you piece of shit!"

The officer reacted quickly; the size of the prison meant that security personnel couldn't afford to allow any situation time to spiral out of control. He stepped back, reached to his chest area, and thumbed the button on his radio receiver. "This is West 307 to 100, I've got a small problem up here on level 3 . . ."

Al cut him off. "C'mon man, fuck! You don't have to do that." However, it was too late. Two more officers arrived within seconds; both men took positions behind the first officer. The first officer then produced a container of compressed Mace and aimed it at Al's face. "I'm giving you a direct order," he declared, "turn around, get down on your knees, and put your hands behind your head."

The energy went out of Al. He couldn't believe that, after all he'd been through this morning, things were actually getting worse. Feeling utterly dejected, he did exactly as he'd been instructed. As soon as he was on his knees, the two support officers approached and cuffed his hands; then they quickly escorted him off the tier and over to the segregation unit. The first officer subsequently resumed his morning inspection. The whole incident took less than two minutes to play itself out; it was a routine that had been repeated hundreds of times over the years. It had gone like clockwork; it usually did.

The young guard in charge of the segregation unit leaned heavily on his recent training while he directed Al in a dispassionate, professional, and mechanical tone of voice, "Strip off your clothes."

Al watched the prison guard search his shirt, pants, shoes, and socks for contraband, then he turned back to Al and issued a series of commands, "Remove your underwear, shake them out, and throw 'em on the chair."

Al did as ordered, and the officer resumed the procedure. "Open your mouth, lift your tongue. Run the fingers of both hands through your hair. Turn around. Lift your arms. Put 'em down. Bend over and spread your cheeks. Okay, stand up. Turn around, and face me." Al continued to obey each humiliating instruction. When the process was over, the officer threw him a pair of coveralls. Al slid into them; and he was immediately ordered into a segregation cell.

"What about my tobacco and papers," Al requested hopefully.

"No smoking in seg," the stone-faced officer replied flatly as he closed the door.

The officer was not quite as unfeeling as he'd let on. He'd been trained in regard to this type of situation; they'd taught him that when normally quiet prisoners suddenly began to act out, it was almost always for a reason. It could be anything—family problems, drugs, a friend's death, etc., or it could be what he now suspected. He'd noticed the fresh blood on the back of Al's underwear, and rape was an all-too-common occurrence at Abaddon!

The officer followed protocol; his first phone call was to the watch commander, to advise him of the situation, and his second phone call was to the health-care unit, requesting that they send up a nurse.

The watch commander entered Al's cell, along with a male nurse; the commander was the first to speak, "Are you having trouble this morning, Allen? Is there something that you want to talk about?"

"No, I'm not, and no, I don't," Al curtly replied.

"Do you mind if I examine you?" the nurse gently inquired.

Al spoke without looking at either of them. "Yes, I do. I've been examined quite enough already this morning, thank you very much!"

Al felt certain that he didn't want or need their attention; what he wanted and needed was to get out of seg before Ike learned of his presence in the unit and concluded that he'd turned snitch. "Look, I'm sorry I swore at the guard," he declared apologetically. "I should've been at school.

"I just wanna return to my cell. Put me back on the tier, and I promise that I'll keep my mouth shut . . . I won't bother anyone."

The watch commander stroked his beard thoughtfully while assessing the situation. Sexual assault was a highly charged political issue; most of the time it went unreported, and the officer was well aware of the fact that administration preferred it that way. Moreover, he truly didn't want the paperwork or the headache. His face brightened a little as he arrived at a decision. "I tell you what, Allen, I'm going to keep you in seg overnight. Since this is not a punitive decision, we'll allow you a shower, reading material, and you can have your tobacco. If you feel the same in the morning, I'll cut you loose.

"Oh ya, and we'll forget about what was said between you and the officer—how do you feel about that plan?"

Al figured that this was about the best deal he was going to get, and he really needed a smoke, "Ya, sure, fine," he agreed.

The watch commander and the nurse gave each other a knowing look while exiting the cell; then the commander issued instructions as the duty officer locked the door: "Shower the prisoner and give him some reading material . . . as well as his tobacco. Cut him loose if he wants to go back to his cell in the morning." He paused and then added, "Oh, and let's not put anything about this on paper, okay?"

"Whatever you say, sir," the officer replied. He didn't like the decision. Deep down he knew that it was wrong, but it wasn't his call, and it wasn't his responsibility. The officer was new at his job, and he needed the work. So he obeyed his instructions. He remained at his post. He did his best to soothe his troubled conscience, and he resisted the urge to open the door in order to comfort Al—by suppressing his own compassion, he enabled the evil Spirit Tree of Abaddon to extend it roots.

CHAPTER 7

STEVE AND SLY

Steve stood patiently in front of the stamping machine, stamping grommets into mailbags, through which a rope would later be threaded in order that the contents of the bags could be secured inside. It was a boring job—kathunk! turn, kathunk! turn, and so on—four grommets in each bag, ten bags to a stack. He tried to be efficient. There was a small bonus for a production level that rose above the required quota, and he needed the money in order to cover travel expenses to and from the prison for his wife and daughter.

Steve sent home nearly every penny that he earned, but he dared not work too hard. Other prisoners had different ideas about the importance of production. He'd already witnessed how overproduction could result in swift and unpleasant corrective action. He walked a fine line; however, production was not first and foremost on his mind this morning.

Steve glanced at his watch; observing that it was eleven fifty-five, he began to shut things down for the noon-hour break. He felt anxious for the opportunity to speak to Sly, and he was certain that the opportunity would present itself during lunch. The shop buzzer rang, and he immediately exited the shop, fast walking in the direction of the dining room.

Steve arrived to find Sly eating in the usual place; Sly looked up, surprised to be approached by a stranger, but he said nothing while Steve seated himself opposite. Steve sat quietly, without touching his food. Sly took a couple of more bites while he tried to remember where he's last seen his strangely silent dinner companion. He couldn't place the face, and he became annoyed, "You gonna talk, or are you gonna eat? 'Cause you sure as hell ain't gonna just sit there and stare at me!"

"Sorry," Steve blurted, "I've been waiting for a chance to talk to you—I'm just not sure how to get started."

Sly chuckled. "Simple, spit it out. And you'd best eat while your talkin', or you're gonna go hungry." He forked another heap of spaghetti into his mouth, then he gave Steve a shrug and added, "Well? C'mon, get on with it!"

Steve threw caution to the wind. "Here's the situation: I'm under a lot of pressure from the guys in the South Block."

"Oh?" Sly commented in a less-than-interested manner.

"Ya, they want me to pack for them, and I don't want to do it."

"Well, then don't," Sly advised.

"It's not quite so simple . . ."

"Surprise, surprise," Sly interrupted, indicating that he'd heard it all before. "Let me guess," he cynically continued, "they've made you the famous offer that you can't refuse."

"Ya, that pretty much sums it up, but it's not just me. They're also threatening to kill my cellmate, Al."

The last comment caused Sly to raise an eyebrow. Something about it didn't ring true. The math didn't add up. The crew in the South Block was more savvy than that. Like all good predators, they knew very well that two are always stronger than one—that two would often support each other in ways that made both more likely to resist. Sly doubted that these guys would involve a second person, at least not without good reason. The usual pattern was to try and isolate the victim. If you pressure one guy, you take a chance on his reaction, but if you pressure two over that same issue, you double the risk for the same reward; and those were bad percentages! It usually didn't go down that way. This situation was clearly out of the ordinary, and things that were out of the ordinary always piqued Sly's curiosity. However, first he needed an answer to the foremost question on his mind. "So why are you telling *me* this?" he inquired.

Steve squirmed and nervously cleared his throat. "Well, I know it's a stretch . . . please don't get mad or think that I'm weird . . . but I saw you watching me and my family in V&C yesterday, and for some reason, I've just got the impression that you might be someone willing to help."

Sly slapped himself on the forehead. "V&C! That's it! I've been sittin' here wondering why your face seems so fresh in my mind. I mean, I know I've seen you around before . . . but your face looks just a little bit more familiar today. Ya, I remember now . . ." His voice faded as he recalled the image, the memories, and the emotions that he'd experienced while watching the young man with his wife and daughter.

Sly suddenly shifted the conversation. "Did you have a good visit?"

"Yes, I did. It was a very good visit! I only get to see them once a month, and I always try to make the most of it."

"Why only once a month?"

"That's all we can afford. I send Shelly what I earn and she saves what she can from her welfare check, and if I'm lucky, it adds up to one visit a month."

A change came over Sly that Steve couldn't account for, but the reason was simple—poverty was a way of life that Sly understood very well; he knew exactly what this family was going through, and he felt deeply moved by the fact that Steve was willing to sacrifice his material wants and needs in order to spend time with his wife and daughter. In Abaddon, this made Steve exceptional! More often than not, the reverse was true—prisoners tended to work their families for money, drugs, or whatever. Sly began to actually respect Steve as a man, and that was also exceptional!

Sly's next words were spoken in a very different tone of voice, almost as one friend to another. "Who's your cellmate?"

"Allan McFarlan," Steve happily proclaimed. "He's a real nice kid. Ike messed him up pretty bad in order to send me a message. Al didn't complain at all! I think he's more worried about me than he is about himself." Steve looked away in order to veil his emotions as he added, "I really don't want anything bad to happen to him!"

Sly reacted immediately to Ike's name. "Ike, huh, I shoulda killed that racist prick a long time ago!"

"You know him, then?"

"Ya, we've met," Sly answered without elaborating; nor did he mention the fact that he was also familiar with the name Allan McFarlan and that he knew Al to be an associate of Ike's crew—Steve's situation was beginning to make a lot more sense!

Sly's face suddenly brightened. "What's your name, friend?" he asked while eyeing Steve's yet-untouched tray of spaghetti.

"Steve."

"Well, Steve, I'll make you a deal—if you slide that spaghetti over here, I'll seriously think about what I can do to help out."

Steve couldn't possibly have passed the food over any faster. "Thank you . . . thank you very much!" he murmured in a voice strained with emotion.

"Don't thank me yet," Sly warned. "I haven't said that I'll help. I'm only saying that I'll think about it—I'll get back to you in a day or two."

"Ya, sure, Sly, no problem," Steve agreed, but his spirits were soaring. He could tell from the tone of Sly's voice, as well as his general demeanor, that Sly absolutely did intend to help. He smiled a genuinely happy smile. "Enjoy that spaghetti. I'll talk to you again soon." Then he rose from the table and returned to the canvas shop.

Sly thoughtfully watched Steve walk away before quickly shifting his attention back to his meal. He'd always had the ability to make the most of life's little pleasures, and it was damn good jailhouse spaghetti!

The hungry man knew that he wasn't right in the head, but he wasn't stupid either. A psychiatrist had once assessed him for the courts as being, among other things, *amoral*. Sly had taken the time to look up the meaning of the term *amoral*. He had then compared and contrasted it with the terms *moral* and *immoral*. He didn't actually understand or think much about the rest of the assessment, all the bullshit about primary and secondary socialization, but he came to understand the *amoral* part and he actually agreed with the psychiatrist. One might reasonably wonder why, having recognized the accuracy of the diagnosis, he didn't attempt to do something about his condition. The truth of the matter was that he simply didn't know how or where to start.

Thinking about the consequences his amorality sometimes caused Sly to laugh and shake his head; at other times, he simply felt frightened. As an amoral person, he often cared deeply about many things; he was just never sure when, where, why, or how his feelings would express themselves. Worse yet, he could never anticipate where those choices might take him. Sometimes the choices he made resulted in a new friend; at other times they resulted in something else; and once they'd resulted in a life sentence. Anything could happen. It was a hard way to live!

Sly finished his meal, carried both trays to the dish pit, and exited the dining room. His thoughts immediately returned to Steve's predicament. True to form, he couldn't understand why he cared, nor could he explain his need to involve himself in the mess. He just knew that he couldn't walk away. "Here I go again," Sly muttered under his breath as he briskly walked toward his cell, which was located on the top level of the East Block, "one of these days this amorality thing is gonna get me killed . . . I'd best take my time and think this through very carefully, before I decide how to handle Ike . . . Steve'll be all right for a for a day or two."

CHAPTER 8

SLY AND RAY

Prisoners sometimes made jokes about the black man tanning in the sun; they quickly stifled themselves when they saw that it was Sly. For his part, Sly loved the sensation of the warm rays on his bare skin—it was like being caressed by a thousand angels. These were the moments when he was able to do his best thinking, and his noontime conversation with Steve had given much to think about.

Sly luxuriously stretched his shirtless torso upon the bench while the last vestiges of late-afternoon sunshine worked magic on his body and soul. He quietly groaned with pleasure as the warmth drove the pain from his aging and aching muscles; however, the temporary respite from the pain also caused him to think about his diminished physical prowess. At fifty-four years of age, Sly could sense that it wouldn't be long until he lost the ability to maintain his social boundaries. His body would fail, the predators would turn on him, and he would be no more. It was the law of nature—survival of the fittest. The end was coming, for sure, but he smiled with satisfaction as he thought to himself, "Not today!"

A shadow passed across Sly's face; he opened his eyes in time to see Ray, the prisoner who lived in the cell next to him, kneel, place a large shoebox on the ground, and begin to industriously dig with a metal cup. "Hey, Ray," he asked in astonishment, "what the hell are you doin'?"

"I'm digging a hole," Ray answered without looking up.

"I can see that much. The question is why?" Sly insisted with a bemused laugh. "Surely you're aware that security takes a dim view of prisoners digging holes in the yard, and it's a big job to get under that wall! Perhaps you should stop and think about this for a minute?"

48

Ray paid no heed to Sly's advice. "I know what I'm doing," he stated flatly. "I'm workin' on a project."

The now-thoroughly perplexed man continued his line of questioning, "Well then, what kind of project are you working on? Does it have anything to do with what's in the box? What is in the box?"

"A ground squirrel."

"A *ground squirrel!*" Sly exclaimed in amazement. "Where'd you get 'em?"

"I snared him out back the baseball diamond," Ray answered proudly.

"Well, you know, Ray, you can let him out of that box. He's perfectly capable of digging his own hole in the ground!"

"He won't be when I get finished with him!" Ray replied with a chuckle.

Sly suddenly felt a strong sense of anxiety. Hesitantly and in a subdued voice, he asked, "Why, Ray, what are you going to do to that critter?"

Ray stated his intentions succinctly. "I'm going to strangle him and bury him in this hole."

Sly was horrified, and he felt a sick feeling in the pit of his stomach. "Why are you gonna do that, Ray?" he demanded to know.

Ray felt inclined to brag about his idea. "I'm gonna bury the dead carcass and leave it in the ground until the flesh rots off of the bones. Then I'm gonna dig it up, boil those bones clean, glue 'em back together, and send the skeleton to the ol' lady so that she can put it in her fish tank—it's gonna be totally cool!"

Sly processed the information slowly; as he did so, his unpredictable conscience began to kick in. Ray continued to expand the size of the hole until he was satisfied that it suited his purpose. However, no sooner had he stopped digging than Sly spoke again. "You better make that hole a little bigger, Ray!"

Ray looked at Sly, looked back at the hole, shrugged, and dug some more; the process was repeated two more times before Ray became completely exasperated. "Just how big do you think this fuckin' hole needs to be, Sly?" he asked in annoyance.

"Quite a lot bigger, Ray."

"Why?"

"Because if you strangle that animal, that's where I'm gonna bury you."

Ray's face went blank. He knew Sly well enough to be certain that he was absolutely serious. He also knew better than to argue with the man. Ray felt angry, hurt, and insulted; he reacted accordingly. "Fuck you! What's wrong with your head? We're supposed to be friends . . . now you're talking about burying me in a hole in the fuckin' yard! That ain't right! This is bullshit, Sly! How the fuck can you say that to me?"

Ray turned on his heel, kicked the shoebox, and then stomped off toward the main building. The shoebox flew through the air, dislodging the lid. The squirrel was thrown clear; it hit the ground a few feet away from Sly, rolled several times, jumped to its feet, ran, and dove into the nearest cover, which just happened to be the hole that Ray had been digging. There it remained, shivering in fear.

Distraught and confused by Ray's outburst, Sly closed his eyes and thought hard about what had just happened. He regretted hurting his friend, but he couldn't see an alternative way of handling the situation. It'd seemed to him as though he had no choice in the matter. "What was I supposed to have done?" he wondered. "I couldn't just sit there and allow Ray to strangle the poor creature!"

It was all too much for the tired man! The world, *life*, felt way too fucking complicated; how could he ever get it right? Sly shook his head and refocused his thoughts; with all of his heart and soul, he wished that he could simply check out, so to speak—no, not suicide, just go someplace safe and secure, somewhere that he could find a measure of peace. He thought about the fishing hole that he used frequent as a young boy. He pictured the grass and the nearby woods that he'd often explored. Then he recalled a long-lost girlfriend with magical eyes and a voice as soft as a summer breeze. He brought to mind all of the comforting and beautiful things that he'd ever experienced in an earnest attempt to transport his consciousness beyond Abaddon's walls. He even pictured the smooth, well-lit hallway that ran from the main building to V&C, which he so much enjoyed to walk, and he chuckled a little when he recalled pretending that it led to an alternate reality.

"Wouldn't that be fantastic!" Sly whispered as he picture himself once again approaching the entranceway to V&C. And much to his surprise, he seemed to actually hear the metallic click of the lock being triggered from within. Next he envisioned the door opening, stepping through the door and onto the soft carpet beyond. It all felt so real; he had no way of knowing that, deep within his mind, he'd breached a barrier and that he had, indeed, passed through to the other side.

Sly was suddenly startled by a sound. "Pssst, psst." He quickly looked in the direction from which it came; it appeared to have come from the hole that Ray had been digging. He looked harder. He was astonished to see the head of the ground squirrel poke up about three inches above the rim and ask, "Hey you, ya you, is it safe?" Sly rubbed his eyes and looked again. The squirrel repeated the question. "Ya, you, I'm talking to you. Is it safe to come out now?"

CHAPTER 9

INSANITY?

There are many types of insanity. In Sly's case, the clinical diagnosis was catatonic schizophrenia. To an outside observer, he appeared to be in an immobile, hypnotic state. The blank look in his eyes gave no indication of his hyperactive mental activity.

Sly was completely unaware of his clinical condition; from his point of view, reality had simply shifted. In his altered condition, the impossible was possible; and right now he was talking to a ground squirrel. Sly spoke in utter amazement, more to himself than in answer to the squirrel, "*What* . . . what in the hell is going on here?"

"Not much," the squirrel replied, maintaining a wary eye on his surroundings. "I really don't wanna hang around too long—no pun intended. I don't feel at all safe . . . I was a bit too close to being strangled! I'll be on my way in a moment. I just wanted to take the time to thank you for saving my life."

Sly sat up and stared at the squirrel in slack-jawed silence. His face betrayed his disbelief. Seeing this, the squirrel began to worry, and he anxiously expressed his concern for Sly's well-being. "Hey, are you gonna be okay?"

"Hard to say!" Sly blurted in exasperation. "I mean, I am sitting here talking to a squirrel . . . and that can't be good! In fact, it strikes me as that very definition of having gone squirrelly. Plus, I think I've lost Ray, one of the few friends that I had in this evil place. To be honest with you, I'm not having a good day at all!"

Pushing fear aside, the squirrel climbed completely out of the hole, reared up on its hindquarters, and looked Sly directly in the eyes. "I see!" he said in a thoughtful and compassionate voice. "I see that you're in great pain. Your needs are extreme, and you have much to learn. I also sense that time is short and that you're not going to achieve your potential in this place."

The gentle creature hesitated; he appeared to be contemplating something important, and then he seemed to smile while apparently arriving at a decision. "You saved my life," he continued, "and one good turn deserves another. I'm not supposed to do this, but if you follow me, I'll take you to a safe place where your needs will be met, and you'll have the opportunity to learn, to grow, and to realize your creative power."

Without further comment, the squirrel turned and leaped back from whence he'd emerged. Several seconds later, his head popped up over the edge a second time. He summoned Sly with a wave of his little paw. "Well, don't just sit there," he insisted impatiently, "c'mon!"

Sly questioned his own sanity while rising from the bench in response the squirrel's urging. "This is by far the craziest thing that I've ever experienced," he mumbled. Nevertheless, with no idea as to what was about to happen, he stood and cautiously walked toward the opening through which the squirrel had again disappeared. His tentative approach seemed to cause the passageway to expand invitingly; it grew larger with each step until Sly reached the edge, whereupon it became a portal, easily wide enough to accommodate his size and stature. Gazing into the portal, the now-thoroughly mesmerized man observed a softly lit, grassy, serpentine path that extended about fifty yards into the unknown. A wide array of beautiful multicolored flowers adorned each side, and there was a uniquely magnificent light emanating from the far end—awe and wonder caused Sly to hesitate.

"Hurry!" an unrecognizable yet somehow familiar voice commanded. In response to the command, Sly stepped through the portal and journeyed the length of the walkway into light.

CHAPTER 10

REALITY?

The sun was setting by the time that the loudspeaker system blared the usual evening message throughout Abaddon: "Clear the yard! All prisoners return to their cells!" The guard in the east tower immediately began to scan the exercise area while, like cattle, the prisoners herded themselves in the direction of main building; he was about to turn away when he noticed a shirtless torso lying facedown on one of the benches; he promptly radioed the central control. "This is 118 to 100, we've got a prisoner facedown on a bench over by the west wall. He appears to be immobile."

The standard protocol kicked in. "Roger, 118, we're on it." Minutes later, six guards in full riot gear—the emergency response team—approached the bench by the west wall. As they drew near, the closest spoke in a loud, condescending, and authoritative voice. "Hey! Wake up! Are you fuckin' dead? Hey, you! Are you sleeping, or are you dead?" He poked Sly a couple of times with his riot stick. Receiving no response, he began to curse and complain, "Fuck, fuck! Why do things like this always have to happen right of the end of our shift! Now we've got paperwork, and we've got to pack this fuckin' guy out of the yard . . . who knows what time we're gonna get home tonight? *Fuck* . . ."

A second officer interrupted the angry tirade. "Is the prisoner breathing, or is he dead? Do you recognize him? Who is it?"

The first officer managed to flip the limp body over on his own. "Holy fuck!" he exclaimed in surprise. "It's Sly." He removed his glove, reached down, and placed two fingers firmly against the unconscious prisoner's jugular. "He's got a pulse. Obviously he's alive. I can't see any blood, and there's no sign of injury." The officer shook his head in confusion. "I don't see anything wrong with him at all, but he sure as hell doesn't appear as though he's gonna be going anywhere on his own!"

By now, all six members of the emergency response team had encircled the bench. "Maybe he's overdosed?" a third officer suggested.

"I don't know, maybe," the first replied contemptuously while reaching for his radio. "But who gives a fuck? Why don't we just get this stupid bastard over to the health-care unit and let them worry about what's wrong with him?" He thumbed the receiver. "ERT to 100. You're gonna have to contact health care. We need a stretcher!"

Fifteen minutes later, Sly was carried into the medical wing of Abaddon. The duty nurse found herself to be equally perplexed by his condition. It took the woman less than five minutes to conclude that, whatever the problem, it was more than she could handle on her own, and she immediately called for an ambulance.

Her actions triggered a second protocol; paperwork was quickly completed. Sly's inert body was handcuffed and shackled in preparation for transport, just in case he happened to regain consciousness along the way, and two officers journeyed with him in the vehicle.

Less than an hour after he was first discovered facedown on a bench in the prison yard, Sly was handcuffed again to a hospital bed; an intravenous needle was inserted into his left arm in order to rehydrate his body, and he was hooked up to monitors that kept track of nearly all of his vital signs. In addition, a nurse drew blood, which was tested for everything that the doctor could think to look for; it revealed nothing out of the ordinary, and as a result, the physician was at a loss for a diagnosis.

Acting on a hunch, he called in a psychiatrist for consultation. The psychiatrist ordered that Sly's brain waves be recorded, which revealed a peculiar pattern of hyperactivity; and as a consequence of the revelation, the psychiatrist diagnosed Sly as a catatonic schizophrenic. The physician agreed with the psychiatrist's diagnosis. They subsequently ordered that a catheter be inserted into Sly, that nutrients be added to his intravenous drip, and that, in addition to everything else, his brain activity be continuously monitored—there was nothing more that could be done.

The two escort officers cursed their bad luck over the fact that supervising a perpetually unconscious prisoner had just become a long-term, boring proposition; from this point forward, there would always have to be at least one guard in attendance, and neither man wanted to be part of the rotation. "This is absurd!" the first officer insisted. "Why waste time, money, and resources on a prisoner with a past like that? It's not as though he's ever going to amount to anything in this world!"

"Ya!" the other agreed. "What we ought to do is turn off the monitors and suffocate the creep!"

Both men laughed; however, the first was of a mind to seriously consider the suggestion.

Their laughter was interrupted by the night-shift nurse, making her initial evening rounds. "Hello, gentlemen!" she sang out cheerfully, mistaking their mirth for genuine happiness. "It's nice to see that you're enjoying yourselves!"

The officers gave each other a knowing look before undressing the beautiful, dark-haired, dark-skinned woman with their eyes. "If I wasn't enjoying myself before," the first muttered under his breath, "I certainly am now!"

The second office ignored his partner's comment. "Good evening to you," he responded loudly, hoping to engage the woman in further conversation. "Are you just starting your shift?"

She sensed their energy but pretended otherwise. "Yes, sir!" the hard-working woman admitted while expertly attending to Sly. "I'm Vivian. I'll be here all night." Feeling at a loss for words, both men watched silently while Vivian replaced the intravenous drip and check her patient's vital signs. Her duties complete, she paused, glanced at both men, and added, "Call me if you need anything." Then she breezed out of the room, preventing further conversation.

"Why do men always have to be like that?" Vivian wondered during her coffee break. She mentally replayed the scene, searching for a clue that might help explain the sordid sexual energy that she'd sensed emanating from both officers; failing in her endeavor, she ended the exercise with a small joke. "I think the unconscious one would probably be the best company!"

It was a prophetic thought!

CHAPTER 11

INSANITY?

The former prisoner stood alone atop a rise from which he could see little more than wilderness. The sun was high in the sky, signaling midday. "Strange," he whispered in surprise and wonder, remembering that the last time he'd checked his watch, it'd indicated 5:17 p.m.

Sly glanced at his left wrist in order to confirm the memory, only to discover that his watch was missing. "Well, whatever's going on here," he announced to himself, "I obviously won't be keeping track of time!"

Anxious to see what else he might not be keeping track of in the near future, the newly liberated man looked back from whence he'd emerged. To his further surprise and wonder, he observed that his point of entry into this new reality now appeared as a normal, door-sized passage.

Curiosity caused Sly to step through the passage; a split second later, he stood frozen in shock! In place of the path that he'd traveled, there now existed a spacious cavern. It was roughly equal to the height of his former prison cell, but with four times the floor space. The surfaces were crude, relatively smooth, and covered with crystals that perfectly reflected the light conditions outside. It seemed as thought it'd been hollowed out of the rock face with a pickaxe, and it was completely empty. Sly took a moment to recover from the shock, then, given that there was nothing more to see, he turned and stepped back out into the sunshine.

Resuming his position atop the rise, Sly now observed a gently downward-sloping, winding path; it was a walkway much similar to the one that he'd first traversed, leading to where he presently stood. To the left and to the right of the walkway existed large, flat, open spaces, each about the size of a football field. These spaces were filled with trees, flowers, and foliage, identical that that which existed in the area surrounding the farm where he'd grown up—a place that he'd much loved! His ears perceived the gentle, familiar hum of bees, competing with butterflies for access to the myriad of colorful blossoms. A soft breeze, blowing from west to east—and up the rise upon which he stood—carried with it the rich scent of flora and fauna. The entire panorama was encircled by a tree-topped, pincer-shaped rock bluff, about fifty feet high, which was parted at the most western point and through which the path led.

Sly's entire being began to quiver with anticipation as he experienced the first sensations of something that he hadn't known for a very long time—*freedom*! His spirit soared while he took the first tentative steps toward the next phase in his journey.

He followed the path until he reached the opening between the two rock bluffs; a few steps more, and he was through the entranceway. Emerging into a large clearing that was surrounded by woods, he paused and stood spellbound by magnificence of all that his eyes beheld.

From atop the external side of the rock bluff on his immediate left, there poured a small but glorious waterfall; it cascaded down and directly into a huge pond of clear water; as it did so, the spray formed a mist over the entire surface that interacted with the sunlight in order to produce a small but glorious rainbow. The rainbow arced from one side of the pond to the other. Directly across from the waterfall, a rapid, gurgling stream emerged, flowing to places unknown. Short grass, flowers, and foliage bordered the entire shoreline. The bottom of the expanse of water was covered with intense white sand; while overhead, there flew all manner of birds that bore witness to the endless miles of surrounding wilderness.

Beside the pond, directly in front of Sly, stood what, at first glance, appeared to be a forty-foot-tall breadfruit tree. However, if it was a breadfruit tree, it was a tree like no other! It seemed to be alive, almost sentient, as its leaves shimmered and danced under the rainbow in the sunshine and the mist. Unlike the white, hard-shelled, melon-sized fruit of a normal breadfruit tree, its bright red, apple-sized offering glowed in an inviting way that suggested that it could be plucked and immediately eaten—that it would be delicious!

Sly advanced and stood under the tree at the edge of the pond. Driven by need, he stripped off the last of his prison garb and stepped into the water. The water temperature was perfect. With each step, the firm, clean granules of white sand seemed to simultaneously massage and cleanse the soles of his feet. He waded in up to his waist and then dove headfirst under the clear water.

The water instantly washed away all of the stink of all of the years of built-up prison filth, his entire being suddenly and unexpectedly began to tingle with life. Seconds later, he surfaced and experienced a sense of exuberance that he'd never felt before.

Overcome with ecstasy, Sly squealed and laughed his pleasure and joy as though once again a child. With a strong kick of his feet, he used his arms to powerfully stroke his way in the direction of the waterfall. Entering the shallows, he came to a stop, rose to his feet, moved forward, and stepped directly under the cascading flow; the sensation was exquisite.

Emerging from beneath the waterfall, Sly casually and peacefully waded the short distance around the edge of the pond until he'd reached his original point of entry. He looked down at the ground beneath the tree and was stunned to see that, in place of his used and worn prison clothes, there was now a clean, white-and-blue checkered long-sleeved flannel work shirt, a pair of blue jeans, and some hiking boots with a uniquely comfortable lining that required no socks. Shaking his head in disbelief, he began to dress himself.

While he dressed, he couldn't help but appreciate the fact that these were clothes that he would've chosen for himself and that everything fit perfectly—the place actually seemed to be responding to his personal needs. Then he suddenly recalled the words of the squirrel, "If you follow me, I'll take you to a safe place where your needs will be met, and you'll have the opportunity to learn, to grow, and to realize your creative power."

What did that mean? Was it the place that was doing all of this, or was he somehow doing it himself? Of equal importance, from where did this seemingly perfect world originate?

Sly suddenly realized that things were not quite perfect—he was hungry. He glanced overhead at the low-hanging fruit and wondered if it might be good to eat. It certainly looked tasty; he reached up and plucked a fruit that appeared to be nicely ripened. Bravely he took a bite, and immediately all of his senses exploded—the sweet nectar instantly rejuvenated him!

Completely renewed by the water and the food, Sly sat down with his back against the trunk of the tree to further ponder the mystery of this strange place. He quickly fell asleep. While he slept, he began to heal in ways that he wouldn't become aware of for a long time.

Sly awoke just as the sun was beginning to set in the west; with inexplicable clarity, he knew that he needed to return to the cave. He smiled during the walk up the incline; his muscles felt strong, lithe, and resilient, and there was no pain at all in his joints. He knew that he could have sprinted the distance with no difficulty whatsoever, but he chose, instead, to simply enjoyed his astonishing physical transformation.

In a day of so many surprises, he entered the cave and found yet another—the cave was no longer empty. Laid out on a bed of soft moss and grasses was an extremely comfortable-looking brown sleeping bag. In the center of the cave burned a small but inviting campfire, with a stool and a modest pile of wood beside it. No longer overly surprised by the strange happenings in this mysterious place, he happily recited the old cliché: "Be it ever so humble, there's no place like home." Though Sly's words were far from original, they were very sincere—it really did feel to him as though he'd come home!

The crystal-lined walls of the cave reflected the setting sun, producing a soft, radiant, atmospheric glow that seemed to embrace Sly's soul. He sat for a considerable period of time, staring into the campfire's dancing flames while he purged his mind of Abaddon.

In his meditative state, Sly reflected on the day's events and asked several questions of himself, "Where am I? Is this real? Am I dreaming? Have I lost my mind?" Then he asked the most frightening question of all: "Am I dead?"

The questions hung on the air with no answers forthcoming, and Sly grew weary. He slowly stood up, walked over to the sleeping bag, stripped off his clothes, and climbed inside—it really was as comfortable as it appeared to be. Sleep had nearly overtaken him for the second time that day when a final question surfaced in his mind: "Where did that little squirrel get to?"

CHAPTER 12

REALITY?

Steve was distraught. Usually he returned from work to find Al stretched out on his bunk, smoking a cigarette and watching his favorite weekday afternoon television show, but not today. Today he'd returned from work to find that Al was missing. Steve was anxious to know what had happened. He asked around. Big Bob, the slob, who, in Steve's opinion, didn't shower nearly enough and who lived three cells down, gave Steve the play by play of the events that had occurred on the tier earlier that day between Al and the prison guards. From Steve's point of view, it made no sense. Why hadn't Al been at school? Hadn't that been his intent when he'd left the cell this morning? Why, then, had he been back in the cell? Equally unfathomable, what the hell had gotten into his head as to cause him to talk to security that way? Steve was fearful that it was all somehow related to the situation with the guys in the South Block and that he might be partially to blame. However, he realized that there was nothing that he could do about it at this point in time. He'd have to wait and see if Al would return. Setting the matter aside in his mind, Steve grabbed his towel and shampoo and headed for the shower.

He completed his shower, made it back to his cell, and dressed himself in time for the 3:00 p.m. count. The loudspeaker blasted the command "All prisoners, stand by for count." Conforming to rules, he stood by the door of his cell in silence as the two security officers passed. With that out of the way, he settled down for the one-hour wait until the usual announcement that the count was clear and that everyone could go to dinner. The announcement came.

Dinner wasn't much—a hamburger patty, carrots, and instant mashed potatoes with apple for desert. He ate everything; having given away his noon meal, he was extra hungry.

The meal completed, Steve returned to his cell for his normal evening routine, albeit without Al's company. He watched some television, wrote a two-page letter to Shelly, and then relaxed in the unusual quiet.

With no one to talk to, he became somewhat introspective, more so as the evening wore on—his past loomed large. Steve began to reflect on what a fool he'd been to believe that he'd be able to jump-start his life with Shelly and the baby with a little bit of easy money.

His older cousin, Bill, had come up with the plan. "I've got a great idea!" he'd said. However, Steve knew for a fact that the idea didn't seem so great to his cousin now. Of the two of them, Bill had paid the far heavier price for their stupidity!

Steve didn't like to admit it to himself, but he was fortunate that the shoot-out had left Bill quadriplegic rather than dead. Under the law, all of the perpetrators of a crime were held responsible for any death that occurred in the commission of a crime. Had Bill died from the security guard's bullet, Steve would probably now be serving time for murder or manslaughter; as things stood, he'd received eight years in prison and Bill had received life, facedown in a hospital bed.

He fought back the tears while he thought about how much he loved his big cousin. He remembered the two of them as teenagers in the old neighborhood—tough streets to have to walk alone. Thanks to Bill, Steve never did walk alone. Somehow the two of them had managed to survive all this time. Now it was over. Chances were that Bill wouldn't live long enough to see Steve released from prison. It hurt so much, and it seemed like there was nowhere to go with the pain.

Shifting his thoughts slightly, Steve wondered if the pain of his loss wasn't somehow connected to the reason that he felt the way that he did about Al. It was hard to say; all that he knew for sure was that he genuinely cared about the little guy. He promised himself that he'd get to the bottom of whatever was going on, and if it was as he suspected, he'd find a way to make those guys over in the South Block pay! "Especially with Sly's help!" he assured himself out loud.

While Steve lay on his bunk, contemplating violence and allowing the Spirit Tree of Abaddon to work on his mind, he had no way of knowing that Sly was already in a hospital bed—at least physically.

CHAPTER 13

INSANITY?

Sly awoke to a morning like no other; three specific sensations arrived with the dawn. First, he opened his eyes and immediately rejoiced in the luxury of his soft, comfortable, and warm sleeping accommodations. Second, he stretched and savored the familiar and delightful odor of charcoal emanating from the previous evening's small, burned-out campfire, and third, he became aware of his hunger—he felt *ravenous!*

Having thus far discovered only one source of sustenance in this strange place, Sly quickly dressed, intent on a return to the tree for a second helping.

Approaching the tree, he was astonished to discover a fishing pole leaning against the trunk. The pole seemed identical in every way to the one that he'd used as a young boy, except that it presently appeared to be new and in perfect condition. At the foot of the tree, there also rested his similarly restored tackle box. Sly stared in disbelief for several seconds, glanced over at the pond, and then began to laugh. "Ah, breakfast!" he declared enthusiastically, feeling every bit as anxious to go fishing as he was to acquire his morning meal; overcoming his astonishment, he reached for the renewed equipment that he'd used so often in the past.

The familiar apparatus felt good in his hands; he opened the box, removed a fishhook, and expertly threaded the fishing line before tying it off. Then he searched for bait. Spying a grasshopper, he caught the insect and quickly skewered it onto the fishhook. Lastly, he attached a small bobber, allowing about two feet of lead line between the floatation device and the baited hook. Hands shaking and heart pounding with excitement, Sly moved to the edge of the pond, whereupon he cast his line twenty feet out and into the water.

Within seconds, the visible portion of his line went tight and began to travel rapidly across the surface; Sly's entire being delighted in the fresh experience of the nearly forgotten sensation, and he set the hook with a deft flick of his wrist. In no time at all, the happy fisherman was kneeling beside the water, holding his glistening breakfast-sized catch.

Sly hesitated, and what happened next was nothing short of miraculous. No sooner had he realized that he had a small problem than there appeared before his eyes, an inch below the surface of the water, a proper fish knife—one edge designed for scaling and the other designed to fillet.

Sly stared in shock while he pondered the appearance of the fishing rod, the tackle box, and now the knife. "How can this be?" he wondered as he reached for the shining blade. "How can things simply appear exactly when I need them? The cynical dimension to his personality suggested that he ought to be concerned, if not frightened by these mysterious happenings, but the practical dimension to his personality simply longed to satisfy his hunger, and the latter won out—he prepared the fish for cooking.

Breakfast in hand, Sly'd just turned in order to make his way back to the cave when a familiar cheerful voice stopped him in his tacks. "I'm impressed!" the squirrel declared. "Your ability to channel creative power in order to meet your own need is developing quickly—the process has begun!"

The implication of this simple yet profound statement nearly bowled Sly off his feet, and it inhibited the conversation that would otherwise surely have occurred. "What do you mean *my* ability? I have no power. I assure you, I'm not doing anything. If I were meeting my own needs, I'd be lodged at the Hilton or in a mansion, not living in that cave just up the hill!"

"Wrong!" his furry friend countered. "You've eaten from the Tree of Life. You've slept under its branches! The power is now in you and moves through you. You are, indeed, creating. However, I told you that the power was developing according to your *needs*, not your *wants*. These are very different things, which can produce very different results. Your initial task during the *healing process* in which you are now engaged is to learn to habitually create to the best of your ability, in order that you may receive according to your need. That is all . . . and, as I said, I'm happy to see that you are well on your way!

"Now, enjoy your breakfast. We'll talk again soon!" So saying, the squirrel expertly leaped from atop the boulder and rapidly disappeared into the nearby foliage.

The mention of breakfast reminded Sly of his hunger; he shrugged and set off for the cave.

He contemplated the squirrel's words along the way; thus, he wasn't all that surprised to discover, on entering the cave, a small fire, which once again burned brightly, nor was he surprised to see a large wooden chest on the ground nearby. Suspecting what he'd find inside the chest, he lifted the lid; sure enough, it contained dishes, salt, pepper, flour, oil, as well as a knife, fork, spoon, and a frying pan—all the things that he required in order to prepare and eat his breakfast.

Sly ate slowly, savoring each bite while reflecting on all that had transpired since he'd first laid eyes on the astonishing creature that had guided him to this wondrous world. "What I really *need*," he concluded, "is to talk some more with that little guy!

"Only this time I'll think to ask him a few questions!"

CHAPTER 14

REALITY?

Ike was coming to the end of what he viewed as being a particularly fine day! Throughout most of it, he'd mentally replayed his morning *adventure* with Al, and doing so had brought him great pleasure.

Then, at 8:00 p.m., he'd received word that they'd taken Sly out of the institution in an ambulance, a turn of events that Ike interpreted as being remarkably good fortune!

His apparent good fortune was trumped at 9:00 p.m. when his mule finally delivered the drugs that should have arrived that morning, and Ike promptly took the opportunity to celebrate Sly's misfortune in proper style.

It was now 10:00 p.m. The happy man was seriously high! Not even the news that Al remained in segregation could dampen his spirits—Ike felt certain that the kid was no snitch.

"Yes, sir! This has definitely turned out to be a helluva day!" he silently assured himself, while reclining on his bed and enjoying the pleasant physical sensation of the barbiturates that he'd taken an hour earlier. "And there's nothing like a good body stone to help a guy to relax!"

Ike briefly thought about Sly. "That cocksucker is lucky that he's in the hospital and that I didn't get to him first," he slurred softly under his breath. "Otherwise, them fuckers would really have somethin' to keep me in prison for!"

His drug-induced opinion of his ability to carry out such a threat may or may not have been correct, but he most certainly need not have been concerned with regard to the second part of his statement—the justice system already considered that it had ample reason to hold Ike in prison for a very long time.

The courts had designated Ike's offense as a *hate crime*. It was something that Ike claimed to be proud of; however, more than anything, it demonstrated how little the system actually understood the man's criminal behavior.

Ike was born with his mother's green eyes and his father's name, Ezekiel Rosenbloom. He hadn't been able to do anything about his eyes, but his name evolved over time. At eighteen years of age he legally changed it to Ike Bisbane. In a sense, the evolution of his name from Ezekiel Rosenbloom to Ike Bisbane revealed the true motives behind his current offense. Had those within the system known where to look—and what to look for—they might well have designated his offense as a *fear crime*.

As is the case with many prisoners, Ike was raised in a tough neighborhood. Fear was a fact of life; children in that part of town tended to be even more cruel, bigoted, and ignorant than their parents. The young boy's first nickname, Zeke the Freak—a play on the name Ezekiel—underscored how socially isolated he actually was. His social isolation was further complicated by the fact that he could never predict which direction the next round of abuse, violence, and bigotry would come from; thus, he grew up hypervigilant, not knowing when or where he'd have to defend himself. Nevertheless, he did defend himself!

Zeke the Freak fought back with his fists. At first he got beat up, and then he started to win. His skills continued to improve until there came a day that he simply didn't lose.

The pugilistically superior young man let it be known that he preferred to be called Ike, and his potential adversaries obliged, at least when speaking to his face. However, behind his back he became known as *Ike the Kike*. It was something that he was aware of but was never directly confronted with—at least, not until his fifteenth birthday. That was the day that he fought Gord in the back alley, behind the store to which Ike had been sent by his father to purchase cigarettes.

Gord was generally considered by his peers to be the toughest member of one of the toughest gangs in the neighborhood. He was hell-bent on proving it every chance that he got. The gang saw Ike coming down the alley with a carton of cigarettes, and Gord bragged, "Watch! I'll take those smokes and drown that Kike in a pool of his own blood!"

His declaration meant that the rest of the gang stayed out of the contest; as instructed by Gord, they watched and enjoyed the show. Indeed, it was a fight that they would all remember, with no clear winner. Afterward, Gord declared that anyone who could fight as well as Ike was a brother, and the rest of the gang agreed!

For the first time in his life, Ike experienced true social acceptance. It was an amazing feeling. Bloodied but happy, he celebrated by dividing the carton of cigarettes among his new friends. From that point forward, it was just him and the gang, and no one ever again referred to him as Ike the Kike.

Emotionally strengthened and socially empowered through his role as a gang member, gang activity consumed all of Ike's time. A week later he dropped out of school; he left his house at 6:00 p.m. the same evening. His father never saw him again.

Then came the day that the gang decided to beat a Jewish boy who'd dated one of the member's sisters. Ike didn't want to participate—he instinctively knew that it was just plain wrong in so many ways and on so many levels. However, he feared that he might lose the acceptance that he'd become emotionally dependent upon, and he was afraid to go back to being the victim—Ike the Kike. So he participated. Along with the others, he savagely beat the young man, almost as though he was trying to kill a part of himself. Over time, through many similar violent acts, that's exactly what he succeeded in doing.

It's a small step from such behavior to a prison cell. Shortly before his nineteenth birthday, a month after he'd legally changed his name to Ike Bisbane, Ike and his buddies beat a black man to death and took that step. A year later, he was sentenced to life in prison. Condemned to Abaddon, Ike continued to hang out with the same type of people, and he was still motivated by fear. However, in some ways, things had evolved. Now he was boss, and those who obeyed his will were similarly fearful of him. It was a vicious spiral of evil that helped to perpetually nourish the Spirit Tree of Abaddon.

CHAPTER 15

INSANITY?

"It's not a *want*," Sly said out loud, "I really do *need* to talk to that squirrel!" He once again recalled the squirrel's words: "I'll take you to a safe place where your needs will be met . . ." and suddenly he knew what to do. Without further hesitation, he set off in the direction of the large boulder by the pond, where he'd last spoken to the little guy. Or, rather, where the squirrel had spoken to him. He simply knew that the squirrel would be there, and this time he wouldn't let him get away without answering a few questions.

Sure enough, Sly found the squirrel waiting exactly where he imagined he would. "Salutations," came the cheerful voice from atop the boulder, "you're learning fast! I didn't expect to see you again so soon!"

Sly nodded. "I think I'm starting to figure this out. I have a genuine need to talk to you, and you have no choice—you have to be here."

"Close, but not quite . . . I don't *have* to be anywhere. Being here for you *is* my *choice*. It's the logical, natural, reasonable, and responsible extension of my decision to guide you to this place. I know it sounds a bit complicated, but let's not get *hung up* on it," the squirrel quipped, as he once again joked about his near-untimely demise. "Just think of yourself as a man on a healing quest and think of me as your spirit guide. Now let's hear some of those questions that I'm sure you feel the need to ask."

Sly gazed at the pond, hesitating for a moment; there were so many questions, he almost didn't know where to start. Finally he decided to begin with the one that seemed to suddenly loom largest in his mind. "Where am I? Tell me where I am!"

"That's the one I was afraid of!" the squirrel admitted. "However, I'll do my best to answer.

"I need you to listen carefully and to be very patient. For my part, I'll try to keep things simple and not be overly philosophical . . . though it won't be easy.

"Set aside whatever philosophies you have about life and allow me frame it for you this way—first, we all come from somewhere, the place we existed before we were born. Let's call that place the first eternity. Second, we're all going somewhere when we die. Let's call that place the second eternity. Third, let's think of your life as the space between those two eternities, and let's think of where you are now as being a little bit of *extra space* that few people ever get to experience—the space to heal and grow that you failed to create for yourself while you were in Abaddon."

"I'm not dead then?" Sly asked.

"No, you're most certainly not dead! However, you're not exactly in your body either."

The squirrel's last comment caught Sly completely off guard. "What do you mean *I'm not exactly in my body?*" he exclaimed. "If I'm not in my body, then where is it? How can I be anywhere without my body?"

"You're here in your spirit body," the squirrel responded gently. "You're corporeal body is in the intensive care unit of the local hospital, outside of Abaddon. It's being monitored, maintained, and cared for by health professionals. They believe that you are in a catatonic, schizophrenic state, and before you ask, *no* you're not going to die . . . at least, not right away . . . I mean, well, we're all going to die sooner or later.

"*Gads!* This is harder than I thought!" Slightly exasperated, the squirrel paused to take a breath before continuing, "What I'm trying to say is that, when the time is right, your spirit body will be able to return to your corporeal body. What happens after that, I cannot say."

Sly sought further clarity. "So, then, for now, I *have* to stay here," he inquired in a slightly rebellious tone of voice.

"No, that's not what I meant to say—*when you're ready* means *when you decide!* You longed for an alternate reality. You followed me of your own free will, and you can go back whenever you want. However, I hope with all my heart that you choose to stay for a while. I can't tell you how grateful I am that you saved my life, and there's so much that I long for you to learn.

Sly carefully considered the squirrel's words. He couldn't imagine why the creature would long for him to learn anything. Nevertheless, he felt inclined to accept. Sly sensed the value of the opportunity at hand—he recognized it as a rare gift that would never again come his way, and he couldn't think of one single good reason for returning to Abaddon! "How long have I got," he asked, "how long can I stay here?"

"You have all the time you need, and all the time you want," the squirrel replied in a very serious tone of voice. "That's one of the really profound aspects of this little bit of extra space. Time here is relative to your needs and to your rate of healing—the faster you heal, the more you can do; and the more you do, the faster time passes. However, there's no correlation between the passage of time here and the passage of time in the outside world.

"Where your corporeal body rests, it's not yet midnight of the first day. Here it's already noon of the second day. You can stay here for weeks, months, even years . . . years can pass in this place with little or no time at all passing out there. Just think of yourself as being safely tucked away in the bosom of the Eternal Present."

At that point, the squirrel stopped and gazed compassionately at Sly, who was clearly overwhelmed with the concepts being presented. "C'mon Sly," he urged, "give yourself a break. You need this, you know you do!"

"Why do I deserve this opportunity?" Sly softly asked.

"I didn't say that you deserved it . . . I said that you need it. You don't deserve it. No one does! You just happened to be in the right place at the right time. Whatever else was going on in your mind, which is something we'll talk about a little later, the fact is, you cared enough to help a ground squirrel. That made you special to me, and I made the decision to guide you here. It's just that simple."

It was a lot for Sly to take in, but he felt mostly satisfied with the explanation. He finally came to his decision. "I'll stay," he declared, "at least for a while. And what I'd really like to do right now is take another swim in that wonderful pond!"

CHAPTER 16

REALITY?

Al could never do good hole time. His emotional and psychological disposition mirrored that of his mother, Julia. He constantly craved multiple forms of entertainment, such as radio, television, food, drugs, music, company, or whatever to help offset the noise in his mind—the memories, thoughts, and feelings that caused him so much pain; and the segregation unit offered very few external distractions.

In the aftermath of the sexual assault, the young man felt particularly small and vulnerable. Seeking an emotional boost, he reached deep into his past, calling on the memories of life with his mother.

His strongest memory was of his first exposure to methamphetamine; it had come at age thirteen—a birthday present from Julia. Al viewed the experience as being his own fault: he'd argued that he wanted to try the drug and ultimately his mother had given in to his demand. Nevertheless, he felt strongly that Julia was to blame for most of what followed.

Money passed through their hands like water; their drug addiction necessitated that they find increasingly creative ways to accumulate additional funds, and his mother planned accordingly.

Initially it was all simple and straightforward. Julia would occasionally turn tricks, bringing men home and keeping them sexually distracted while her son picked their pockets. However, this proved to be a little too dangerous for comfort, so Julia came up with an alternate idea.

She began to pay attention to the coming and going of the other families in the trailer park, keeping track of which homes would be empty as a result of vacations or holidays. She'd pass this information along to Al, and her son would take advantage of the opportunity to burgle each temporarily vacant residence.

Al was neither then nor now adverse to his role in any of his mother's schemes; it was Julia's priorities and her secret agenda that eventually came to perpetually disturbed the boy.

In terms of priorities, Julia always seemed to be more concerned with herself than with the well-being of her son. Al's blood ran cold while the memory of her often-repeated words now flooded his mind. "Whatever happens," she'd habitually insisted, "don't let them know that I set it all up—keep my name out of the picture.

"Don't worry, son—you're a juvenile. They can't lock you up for long. I'll get you out of jail, no matter what! All you have to do is make sure that they don't put *me* back in prison!"

Al obeyed; he always protected his mother, and he had plenty of opportunity to do so!

The bitter man's hollow laugh echoed within his Spartan segregation cell as he recalled believing that he was the world's worst criminal. No matter how careful he tried to be, somehow the authorities always found a way to track him down. It took him a long time to figure out why he kept getting caught.

Throughout it all, Julia also kept her word. Two times Al ended up in juvenile hall, and two times his mother got him out of juvenile hall, sentenced only to a period of probation.

It wasn't until he was seventeen that he uncovered her secret agenda—Julia habitually used the tips line in order to turn him in for the reward money, then she used her influence as a snitch to get her son out of juvenile hall.

How well he remembered the emotional shock of rounding the corner to discover his mother on the phone with the authorities, reporting his most recent break and enter. He'd walked out in anger that night, and he hadn't been home or spoken to the woman since.

Tonight Al reached for the memory of his mother not for maternal consolation but rather for the anger that he knew it would generate— anger that would energize him and give him the strength that he needed to get through the difficult period ahead. "Yes," he hissed while reflecting on his plans to further betray Steve in order to exact his revenge on Ike, "Mother taught me well."

CHAPTER 17

INSANITY?

Sly climbed out of the water and hungrily reached for a piece of fruit from the Tree of Life. Glancing in the direction of the boulder, he was surprised to see that the squirrel was still there, curled up and seemingly enjoying the sunshine. "Hey!" he called out in surprise. "Whatcha doin'? Why're you still here?" He paused for a moment with a confused look on his face and then added, "What's your name, anyway? Do you have a name?"

The squirrel responded in a tone of voice that was obviously appreciative of the question. "Well, yes, I do; and thank you very much for asking! However, the truth is that no human tongue can pronounce my name and no human ear can understand its meaning." Then he smiled, "Nevertheless, you can call me Lucky . . ."

Sly unintentionally interrupted with a laugh. It was a gut-busting belly laugh that emerged from way down deep, and a laugh that he hadn't laughed in many years. It simply struck him as being so damn funny that the squirrel from the shoebox would call himself Lucky.

Lucky recognized laughter as a necessary step in the healing process. Feeling secretly pleased with Sly's emotional leap forward, he playfully feigned that his pride was slightly injured. "Well, I'm glad that I'm able to amuse you!"

Still barely able to control his laughter, Sly managed to squeeze out, "S-s-sorry . . . I don't mean any offense!"

"None taken. Now as to your first question, I'm still here for two reasons. One, like you and I love the sunshine, and two, I know you well enough now to realize that there's at least one more question on your mind that you won't be able to get through the night without asking. I figured I might as well hang around and help you out. So go for it . . ."

Sly seized the unexpected opportunity, "Well, now that you mention it, I would like you to clarify something for me—am I dreaming? Am I hallucinating? Does this place originate in my mind or elsewhere? Is it real? Is this really happening? Please, I need to understand!"

Lucky took the time to carefully gather his thoughts before answering; he knew that whatever he said next would be critical to Sly's recovery. And then he slowly began, "Only you can decide what is real. Only you have the power to define your own reality. Moreover, it is paramount that you always be very careful when you define something as being real or not real. You must have a very good reason for defining something either way. The truth isn't always what it appears to be, and what is defined as being real, or not real, will always be real in its consequences. In that sense, this place is as real or not real as anything can possibly be. That is to say, there are serious consequences to whichever choice you make!

"The energy that created this place originates from the Tree of Life. When you first arrived, the tree clothed you, fed you, and sheltered you. It did for you what you were not yet ready to do for yourself. The tree does for us that which we cannot do for ourselves in order that we may have the opportunity to do what we can . . . to do what we must, if we are to achieve our potential.

"Like I said, you've eaten from the tree. The energy is now in you and flows through you. As you grow stronger in your recovery, you will create in ever more meaningful ways. It's an emotional and spiritual journey that will take you to a wonderful place.

"That's not to say that it's an easy journey. It's not! However, it's definitely one worth taking, and I beg of you to accept the reality of this opportunity."

Sly was taken aback by the intensity and the sincerity of Lucky's words. He responded with equal intensity and sincerity, "So I shall, my friend, so I shall!"

A spontaneous afterthought quickly surfaced in Sly's mind. "I hope that there's a lot of fish in that pond. It doesn't appear to me as though there's a wide variety of things to do around here. I suspect I'll spend considerable time fishing."

Lucky laughed, "There are exactly 153 fish in that pond."

"One hundred and fifty-two," Sly countered, "I caught one this morning."

"No, 153," Lucky corrected. "It has been so from their beginning. They live in the shelter of the tree. Though they exist as individuals, they were created united in spirit for a single purpose. There will never be more or less than 153. I know that you don't understand, but let us just allow this to be the mystery that it's always been.

"The good news is that you can fish until your heart's content. Their numbers will never be depleted. The better news is that, soon you will have a whole lot more to do than sit around fishing. You're very close to the next stage in your healing journey."

Lucky suddenly glanced over his shoulder as though hearing a voice. "I must be on my way," he added apologetically, "there are others who need my assistance.

"You have a fine afternoon. We'll talk again in the near future." Without further explanation, he leaped from the boulder and scurried off to attend to something that was clearly important to *him*.

CHAPTER 18

REALITY?

If there was one type of prisoner that Ike hated more than any other, it was rapists—skin hounds, skinners, pedophiles, baby fuckers. Whatever the term used to describe them, whatever they were labeled, whatever they'd done, for whatever reason, it didn't matter. Ike hated them all! He hated them even more than he hated snitches; and at the moment, he was incredibly irate to learn that a skinner had moved over to the third level of *his* block. Worse yet, this one was rumored to be both a skinner and a snitch!

Phil shuffled his feet and waited patiently for Ike's response to the news.

Ike hesitated, thinking that he should just go down there and send the creep back to the block that he came from, by way of the hospital. "Where's the rat bastard now?" he snarled.

"I saw him heading over to the chapel. I think he's in one of those programs . . . I don't know, some sort of religious shit!"

Ike grunted his acknowledgement and disgust. *Christians*, they were the third category of prisoner that he hated! "Strike three, you're out, *creep*!" he silently promised himself.

"What are you gonna do, Ike?"

"It's not what I'm gonna do—it's what we're going to do. The skinner wants to wrap his arms around Jesus, and I'm thinking that we need to think up somethin' real special to help him accomplish exactly that."

Phil silently began to panic. "I don't like the sound of this," he told himself, "no, sir! I don't like the sound of it at all!" However, he wisely kept his mouth shut; the old convict knew very well that he was only one of fifty prisoners on the tier, two hundred on the block, and that Ike called the shots. Preoccupied with self-preservation, he arrived at the only conclusion possible. "I'm not gonna risk my freedom, my future, or my life by speaking up on behalf of a fuckin' rapist!"

Ike arrived at a decision. He interrupted Phil's thoughts with a hearty slap on the man's back, "I'll tell you what I want you to do—I want you to find me four guys that we can depend on to follow orders, four guys who know how to keep their mouths shut.

"Make sure that they're lifers. Take your time. Pick four big, strong guys. Feel them out carefully. When you're sure that you've got the right caliber muscle, you bring 'em to me and I'll take it from there . . . ya hear me?" Then he grinned from ear to ear as though he'd just presented Phil with a winning lottery ticket.

Ike observed the look of concern on Phil's face; his grin faded a little while he mentally groped for a way in which to alleviate the man's fears. Finally, he continued as though Phil's well-being had been foremost in his mind all along, "Oh, by the way, my friend, there's nothing for you to worry about. I know that you're gettin' out in a couple of years. You just do what I tell you to do, and I'll make sure that no matter what, your name is kept out of it—that you're protected, and you know that you can trust me, right?"

The irony of the situation existed in the fact that Phil's distrust of Ike was precisely the reason that he intended to obey. Phil didn't trust Ike about anything. Ike had spoken as though he was a friend, but Phil was perfectly aware that Ike would turn on him in a heartbeat if he disobeyed. "Sure, Ike," he promised, "I'll get right on it."

With those final words, his stomach churning, Phil turned and quickly made his way back to his cell so that he could vomit.

Ike watched him leave, and then he began to laugh while he mentally completed the script to the horror show that he had in mind, staring the unsuspecting skinner.

CHAPTER 19

INSANITY?

Sly walked away from the vicinity of the tree, intent on exploring the northern area directly in front of his cave. However, as he retraced his steps along the now-familiar trail and emerged from between the two rock bluffs, he was stopped dead in his tracks by a sight that he'd been certain that he'd never see again. There, in the center of the previously empty northern field, sat the ramshackle farmhouse in which he, his grandmother, and father had lived for most of his young life. "It can't be . . . ," he murmured to himself, "it *can't* be real!"

He approached the house with the fixated intensity of a thirsty desert wanderer nearing an oasis that he feared to be a mirage. Drawing closer, he detected a familiar and welcome aroma—the scent of fresh-baked apple pie! Pausing a moment to deeply inhale the memories, he was slightly startled by the opening of the door. There, framed in the doorway, appearing angelic in the gentle glow of the early afternoon sunlight, stood his beloved grandmother.

The elderly woman immediately ambled forward in her unique high-speed gait that Sly remembered so well. Tears flowing, she wrapped him in her arms, hugged him tight, and then repeatedly kissed his face.

"C'mon boy," she urged while guiding him in the direction of the farmhouse.

"Ma," he whispered, "it's so good to see you again."

"It's a blessing to see you as well, boy," she responded as the two entered the kitchen. "Why don't you sit down and have some of your ol' gramma's warm apple pie."

Ma somehow always knew when to talk and when to remain silent; in silence she cut a generous slice of pie, added some cheddar, and placed both in front of her only grandson. Then she sat quietly across the table, giving him the time that he needed to emotionally adjust to his new reality.

Sly took a few minutes to absorb his surroundings—he observed the familiar wood stove next to the wall, wood and kindling stacked within the metal box beside it; the kitchen sink across the room, with its hand pump, ready to produce clean, cold, pure water; and he became overwhelmed by the simple fact that everything appeared to be exactly as it'd been so many years ago. "Everything is exactly the same as I remember it!" he exclaimed in disbelief. "How is that possible?"

The astonished man's demeanor was then transformed by a further memory. "How can you be here?" he added in a subdued voice that echoed the pain he'd experienced at his grandmother's funeral. "You died—passed away—when I was just a boy!"

Ma smiled. "First of all, this is your home. I wouldn't go changing things on you. second, you're only half right about me—I didn't die, *I only passed away*. I went somewhere else, and now I'm here.

"The tree makes my being here possible. You make my being here necessary. I'm all that remains of your past that still anchors you to your humanity. I'm the next component of your healing process.

"Now, Sylvester, why don't you eat that pie while it's still warm?"

Sly reacted to being called Sylvester. "You know I always hated that name, Ma," he mumbled uncomfortably.

"Yes I do, but I've never understood why. Tell me, son, why do you hate your name so? It's the name that your father gave you. It seems like a perfectly good name to me. Why do you hate it?"

"I hate it because it sounds like the name of a share cropper's son!" he answered without thinking. No sooner had he spoken the words than he felt a wave of shame that caused him to look down at the floor, thereby avoiding his grandmother's eyes.

Ma correctly interpreted the meaning of his downcast gaze. "No, boy, don't let the shame defeat you," she urged, "you've allowed that for far too long. Work with it. the best way that I know to change the way you feel about anything is to change the way that you think about. so take some time and think about your father.

"You know it wasn't easy for him to raise you alone. Between the fields and the cotton gin, he didn't have much time for you or himself, but he never quit and he always thought of you first. He worked day and night to provide a home for you. We might not have had the best of food and clothes, but thanks to him, we always had what we needed. Tell me, son, given all that you've seen of life so far, aren't you just a little bit proud to have had a father like that? Aren't you just a little bit proud to carry the name that he gave you?"

Seeing the look on his face, she quickly added, "Now don't you go being too hard on yourself. That doesn't help, either! Apply to yourself the same level of understanding that you're now beginning to apply to your father. Know that it's your years of experience that now helps you to open your eyes to this new wisdom—it's the experience that makes the difference.

"You did the best that you could at the time. All children have status and peer acceptance issues. It's perfectly normal. It's just long past time for you to let all that go. Don't stay stuck in the mud, but don't beat up on yourself either. Choose the middle path, the one that leads to healing."

Sly listened in thoughtful silence, carefully processing each word, then he deliberately picked up his fork and began to eat. He chewed slowly, savoring the sweet fruit and tender flakes. When he was done, he stood up, came around the table, leaned over and kissed his grandmother softly on the cheek. "My name is Sylvester Bartholomew Alexander," he announced proudly, "and it's good to be home!"

CHAPTER 20

REALITY?

Steve awoke to the strange sensation of being alone in his cell. As difficult as it had been to be double-bunked, he'd grown used to the energy of another human being within the confined space, and he was surprised at just how much he missed it!

He was enjoying his second cigarette along with his first cup of coffee when Al appeared at the door. Steve joyfully leaped from his bunk, ran over, and threw a huge bear hug around the younger man. "What the hell happened to you, brother! Come on in and tell me all about it," he demanded excitedly.

Al entered, walked across the floor, leaned his back against the wall near the head of the bed, and slid down the wall until he was seated on the floor beside Steve, who now sat on the edge of the bottom bunk.

"Too much stress, my friend, way too much stress," Al deceptively explained. Then he continued with an outright lie, "I came back to the cell on account of the fact that I forgot my cigarette papers on the bunk. I decided to roll a smoke and make myself a cup of coffee for the road.

"I was about to head off to school when the goon with the attitude showed up. I guess the stress of everything just got to me—I lost my temper and said a few things that I shouldn't have. One thing led to another, and the next thing I knew I was being threatened with mace before being hauled off to segregation."

Steve listened thoughtfully, and he noted that Al's account didn't quite square with Bob the Slob's version of events, but he chose not to doubt his friend. Steve had no reason to suspect that anything was terribly amiss, and he was so damned happy to be reunited with his cellmate. "Forget about it, guy," he urged the young man. "Don't you worry about anything. You're gonna be fine now. You just relax, have a shower, and do what you need to do. We'll have a good talk when I get back from work." So saying, he reached over and patted Al on the shoulder before rising to casually saunter off to the canvas shop.

Steve arrived at the canvas shop, only to have his day promptly take a turn for the worse—the shop was buzzing with speculation as to why Sly had been taken out in an ambulance the previous evening. "NO FUCKIN' WAY!" the devastated man screamed inwardly. "You've gotta be fucking kidding!" However, outwardly he managed to maintain his composure while making his way over to the grommet press in order to begin his daily routine.

Steve thought about Sly intermittently throughout the day; he alternately speculated as to how much time he had, should it turn out that Sly was, indeed, down for the count. With a full month remaining until his next family visit, Steve concluded that he had at least a week to come up with a plan B for dealing with Ike and the boys.

Next he tried to imagine what it might look like to have the South Block crew come after him; the possibilities were terrifying, and toward midafternoon, he began to search for material that he could use to fashion into a weapon, just in case it came down to that level of violence.

His search was rewarded when he found a twenty-inch length of heavy-gauge wire. Steve discreetly managed to use the grommet press to double one end of the wire over twice, creating a six-inch handle, which offered a firm grip, and left eight inches for penetration. This done, he slipped it up his pant leg and into his sock so that he could take the weapon back to his cell and sharpen the point on the cement floor. He felt pleased that he'd managed to do it all without being detected. More importantly, he now felt ready to deal with Ike. "There's no way that I'm gonna go down without a fight!" he confidently promised himself.

Steve refused to allow himself to further consider the consequences of the violence he now anticipated—how it would affect Taba and Shelly. He pushed the issue aside by telling himself that he wouldn't be any good to them dead either.

He wasn't fooling himself; he simply couldn't see a better way forward. That is to say, he felt trapped, and this seemed to be the best of a number of really bad options. True enough, there was the fact that he was becoming seriously angry with the entire situation, and that made violence seem more appealing. Nevertheless, he continued to hope for a miracle—Steve actually prayed a silent prayer as the workday drew to a close, "Please, Lord, let Sly be okay. Bring him back soon. He really is my best hope for getting out of this place in one piece."

CHAPTER 21

INSANITY?

For three days, Sylvester had spent nearly every waking hour talking to his ma. It'd also been three days of homemade food, memories, long walks, and healing. "Always healing," he silently marveled while enjoying the warmth and the crackle of the wood stove. "But that's why I was guided here!" he gratefully admitted out loud.

Ma mistook the comment for a question. "What's that you say, son?"

"Nothin', Ma. I was just thinkin' out loud."

He watched her shuffle around the kitchen while preparing dinner, and he was suddenly struck by a silly memory. "Hey, Ma," he called out, "do you remember how, when I was three years old, I used to cling to your to your leg while you dragged me around the kitchen on your slipper?"

"Do I ever! There were days when my hip was so stiff and sore that I could barely stand, but it sure did make you laugh. My lord, how it used to make you laugh!"

"I had no idea that I was causing you such pain."

"Why do you think that I used to give you that dust mop and send you out to catch grasshoppers? Sometimes I just needed a rest, but it wasn't so bad—hearing your laughter made it all worthwhile."

Sylvester smiled. "I always thought that you simply admired my skills as a great grasshopper hunter!"

There followed a brief period of silence while they both enjoyed the memory. Then Sylvester changed the topic of conversation. "Why is it that we were never allowed to talk about my mother? You know, to this very day, I don't know how she died! Dad always got so mad when I mentioned her!"

"It was cancer, son—leukemia," Ma answered softly, "We didn't have the money to get her the treatment that she needed. It was a slow and ugly death that nearly broke your father's spirit. To be honest, I don't think that he'd have made it, except for the fact that he promised her that he'd take good care of you. He was so lonely after she died, and I think that he was always ashamed that he wasn't able to do better for her. He carried a lot of emotional pain."

Sylvester thought about Ma's revelation for a minute and then spoke in an equally soft voice, "I think that's pretty much the way I felt when I had to watch him die."

"That damn cotton gin," Ma cursed, "sooner or later, those fibers get to everyone who works there! It was a hard thing to watch him cough himself to death like that. No wonder you came back and burned the damn place down."

Sylvester was startled and emotionally shaken by the memory. "I was drunk, Ma," he countered. "I was drunk and I was angry . . . so very angry over what that place did to him." Tears began to stream down his face as all the memories of that night flooded back. "It never even occurred to me that someone might be in there, let alone two kids.

"What were those kids doing in there so late at night, Ma? They shouldn't have been there! They should've been home, in bed . . ."

Sylvester's grandmother shook her head sadly. "My poor boy, you shouldn't have burned the place, and they shouldn't have been there. That's a fact. It was a terrible thing!"

"I know it was, Ma," he agreed sadly. "I'm so sorry . . . so very sorry!"

"I know you are, son, and now you have to forgive yourself. I know I've said it before, but I'll say it as many times as you need me to—give yourself the same level of understanding and compassion that you're learning to give to others. It's time to accept the fact that we were all doing the best that we could. Learn from the experience and move on."

Sylvester shook his head, "To tell you the truth, Ma, I don't believe that I was doing the best that I could. I don't believe it at all, but I accept the wisdom of your words, and I'll try hard to take your advice—I'll try to learn from it. Now if you don't mind, I think I'm gonna take a walk. There's a friend of mine down by the pond that might be able to help me."

Ma ambled over and gave him a hug. "I'll be here when you get back, my sweet boy," she promised. "You take your time."

The previous three days had left Sylvester unprepared for the pain and sorrow that he now felt. He walked very slowly in the direction of the pond; he needed to talk, and he knew that Lucky would be there.

"Hello, my friend!" Lucky greeted cheerfully as Sylvester approached the rock that the squirrel so often used to rest upon while enjoying the sunshine. Then he hesitated, noting Sly's despondent demeanor. Without waiting for a response, he added, "You're sad. Come, sit and talk with me for a while . . . tell me what's wrong!"

Sylvester sat on the grass at the foot of the large rock, placing himself at eye level with his friend. "I was having a wonderful day," he began. "In fact, these last three days have possibly been the best days of my life. Then I somehow got onto the subject of the night that I burned down the cotton gin, and now I feel like drowning myself in that pond."

Lucky nodded. "That's a cancer that's been eating at you for a long time."

"Ma says that I need to learn from the experience and move on."

Lucky nodded a second time. "She's a wise woman!"

"I want to take her advice, but something is wrong. I feel in my heart as though there's a lot more to learn and that I'm just not seeing it. How can I learn and move on if I can't see the whole truth?"

"That, my friend, is exactly what I'm here for," the squirrel assured Sylvester. "I'm here to help you see the truth that's written on your heart as well as the many truths in your life that have been obscured by lies and self-delusion."

Lucky paused for a moment to organized his thoughts, then he continued, "There has never lived a sane man or a women who chose to cheat, steal, rob, rape, murder, commit arson, or any other type of evil who didn't know deep down in his or her heart that it was wrong. But there's a means by which we sometimes delude ourselves into believing otherwise.

"Let's recall the day that you saved my life. Do you remember? Yes, of course you do, but are you really aware of what you were thinking and feeling at the time? Or even what you were actually saying to Ray?

"Now don't get me wrong, I'm truly grateful for what you did. But having someone's gratitude for doing something does not automatically mean that it was necessarily the right thing to do, that you did it for the right reasons, or, of equal importance, that you went about it the right way.

"You saved my life, but you also threatened to bury your friend in a hole in the ground . . . you threatened to kill him! You threatened to kill your friend, and you justified it with the idea that you were saving a ground squirrel—me! Looking back at it now, does that make a whole lot of sense?"

"No!" Sylvester instantly replied, with a shake of his head. "No, and I didn't feel good about it back then either. It just seemed like I had no choice in the matter."

Lucky nodded his head for a third time. "That's the thing about evil—it rarely identifies itself as such. It's extremely rare for a person to say that I'm going to do this evil thing because I'm an evil person and I want to hurt someone. The evil action is nearly always clothed in a some sort of veil of self-deception, made up of any combination of things . . . such as righteous indignation, gang loyalty, revenge, self-preservation, or whatever. In so doing, it nearly always manages to obscure the underlying motives. That's how it gets its power—the intellectual sleight of hand enables people to tell themselves that they're doing one thing when they're actually doing something else, and it often leaves the person feeling as though he or she has no choice in the matter. The end result is always suffering and misery.

"You must learn to strip away the layers of self-deception and to see things for what they really are. For example, what you said to Ray was arrogant, threatening, and abusive. You left him feeling shamed and humiliated. Moreover, to threaten to kill someone is truly an evil thing.

"It probably wasn't even necessary to make such a threat in order to save my life. I can't say for certain, of course, but I'm betting that you could simply have explained to Ray that you love animals and then asked him not to carry out his intentions. Given that he's your friend and someone who has a healthy respect for you, he would most likely have set me free. Either way, you didn't even give him a chance before dropping the *kill bomb* on him, by way of such a threat. And now, as you noted yourself at the time, he's really hurt!"

A quiet minute passed before Lucky summed up his thoughts on the matter. "I'm guessing that you had some serious emotional stuff going on in the background that day."

"As a matter of fact, I did," Sylvester admitted thoughtfully. "I'd promised to help someone with something that was probably far too big for me at this stage of my life. It involved a guy named Ike—a real piece of work that I've butted heads with before. I was feeling old, tired, and insecure. I think that I might have been using Ray to prove to myself that I still had some degree of personal power and I hid my motives behind a veil of righteous indignation, based on my love of animals. Yes, I see that now!

"It was my hatred of Ike that was foremost in my mind." Sly stopped abruptly; then, with an amazed look on his face, he continued, "That's the first time that I've thought about my dinner conversation with Steve in those terms. Up to this point, I've been telling myself that I wanted to help a young man in trouble, but I was at least equally motivated by my hatred of Ike!

"I think I'm really starting to understand what you're getting at. I may or may not have been doing the right thing in choosing to help Steve, but I was certainly doing it for some of the wrong reasons and I was definitely set to go about it in a self-destructive way. I concealed my true motives beneath a cloak of nobility and self-sacrifice, hiding them from the world and myself!"

Lucky became very animated in his response. "Especially from yourself!" he exclaimed excitedly. "That's why evil has so much power, and the only way to neutralize it is to peel back the layers of self-deception. That's what enables you to take control of your life and that's what enables you to really learn from your life experience.

"Now with that new level of insight, why don't you take a day or two to think about what was happening, what you were really feeling and doing the night that you set fire to the cotton gin. See if you can peel back the layers of self-deception that you sense are there. If you can do that, then you'll truly be in a position to learn and to move on, as your grandmother wants you to do."

Lucky could easily see that Sylvester was emotionally exhausted. "Go home," he advised kindly, "you've had enough for one day. I'm sure your ma's got some warm apple pie waiting for you, and we have all the time in the world to work through this issue."

CHAPTER 22

REALITY?

Al was as shocked and dismayed as Steve had been to learn that Sly'd been hospitalized. More than that, he was out and out despondent over what it might mean in terms of his planned revenge on Ike. "What're we gonna do?" he asked, while the two of them sat alone in the cell.

"Don't worry about it," came Steve's strangely calm reply, "I've got a backup plan."

Al's despondency quickly transformed to secret joy when Steve proudly produced his partially completed homemade weapon. "I need your help," Steve stated flatly. "I need you to keep an eye out while I sharpen this thing."

"Absolutely, buddy!"

Al promptly rose and casually stood by the cell door, watching for unusual activity on the tier. Steve used the corner between the cement floor and the wall to hone the tip to a fine point. He worked with long, careful, deliberate strokes, which maximized the grinding action and minimized the noise; he was intent on doing a good job—Abaddon was working its *magic* on his soul. The more that he thought about the situation that he and Al were in, the more he felt inclined to use the weapon. If and when the time came for him to do so, he wanted to be sure that it would achieve the desired effect.

Al grew ever more excited with each pass of the tip across the abrasive cement surface. He'd about given up on the possibility that Steve would ever pack drugs, but he was beginning to see in Steve's new behavior a myriad of possibilities that would facilitate revenge on Ike—with or without Sly's help, this situation was definitely filled with potential; but first he would need to reel Steve in just a little bit more.

He looked over in Steve's direction, took a long drag off his cigarette, and exhaled slowly. He spoke in a seemingly thoughtful, introspective, and casual way, "I'm gonna need one of those myself."

"Why?" Steve asked, feeling slightly alarmed.

"We're in this together, brother. You're the best friend that I've ever had. I can't leave you to handle it all on your own. Besides, those guys could come after either one of us, at any time. I need to be able to protect myself too!"

Steve considered Al's words as he proceeded to wrap the handle of the *shank* with masking tape in such a way that it would enable a firm, nonslip grip. Task completed, he tore a small hole in the foot of his mattress and inserted the completed work into the center of the foam. It wasn't the best of hiding places, but he was thinking that it wouldn't have to be there long. Finally, he turned to Al and said as much, "I have no intention of allowing this situation to drag out—as soon as I have some idea as to what's going on with Sly . . . as soon as I'm sure that violence is inevitable, I'm gonna catch those motherfuckers by surprise. In the meantime, you know where the weapon is. If need be, use it to defend yourself. Otherwise, you just let me take care of things. You've been through enough already. There's no reason for you to get yourself hurt. I love you too, brother . . . you let me do what needs to be done!"

Steve's words were, of course, music to Al's ears. Al was actually hard pressed to keep himself from gleefully tap dancing around the floor; however, in a further display of unusual self-discipline, he solemnly added, "You're the boss, big brother. You know where I stand." Then he walked to the table, rolled Steve a cigarette, passed it over, and held out a lit match.

"Thanks," Steve mumbled appreciatively before flopping down onto his bunk. He flipped on his television set. "Now let me see if I can find something on this damned tube that will help to take my mind off all the bullshit that we've been through in the last couple of days."

CHAPTER 23

INSANITY?

Sylvester didn't go straight back to the farmhouse as Lucky had suggested he should. Instead he made his way up the grade to the cave, where he knew a fire would be burning. He smiled upon entry—it brought him great comfort to see the dancing flames and all that the familiar area contained. He sat down on the stool, tossed a small piece of wood onto the fire, and focused his thoughts on the complicated and interlocking events in his life that had culminated with him burning down the cotton gin.

The first image to come to mind was that of a short-haired thirteen-year-old boy dressed in shiny black shoes, gray slacks, and a long-sleeved white button-up dress shirt. That had been his father's idea of how a proper young student ought to look while attending classes. However, the year had been 1967; his formal attire, set against a backdrop of colorful clothing worn by the other students, caused him to stand out as though he were a being from another planet. It wasn't hard for him to see that his father had meant well. He just wished that his father could have understood how difficult this seemingly small thing had made life for his son.

Social status and peer acceptance were the issues which had plagued Sly for as far back as he could remember. Other students didn't seem at all prepared to accept him as he was. It would have been difficult enough just being a poor, black share cropper's son; but dressed like an FBI agent, he was bound to become a target of ridicule.

Grade 7 had been the worst; there were so many fights, and he'd been suspended so many times that, looking back, he didn't know how he'd managed to get through the year without being permanently expelled. However, it all changed in grade 8 when he tried out for the football team.

Sylvester turned out to be a natural athlete, and football proved to be his ticket to peer acceptance. His presence as quarterback on the field was usually the difference between winning or losing; as a big fish in a small pond, he soon learned that he could actually control the outcome of the games. The temptation of easy money and all the came with it quickly followed; it was a temptation that seemed too difficult to resist, and it wasn't long before he was placing bets and shaving points. The money led to an increase in popularity, girlfriends, gambling, drinking, and parties, which resulted in the need for more money—a dangerous spiral! However, for a while it seemed as though he had everything that he'd always wanted. Then he got caught. Overnight, he once again became the poor black kid that no one wanted to associate with. Except that this time he had the additional baggage of a reputation as a gambler and a cheat.

Drinking and gambling were now an integral part of the man that he was becoming, and he was a better drinker than he was a gambler. He did all right at playing poker—not well enough to get rich, but well enough to make a living, and he decided that this lifestyle was much preferable to that which awaited a share cropper's son. So he dropped out of high school, abandoned Susan, his then-pregnant girlfriend, and spent several years drifting and plying his trade. When he was winning at poker, he had all the friends and companionship that money could buy; and when he was losing, he endured long periods of gut-wrenching loneliness. During such times, he would often think about Susan and wonder whatever became of her and the child.

Once, flush with cash, Sly'd returned home for a visit, just to prove to the hometown crowd that he wasn't the loser that they all seemed to think him to be.

He'd looked for Susan on that trip. Former schoolmates informed him that she'd given birth to a baby girl and that she and her family had moved away, seeking a new start in life. No one seemed to know where they now resided.

That night he'd drowned his memories of Susan in alcohol and he'd buried his emotions within the newly built town casino; it's where the nightmare began, so many years ago—the night he'd set fire to the old cotton gin.

He'd started out early in the evening, feeling lucky, with lots of money in his pocket; but emotions and alcohol impaired his judgment. He tried too hard to win and thereby impress the crowd. By late evening, he was broke. His attempt to borrow money from former associates was rebuffed and ridiculed. "Why don't you see if they'll hire you down at the old cotton gin," they'd cruelly suggested. He left the casino that night feeling lonely, isolated, and ashamed.

Sly had used the last few coins in his pocked to purchase a bottle of cheap wine, and by two in the morning, he'd made his way to the cotton gin—the symbol of everything that he hated.

Throughout the many years that followed, Sylvester'd told himself—and anyone who'd listen—that he'd burned the cotton gin down because of what it'd done to his father. He even bragged that he'd ensured no one else's father would ever cough himself to death as a result of working there. He repeated that lie for so long, he actually came to believe it, but not tonight. Tonight he chose to face the truth. "I acted out of anger and shame," he whispered. "The issues that night were the same as they'd been when I was thirteen years old—it was all about social status and peer acceptance. I was driven by a sense of self-loathing, a desire to destroy all that I hated about myself, my life, and those who'd rejected me . . . my father's suffering had nothing to do with my behavior. I simply wanted to set flames to my old life and never look back, but all that I succeeded in doing was to become an arsonist and a child killer.

"Yes, I need to face the truth, and it's time to accepted myself for who and what I am."

Sylvester found his self-confession to be uniquely comforting; he felt strangely free as he made his way to the sleeping bag where he'd spent the first night in this strange place. He slowly undressed, climbed into the soft bedding, and closed his eyes. Succumbing to sleep, he sensed a change deep within his soul, and he knew that he'd never be the same.

CHAPTER 24

REALITY?

It'd been three days since Ike first directed Phil to find four big, strong, obedient lifers who would be willing to do *something special.* Prisoners of such caliber and description were not all that common, but with eight hundred inmates to choose from, Phil felt reasonably confident that he could achieve the task; and as he watched Alex perform in the weight-pit, he felt reasonably certain that he'd found the first of his yet-to-be assembled team.

Twenty-seven-year-old Alex clearly wanted to be the center of attention; his need was evident in the way that he loudly counted off the repetitions of each bench press, all the way to twenty-one. Twenty-one reps was a lot for five sets, but especially remarkable, given that he was using 205 pounds! The grunting, the counting, and the clanging of the weights resulted in quite a show! It was an unusual display of strength, stamina, and macho behavior intended specifically to impress his audience, and it was working well. Alex beamed his pleasure while onlookers cheered the completion of each set.

Though Alex was only five feet nine inches tall, 195 pounds, he was definitely big and strong enough to get the job done. Phil felt certain that Ike would like him; and Alex resided in the South Block—Phil reasoned that prospective candidates would be much easier to gather for the purpose that Ike had in mind if he selected exclusively from the South Block. He further reasoned that, as residents of the South Block, prospective candidates might also feel more inclined to participate in Ike's plan.

Phil knew a little about Alex's background; he knew that he was serving some sort of life sentence, he knew that he had five years in on that sentence, and he knew that Alex'd won several fights involving formidable opponents—fights that he'd started in what had obviously been an attempt to make a name for himself. Alex appeared intent on convincing other prisoners that he wasn't afraid of anything, and Phil instinctively understood that this would make him easy to manipulate. The only thing that Phil was unsure of was whether or not Alex would do as he was told and then keep his mouth shut about it.

Phil decided to feel him out. "Hey! Alex! Got a minute?" he hollered as soon as it appeared that the young weight lifter had completed his workout.

The surprised man looked out from under the towel that he was applying to the top of his head, and he instantly recognized Phil as a respected member of Ike's crew. "Sure," he answered through a jovial smile that revealed uneven, tobacco-stained teeth, "I've always got time for you good ol' boys!"

Alex meant it; he was delighted to be noticed by anyone directly associated with Ike; however, he was also a little nervous as to why he'd been noticed at all.

Phil suppressed the urge to laugh at Alex's swaggering approach, so typical of young, jailhouse weight lifters. He momentarily averted his eyes in an attempt to shake off the somewhat-mesmerizing effect of glistening sweat on his clean-shaven white head; then he met Alex's gaze with a reassuring smile.

The smile had the desired effect. Reassured, Alex spoke casually, as though he and Phil were old friends. "What's goin' on, big guy? How's Ike these days?"

"He's good! Always on top of his game, if you know what I mean? In fact, right now he's workin' on somethin' special . . . real special, and he's lookin' for some special people to help him out with it." Phil paused a moment, looked around for effect, and then he added, "You seem to have a lot of respect around this place. I'm thinkin' that you might be one of those people!"

Alex promptly puffed himself up like a prairie chicken during mating season. "*Hell yes!*" he replied, "Hell yes . . . if Ike's lookin' for solid brothers for *anything*, I'm your man! I don't care what it is. I'd consider it a right privilege to be of help to you boys! Yes, sir! You can call on me anytime, for anything!"

Phil was more that slightly taken aback by Alex's overwhelming display of enthusiasm, especially given the fact that he didn't even know what he was volunteering for! Nevertheless, he felt inclined to take him at his word.

Thinking long term, he decided to lay down a little bit of cover for himself, just in case things went wrong, "To tell you the truth, I'm not even sure what it is that's Ike's up to. He just asked me to find him a few good ol' boys that he can depend on. But if you're really interested, you come up and see him over the dinner hour, and I'll let him know that you're comin'. How does that sound?"

"Fuckin' fantastic!" Alex exploded enthusiastically. "You *know* I'll be there! Yes, sir! Man, that makes my day!"

The two men shook hands. "All right then," Phil acknowledged, "we'll watch for you as soon as the count is cleared. You have yourself a fine afternoon." Then, intent on walking a few laps before dinner, he abruptly strode away in the direction of the yard.

Phil was on his second lap when he suddenly stopped in midstride, gave his head a shake, and spoke aloud to himself, "Where the fuck do these guys come from? I know there's very few well-adjusted, upper-middle-class kids in these places, but that fuckin' Alex is just too much!

"I swear, when I get out of this fuckin' shit hole, I'm stayin' out! I've had enough of these morons!"

It was the same promise that he'd made to himself prior to his last release, and it was a promise that the Spirit Tree of Abaddon found infinitely amusing!

CHAPTER 25

INSANITY?

Sylvester stopped hoeing the garden long enough to wipe his forehead and sip from the glass of cold, sweet iced tea that his ma had served as a reward for his efforts. She'd been so pleased to see him working to produce fresh vegetables for the two of them, and he was more than happy to do it. The hard work, under the warm sun, with a flower-scented breeze in his face felt good—it produced a profound sense of freedom and satisfaction.

Sly smacked his lips in appreciation of the tasty drink, reached for his hoe, and returned to the task at hand. He smiled inwardly as the sharp blade once again bit into thick, rich, productive soil.

Everything here seemed so perfect. There was lots of sunshine, yet just enough rain to nourish the soil. There were butterflies, bees, and grasshoppers but no mosquitoes or black flies. There were fish in the pond; however, one could swim in the cool, clean water without fear of leeches. In short, the entire place seemed to exist and develop in relation only to the things that seemed to him to be good in life. Best of all, his power to participate in the development of these things seemed to be growing; it had been rapidly doing so since the night that he now thought of as being his night of remembrance and self-honesty.

"How long ago was that?" he wondered, and then paused, mildly perplexed at his inability to answer his own question. It wasn't so much that he'd lost track of time as it was the fact that he simply no longer felt much of a need to be aware of it.

Sylvester thoughtfully surveyed his garden. "Given that this is our second crop of vegetables," he reasoned, "I must have been in this world at least three months!"

Then he laughed. "Why do I care?" he silently asked himself. "Wherever I am, whatever kind of place this is, I'm truly happy. Why not simply forget about everything and stay here forever?" The more he thought about it, the more he liked the idea—not only was he increasingly comfortable living in what he'd come to think of as being Lucky's World, the power to create was becoming a pleasure *in and of itself.*

True, his power was limited; much to his chagrin, he couldn't simply create as he pleased. He'd tried; he'd imagined a bottle of fine whiskey in the cupboard above the sink and hurriedly opened the door, only to find nothing more within than the usual contents. Thus, he'd been forced to concede that whiskey was a want, rather than a need. However, other things did routinely appear.

The appearances always occurred in the way they'd done so on the day that he'd found the fish knife. The things that he really needed simply manifested accordingly—the tool shed out back, the garden equipment, seeds, etc. All these things had been created by acknowledging his own legitimate need, and the increasingly frequent manifestations had each been accompanied by a wave of joy and appreciation.

Though he'd been unable to make the vegetable garden appear, everything that he required to seed his garden was readily available. Apparently, when it came to growing vegetables, he had to do the work himself, and that suited him fine! The freedom, the tools, and the time to do the work was blessing enough. Every aspect of each activity within Lucky's World blended seamlessly into one deeply satisfying experience, and he could see no reason why he'd ever want to leave!

Sly had just finished hoeing the last row when he was suddenly struck by a strange thought. "Isn't the very act of farming vegetables itself a way of creating?"

He pondered this thought while putting away the garden tools, and the subject continued to be foremost in his mind as he took up the basket that his ma had asked him to fill with fruit from the tree. Ma wanted to see if she could make a pie from the sweet fruit, and Sylvester was eager to assist. In the back of his mind, he could actually imagine what such a pie might taste like, and he instinctively began to salivate without being fully conscious as to why.

As he walked the path in the direction of the tree, the issue of the different ways in which people create—in nonmagical ways—continued to occupy his conscious thoughts. "How much power do we have?" he wondered. "How big a part do we play in the creation of the world in which we live?"

These two questions were abruptly displaced by an astonishing event—emerging from between the rock bluffs, Sly's attention was immediately drawn to the sound of splashing water. His Abaddon-honed instincts caused him to quickly crouch near the rocky outcrop. From his place of semiconcealment, he watched in utter amazement as a slender form knifed gracefully across the surface of the pond. The swimmer neared the shore, and a naked woman rose from the water.

Sylvester continued to observe while the unclad beauty waded toward a pile of clothing that was neatly laid out beneath the tree. "Now that's what I call creating!" he heard himself whisper.

He watched breathlessly while she paused in the sunshine in order to wring the moisture from her shoulder-length jet-black hair. Already hopelessly captivated by the sight, Sly was now further mesmerized by the sparkling droplets of water, which formed glistening, shimmering rivulets the full length of her exquisite curves. It was a dreamlike experience—a vision that rendered him completely unconscious of his voyeurism.

Increasingly certain that he'd somehow created the woman of his dreams, Sly shamelessly followed her every move with his eyes; he was nearly ready to stand up and call out when, now fully clothed, his dream woman turned and walked quickly down the path, disappearing into the nearby woods.

The speed with which she'd vanished left him dumbfounded, and he immediately began to doubt his previous assumption. "Where did she come from?" he wondered. "Did I create her? If I didn't create her, who did? More importantly, where did she go? Is it possible that the world beyond the area that I've already explored is populated?"

His thoughts were interrupted by soft laughter—it was Lucky, perched on his rock, obviously very amused. "Tell me, my friend," his cheerful voice rang out, "do you honestly believe that you have the power to bring such beauty into the world?"

Sylvester tried hard to hide his embarrassment as he rose from his place of concealment and approached his friend. "Well, then," he countered indignantly, "if I didn't create her, who did?" He sat down on the grass, paused thoughtfully, and then added, "Where did she go?"

Lucky shook his head. "I'm sorry, I can't answer either of those questions; but I've got a feeling that, sooner or later, you're going to find a way to answer them for yourself."

"You can bet on it!" Sylvester sincerely affirmed.

Lucky became much more serious, "Be that as it may, I'm here this evening to discuss a different subject—I'm here to talk to you about creation from a slightly different perspective.

"Just a short while ago, you were on the edge of a breakthrough in the next step of your healing journey. That is to say, you were starting to think about the nonmagical ways in which people habitually create . . ."

Sylvester couldn't help but interrupt, "How can you possibly know what I was thinking?"

The squirrel shrugged unapologetically. "I know what I know, I cannot tell you how! Nevertheless, I sincerely hope that it won't prevent you from listening to what I have to say about the creative process."

Sylvester nodded his acceptance, and Lucky continued as though the interruption hadn't occurred, "On the subject of creation, I want to give you something very serious to consider, maybe the most serious issue that you're ever going to think about."

He waited a moment to be certain that he had Sly's full attention, and then he poured out *his* wisdom, "Whether you realize it, or not, you are a full participant in the ongoing creation process. You always have been. That is also true of everyone who is living, has ever lived, or ever will live, and it is true of every living thing on this earth.

"It works like this: First the trees, grass and flowers were created, but the process didn't stop there. The trees, grass, and flowers have within them the power to recreate, to procreate, in perpetuity. In that sense, they continue to be partners in the ongoing creation process, and they will remain so until the end of time.

"Likewise, fish, animals, birds, and insects were all created and then given the power to recreate, to procreate. Thus, they too are full partners in the ongoing creation process, and they will continue in the same manner until the end of time.

"Then people were created. As with all living things, they have within them the power to recreate, to procreate. However, they do much more—they recreate socially, culturally, spiritually, intellectually, and emotionally. They do it for good purposes, and they do it for evil purposes. They take steps to preserve these different creations, and they add to them over time, causing their creations to either grow or decline, sometimes transforming their very nature. In one way or another, every single thing that you say or do in your entire life contributes to this ongoing creation process.

"This is just as true when it comes to great works of art, things of beauty, or any other wonderful endeavor to which you contribute, as it is of the violence, hate, and destruction that all too many people prefer . . ."

"Wait a minute," Sylvester interrupted a second time, "how can destruction be part of creation? Aren't they opposite and mutually exclusive concepts?"

"No," Lucky patiently explained, "they're just different ways of creating, for different purposes . . . that is to say, for good or for evil. Evil destroys in order to manifest itself in the world. Good creates without destroying for the sole purpose of being what it is. Evil grows itself at the expense of others. Good leaves room for others to grow. However, both are definitely part of the ongoing creation process in which we all participate.

"Abaddon is the perfect example of evil's power to create—as society's response to crime, the prison is, itself, the result of the harm and misery inflicted by human beings upon other human beings, and once built, it takes on a life of its own. It begins to feed on further harm and misery—the behavior and experience of those who come under its influence.

"Violence begets violence. Fights, murders, sexual assaults, riots, or the like bring about the inevitable changes. Abaddon begins to grow. Better technology is installed. Budgets are expanded. New security measures are taken. High security wings are built. More staff are hired . . . and so it goes . . . and so it grows!

"The bigger and uglier that it gets, the more it impacts on the individuals within. And the more impact that it has on each individual, the more likely those individuals are to succumb to its power, thereby contributing to its growth. In that way, Abaddon quickly transcends the sum total of its constituent parts, becoming a self-perpetuating cultural entity—evil creating evil.

"Individual will is crushed by the overwhelming enormity of the experience: that's Abaddon's ultimate destructive power. However, its growth remains dependent upon the actions, attitudes, and behaviors of all those who are in any way involved or connected to the existence of the prison."

Lucky stopped and looked hard at Sylvester, "Do you understand what I'm saying?"

"Yes, I do," Sly answered softly, "I've lived it for a very long time!"

Lucky nodded sadly. "I know you have, my friend, but now I want you to think more deeply about what you've lived. Specifically, I need you to take a few days in order to consider the consequences of the different ways in which you've created within the context of Abaddon—try to identify your contribution to an evil creation.

"I know it won't be easy, but try to understand the manner in which you are both the product and the producer of all that you have experienced in that terrible place. And remember, it's not always about the things that you've done . . . sometimes it's about the things that you've failed to do.

CHAPTER 26

REALITY?

Phil was seated at a table in the prison library, skimming an edition of the morning newspaper, or what was left of it. Throughout the day, prisoners habitually ripped out sections of the paper—articles that they were particularly interested in. Those who failed to arrive early enough invariably found very little left to read. Such was the case this evening, but Phil wasn't thinking about that. In fact, he wasn't interested in reading anything at all. He'd come to the library seeking a quiet place to sit and reflect on recent events.

The aging prisoner's conscience was somewhat troubled. He felt as though he ought to do something to prevent Ike from following though with his plan. Though he wasn't certain what Ike had in mind, he was confident that it would result in serious harm or death, and he very much desired to avoid becoming involved in either outcome. However, there seemed to be no way out.

The frightened man thoughtfully ran his gnarled knuckles over the front of his balding, sixty-three-year-old, gray head, mentally searching for an alternative way forward. "What choice do I have?" he wondered. "How can I possibly stand up to Ike?"

He recognized himself as a career criminal. Indeed, he'd often joked about serving life on the installment plan, well aware that the joke was on him.

Phil had served more short sentences for small-ball crime than he could keep track of. Deep down, he knew that his chances of getting out of prison—and staying out—were slim and none. Moreover, in his experience, there'd always been prisoners like Ike, and there always would be. Whatever decisions he now made would remain decisions that he'd have to live with upon his return to prison, and survival was paramount. Thus, his thought process was actually shaped by his direct experience of Abaddon's culture of violence and hate. The influence of the Spirit Tree was such that the fact that his participation in Ike's plan was in conflict with what was left of his conscience became little more than a psychological nuisance—something that he'd have to overcome.

The inevitable conclusion now loomed large in his mind. If his future well-being was dependent upon his present willingness to involve himself in violence, then so be it!

The conclusion necessitated an adjustment to his thinking in order to alleviate his nuisance conscience. "Why should I care about what happens to some skinner?" he silently asked himself. "Isn't the world better off without him in it, anyway?

"Sure it is! Killing the scumbag is just another method of protecting women . . . the only sure method of protecting them! Hell, we'll probably all get a fuckin' medal." He continued with this train of thought until all of his fears, misgivings, past actions, and future intentions on the subject were veiled beneath a cloak of righteousness. At that point, he no longer felt motivated by fear and self-interest nor did he feel as though a pawn in an evil endeavor—he actually began to view himself as a knight in shining armor!

No sooner had he arrived at this point of view than another noteworthy South Block resident—a prisoner with the nickname Lefty—entered the library and sat opposite him at the table.

Phil wasn't at all surprised to see Lefty sporting two freshly blackened eyes. Prisoners jokingly called him Lefty for the same reason that a dark horse is sometimes called Snowball or a white horse Midnight. Lefty was a big, strong kid but just about the worst fighter to ever walk into a place like Abaddon; and he was particularly awkward with his left, hence the nickname. Lefty tried hard. He was a lifer, and he wanted to make a reputation for himself as much as the next guy. He'd fight anybody anywhere. However, his unfortunate habit of throwing punches from too far away and blocking those of his opponent with his face tended to put him at a distinct disadvantage.

Phil struggled hard not to laugh but was forced to smile as he greeted the obviously despondent younger man. "Hey, Lefty, how ya doin'?"

Lefty bristled inwardly at Phil's vaguely condescending tone of voice. He cast an appraising eye over the slightly decrepit body across the table, which obviously hadn't been properly exercised in more than a dozen years. "Now here's someone that I don't have to take any shit from," he assured himself, "I can definitely kick this old man's ass!" However, recalling that Phil was hooked up with Ike, Lefty rapidly pushed the idea far from his mind and answered the question. "Shitty, old man, I'm doin' real shitty. I got into it with Dean this afternoon . . . over my television being turned up too loud. I damn near had him beat, but he got lucky! Oh well, maybe next time . . ." His words trailed off, and a faraway, wistful look appeared in his eyes.

Recognizing a certain vulnerability in the look, Phil began to think about Lefty's potential in a different light. The man was definitely no fighter, but he was certainly big and strong. "How old are you?" he suddenly asked.

"I'm twenty-seven. Why?"

"No offense, big guy, but you're a young man. Every time I see you, you're all busted up. I'm thinkin' that maybe you're goin' about things the wrong way. If this continues, you'll be a broken-down old fucker like me by the time that you're thirty-five."

"So what? What do you care?" Lefty snapped back defensively.

Phil chose his words carefully. "Well, I'm just sayin' that it doesn't have to be like that," he responded gently, "there are easier ways to get respect around this place . . . real lasting respect . . . the kind of respect that stays with you for the rest of your life!

"My only question to you is, are you interested? Or do you wanna just keep on goin' the way you're goin'?"

Slightly embarrassed by Phil's words, Lefty took a moment to focus on the pain in his body, and he realized how tired he was of being battered and bruised. "You've got my attention," he admitted in a humbled tone of voice, "I'm definitely interested!"

Having minutes earlier reassessed his own role in Ike's plan and subsequently determining it to be a noble endeavor, Phil now felt less concerned about laying down cover for himself—he saw no reason to feign ignorance as to Ike's objective. "Nice!" he declared enthusiastically. "I'll tell you what, why don't you come over and have coffee with Ike 'n' me tomorrow mornin', right after the nine o'clock count.

"Ike's workin' on somethin'. If you decide that you wanna be a part of it, you'll have all the respect that you ever hoped for. *I guarantee it!*"

"Sure," Lefty agreed wholeheartedly, "I'll be there."

Phil extended his hand across the table. "Okay, my man, I'm outta here. I've got some things I gotta do. I'll see you tomorrow morning, then."

The two shook hands. Phil rose from the table, giving Lefty a brotherly pat on the shoulder as he walked away.

The pat on the shoulder caught Lefty off guard, generating an unexpected sense of fraternal intimacy with the older man. "Maybe that fucker ain't so bad after all!" Lefty speculated, and reflecting on Phil's promise, he concluded, "This could turn out to be the best thing that ever happened to me!"

CHAPTER 27

INSANITY?

Sylvester finished preparing a sandwich for lunch. He wrapped the meal in a cloth napkin, stuffed it in his jacket pocket, and headed out to the southern field. He was anxious to catch one of the half dozen horses that he'd discovered grazing there when he'd looked out the window this morning.

The farm was becoming seriously active with animal life—chickens out back, a milk cow in the barn, and now horses. Caring for all of those animals, as well as working in the garden, definitely constituted an honest day's work, but today he intended to take a break in order to go riding and exploring.

Sly checked the shed for riding gear. Sure enough, he found a suitable length of rope, a comfortable-looking saddle, and a bridle. With all three bundled in his arms, he strode purposefully out to the field to select his mount.

The horses were all magnificent. However, his eyes quickly settled upon a spotted Appaloosa mare that appeared to him to be both energetic and gentle. So much time had passed since he'd last been on horseback that he didn't dare consider the roan stallion with the wild look in his eyes. "I'll get around to you later," Sly promised the horse. "For now, I just need a dependable ride. I'm much more anxious to see that beautiful woman again than I am determined to ride a stallion!"

He was in the process of fashioning a lasso out of one end of the rope when, to his surprise, the mare walked right up and sniffed beside his ear. Pleased and assuming that he'd chosen well, he reached down for the saddle and attempted to place it on the mare's back. He missed;

the nimble-footed creature sidestepped, causing the saddle to fall to the ground. Puzzled, he looked at the mare, then at the saddle, and began to laugh. "I know what's wrong," he admitted apologetically. "Sorry, girl, it's definitely been too long since I've done anything like this."

Sly returned to the shed and retrieved the previously overlooked thick, comfortable saddle blanket. Sure enough, with the blanket in place, the mare stood patiently while he positioned the saddle and fastened it tight. Next came the bridle, which she also accepted without incident.

He hesitated before mounting, smiling as he sensed their unity of spirit. Then remembering that the left side is the right side from which to mount a horse, he placed his foot in the stirrup and hauled himself up into the saddle.

Sylvester had long forgotten the sheer joy of being united with such raw power. His ride was gentle, but she was no child's pony. She was a big, strong, and energetic animal, and each step transmitted the ripple of her muscles throughout his entire body. Twice he walked her up and down the path between the fields; on the third trip, he brought her to a trot, and the fourth trip, they took at a full gallop. Slowing once again to a walk, exhilarated by the experience and satisfied that they were in sync with each other, he then directed her quick, high, proud steps through the entrance between the cliffs.

Sly felt emotionally intoxicated by both the experience and his expanded sense of freedom. His heart pounded with excitement as he crossed the creek on the far side of the pond and entered the woods at the edge of the clearing.

For the first two miles, he relaxed, enjoying the scenery. He was tempted to continue on and explore the densely wooded foothills that preceded the snow-covered mountains in the distance, but he remembered the beautiful woman. He doubted that she would have walked such a distance, if, indeed, she was traveling on foot, and he very much wanted to see her again. So he doubled back to the point where he'd first entered the woods and began a zigzag search pattern that extended twenty-five yards on either side of the path, crossing the path every fifty yards.

Sly's eyes searched the ground for footprints while his mind drifted back to his earlier conversation with Lucky. Obedient to the squirrel's suggestion, he now began to recall many of the different situations that he'd encountered while at Abaddon. In doing so, he tried to imagine how his actions, or nonactions, had affected people, circumstances, and events—his role and contribution to what Lucky had referred to as the ongoing creation process.

He immediately encountered a problem. No matter what he thought about, he could always identify both good and bad consequences resulting from each and every action. True, there was often more of one than the other; however, both were always present, and the outcome was seldom predictable. Even more confusing, he'd sometimes taken the exact opposite decision, in very similar situations, with the result being the same—both good and bad consequences.

Sylvester's thinking came full circle. He once again began to question the basis of his decision-making process. Only this time he realized that the issue was far bigger than simply never knowing when, where, or what he would choose to care about in any given situation. Although it was evident that, in the past, his decision-making process had been entirely dependent upon how he'd been feeling at the time—and that his ever-changing feelings were part of the problem—his inability to foresee the outcome of his choices left him feeling even more confused.

"How can I be sure of doing the right thing, for the right reasons," he asked himself out loud, "if I'm motivated solely by my feelings? And if I can't predict the outcome of my choices, then how can I ever make any decision?"

Sly was surprised when the mare stopped of her own accord. They'd arrived at the point in the trail where they'd first doubled back, and she seemed to be sending him some sort of message. He noted the sun high in the sky and started to laugh. "Is it lunchtime already?" he asked while sliding from the saddle. The Appaloosa seemed to agree as he removed her bridle so the she could graze, and she paid him no mind while he sought a place to enjoy his own meal.

Sly settled atop a comfortable, warm rock that was bathed in sunshine. He unwrapped his sandwich. "That's two big zeros," he announced to the mare before taking his first bite, "there's no trace of the woman, and I have no idea why Lucky wants me to think about this stuff."

The silent companions enjoyed a lengthy afternoon break before returning home. Sly dismounted near the shed, stripped off the saddle, and worked the mare over with a currycomb. Then he released the gentle animal to happily wander off with the rest of the herd.

Ma was waiting for her grandson when he entered the house. "Where you been, boy, I was worried about you!"

"Sorry, Ma. I got up and noticed the horses, and I couldn't resist an early morning ride. I didn't want to wake you, and I was anxious to try and find something . . . someone."

"Oh?" his grandmother inquired with a raised eyebrow. "Do tell!"

"It was a woman. I saw her down by the pond yesterday. She was so beautiful. But she vanished into the woods before I had a chance to speak up and introduce myself.

"I spent the entire morning looking everywhere for some trace of her or some indication of where she'd disappeared to, but I couldn't find anything," he admitted sadly.

"Well, don't give up hope, son. If the two of you crossed paths in this place, it was undoubtedly for a reason. The big picture will reveal itself soon enough.

"Now would you like a late lunch?"

Sly shook his head. "No thanks, Ma, I took a sandwich along with me. It's been quite a morning, and I'm kinda tired. I could use an hour's sleep!"

"As you please . . . however, when you wake up, maybe you can think about gettin' started on that chicken coop we've been talkin' about— them chickens are constantly under my feet . . . plus they're making an awful mess!"

"You bet," he promised as he made his way to his room, "I'll see you in an hour."

Sylvester slept soundly. However, he dreamed. He dreamed a most vivid dream. He dreamed of a beautiful, ebony-skinned woman with warm, wise, passionate brown eyes and shoulder-length dark hair. He dreamed that she stood over him while he slept, and he felt her caress his body.

He tried desperately to move and to speak, but he was unable to do so. She was literally the woman of his dreams, yet he remained helpless to communicate.

CHAPTER 28

REALITY?

Vivian had been a night-shift nurse for thirteen years. In some ways she was a hard woman. She could administer a needle, change a bedpan, clean up vomit, or strip bloodied bedding without flinching. At age thirty-three, she remained very beautiful, but her no-nonsense attitude toward her job, life, and men in general tended to frighten potential partners. She sometimes joked about how often she was "between boyfriends." To date, no one had stayed with her long enough to discover what a truly gentle, loving, and spiritual human being she actually was, and it saddened her to realize how few people there were in the world who were willing to spend the time to get to know her. She was a little bit lonely, but mostly she was tired of the same old superficial attitudes; emotional fatigue had resulted in a decision to remain "between boyfriends" for the foreseeable future.

Abaddon's evening-shift hospital duty guard watched from across the room while Vivian expertly washed Sylvester's inert body, changed the sheets, and checked his vital signs. Outwardly, she appeared very professional; however, inwardly, for the first time in her career, she was actually feeling just a little bit self-conscious—this was the second time that she'd tended to the helpless prisoner, and she'd dreamed about him after the first time.

Her dream hadn't been so much about her patient, at least not at first. She'd initially dreamed that she'd been swimming in the most wonderful of places—a deep, clear, warm pond with a waterfall at one end and a magical rainbow above. The sand had been ever so clean and white, with the strangest tree growing near the shore. It wasn't until she'd emerged from the water and donned her clothing that that she'd noticed the man—someone that she couldn't quiet recognize—semiconcealed near the rock cliff. Slightly frightened, she'd quickly hurried off in the other direction, awakening as she entered the woods, only to find herself safe and secure in her own bed.

Vivian felt self-conscious because she presently recognized her catatonic patient as being the man in her dream.

Curiosity began to overcome her discomfort. She took a moment to appreciate the chiseled features of Sly's distinguished face before whispering the obvious question: "How did you manage to appear in my dream, handsome man?" Gently wiping his forehead a second time with a damp facecloth, she added, "More importantly, what horror has caused you to want to retreat from life in this way?"

The security officer—a self-identified man of faith—overheard her whispers and wrongly assumed that she was praying. "I wouldn't waste my time, if I were you, miss," he declared abrasively, "that one's gonna burn in hell, for sure!"

Vivian was startled by the rude misinterpretation, and she quickly became annoyed by his attitude. "What makes you so certain about that?" she asked pointedly.

The officer failed to notice the warning in her tone of voice; he answered as though he saw himself as being the ultimate spiritual authority on all prisoners. "Because he's an arsonist and a child killer, and that's the only place for such people!" he assured her.

"Well," Vivian countered sternly, "perhaps he's lucky that you're not the one making the decision."

The officer promptly pursed his lips and turned away in anger. Like so many people in the modern world, he didn't much care for the truth when he heard it—not if it contradicted his own opinion!

Vivian turned her full attention back to her work. She checked the patient's chart one last time before leaving, and she noted his name—Sylvester Alexander.

She thought about her unusual patient and the strange dream that she'd experienced as she continued her rounds, but soon the demands of the night shift pushed all else from her mind. It wasn't until she was home, fed, showered, and tucked safely away in bed that her thoughts returned to the man who'd appeared in her dream. "Sylvester Alexander," she murmured as her consciousness slipped beneath a blanket of sleep, and she cried out in delight when she surfaced, once again, in the pond beneath the rainbow.

CHAPTER 29

INSANITY?

Sylvester stopped to wipe the sweat from his brow before moving on to dig a hole for the next fence post. There seemed to be no end to the work on the small farm. First there'd been the chicken coop that Ma had asked for. Next he'd built a barn for the milk cow. Now, on account of the milk cow, as well as a modest herd of hungry horses, his vegetable garden was in serious jeopardy; it needed a high, sturdy fence to protect it from the marauding grazers. As with all of the projects that he'd undertaken, the materials had been readily available; nevertheless, he had to do the work himself, and building the fence was proving to be a harder task than he'd anticipated!

The Appaloosa—which only today Sly'd decided to name Shylow—frisked nearby. She occasionally kicked up her heels, pretending to be afraid of butterflies, all the while watching and waiting for an opportunity to dart into the garden for a mouthful of tender lettuce leaves. Sylvester repeatedly feigned anger, shooing her away, but the truth was that he'd become so fond of the mare that he was tempted to allow her to do as she pleased. Shylow sensed his disposition and appeared to be deliberately teasing him.

Sly glanced up from his work in time to see her make yet another dash for the tasty garden treat. "To heck with it," he mumbled before turning his attention back to constructing the fence. "I'll have this job done by the end of the day. She won't eat the entire garden . . . and I can always plant more lettuce!"

A familiar cheerful voice from atop the most recently installed fence post interrupted both his self-talk and his work, "Hey, Sylvester, why don't you take a break . . . you look like you could use it!"

"Lucky!" Sly happily exclaimed in surprise. "How good to see you again! I've got a ton of things on my mind that I've been wanting to find the time to talk to you about."

The squirrel nervously looked around as though watching for something—or someone—before answering, "I'm sure you do, but time has temporarily become a luxury, and I need you to listen up!"

"I'm all ears!" Sylvester assured him, always ready to accommodate his friend's needs.

Lucky quickly came to the point. "You're progressing much faster than I ever imagined possible," he declared. "That's good, but it's also resulted in a kind of a problem . . . you see, the thing is, particular types of people are always drawn to each other, no matter what. You're growing. You're emotionally and spiritually stronger with each passing day, and such strength is synonymous with personal accessibility. That is to say, though your growth, you've become emotionally and spiritually accessible to others. And as a further result, your ability to attract a kindred spirit has increased dramatically."

The anxious squirrel paused for a moment to organize his thoughts before continuing, "Again, as I've said, that's all good. However, it seems to have led to a complication that I never anticipated might occur at this early stage in your development.

"As you know, you're here, but your corporeal body is elsewhere. Without realizing it, through your corporeal body, you're drawing someone out of her world and into your world in a very powerful way. Likewise, she's exerting a profound influence on you."

"You mean the woman in my dreams," Sylvester guessed.

"Yes and no . . . first, you saw her from a distance, then in your dreams, and very soon she's going to come walking right up that path."

"FANTASTIC!" Sylvester's voice rang out in delight. "That is absolutely fantastic!"

"I hope so," Lucky replied in a decidedly less enthusiastic tone of voice. "To be truthful, I'm afraid that you're not quite ready for this. It'll be very difficult for her to get to know you when you don't yet fully know yourself. Still, I have to accept that things are happening this way for a reason. I just urge you to be very careful as to how you proceed.

"I don't know how long she'll choose to stay, but come on down to the pond and talk to me whenever you need to. I'll be waiting . . . good luck!" So saying, he leaped from the fence post and disappeared into the underbrush.

Vivian took a few minutes to enjoy the luxurious water. It was a strange way to awaken; but not for that reason less glorious. In due course, she emerged from the pond to dress herself in the clothing that she was certain would be laid out beneath the tree.

Sure enough, she found the garments neatly piled, exactly as before—gray pants, black boots, and a white pullover top, of the same type and material that she'd worn on the previous occasion. The fit was perfect. Comfortably attired, she instinctively reached for one of the low-hanging fruit that seemed to invite her attention.

Vivian hesitated. Her practical nursing experience warned her not to eat anything that she couldn't readily identify as being safe, but her instincts trumped her reservations, and she took a big bite. The first bite was quickly followed by a second, and then a third, until she'd entirely devoured the most incredibly delicious meal that she'd ever eaten.

The nourishing power of the fruit immediately began to energize the woman in astonishing ways—her spirit soared!

The moment of ecstasy was interrupted by a startling thought: "What if I'm being watched?" She nervously glanced in the direction of the place where she'd last observed her intrusive hospital patient; the glance was followed by a sigh of relief when she discovered herself to be alone. However, her sense of relief very quickly turned to disappointment as she realized that she actually wanted to meet the man in *her* dream. "I'll bet you're around here somewhere," she declared out loud before striding determinedly up the path in the direction of the rock bluff.

Arriving at her destination and finding nothing, she continued on through the entranceway, emerging within the natural enclosure. There her eyes beheld a sight beyond belief, even for a dream—from a distance, it appeared to her as though a squirrel sat atop a fence post, conversing with a man that she'd last seen in a hospital bed! "Note to self," she whispered incredulously, "remember to request a work transfer to the psychiatric unit . . . This calls for professional help!"

She looked away, and when she looked back, she was relieved to see that the squirrel had disappeared. Bravely she proceeded up the path in order to meet the man whom she'd been caring for during her working hours.

"Hello, Sylvester!" she greeted cheerfully as she approached. "I'm Vivian."

In spite of Lucky's warning of her arrival, as well as Sly's own genuine desire to meet the woman, he simply stood there, speechless.

"What's the matter, big guy?" she inquired mischievously. "Don't you recognize me with my clothes on?"

"Oh wow!" he sputtered. "I'm so sorry about that. At first I had no idea that you were there, and then I didn't know you were a woman . . . I mean, you were in the water, swimming. It wasn't until after you stepped out of the water that I realized . . ." His sentence trailed off as words failed him. Exasperated, Sly opted to apologize a second time. "I was so surprised, I just didn't know what to do, and I'm truly sorry. I hope you can forgive me," he added hopefully.

Vivian accepted the apology and attempted to reassure her new friend. "Easy now, it's not like I haven't seen a whole lot of you as well."

"What do you mean?" Sylvester asked suspiciously.

Vivian paused, momentarily confused. "Don't you know that I'm one of the nurses attending to you while you're in the hospital?" She could tell from the expression on his face that he had no idea as to her professional role in his life. "It's true," she insisted, "I've been feeding, bathing, and watching over you for four days now."

"Four days!" Sylvester exclaimed in amazement. "Really, only four days?"

Vivian misread his meaning. "Well, I realize that it's not a whole lot of time to get to know someone . . . especially given that you're unconscious . . ."

"No, that's not what I'm saying," Sylvester quickly assured her, "from my perspective, I've already been in this place for several months.

"It was explained to me that time passes here differently, but it's still hard to believe . . ." Once again his voice trailed off, this time as a consequence of her earlier statement resurfacing in his mind. "You've been feeding, bathing, and watching over me," he echoed in surprise.

Slowly but surely, the light of understanding began to illuminate the mystery of her presence. "So that's why you were in my dreams," he reasoned out loud, "you really were standing over me, but you were bathing, not caressing . . ."

His reasoning was interrupted by Vivian's sudden outburst of laughter. "Caressing." She giggled. "That must have been some kind of dream!" Then, noting his embarrassment, she shifted the subject. "This is some kind of dream that I'm having as well!"

"Dreaming, sleeping . . . of course!" Sylvester continued, happy to set aside talk of caressing. "That's how you've been able to enter this world . . . you must be at home, right this minute, sleeping in your own bed."

He became animated with excitement. "If more than a month can pass here with only a day passing out there, then overnight out there is likely to be more than two weeks in here . . . if you want it to be? We could have lots of time to get to know each other," he hinted in a hopeful tone of voice.

"I can't think of anything that I could possibly enjoy more," came the woman's unequivocal reply, and Vivian meant it with all of her heart.

CHAPTER 30

REALITY?

Rick was in trouble. His drug debts were piling up; his gambling debts were even bigger, and his family was weary of sending money in order to facilitate his self-destructive behavior—he'd been financially cut off.

This was serious trouble! His family had been his only means of keeping his head above water, and the people that he owed money to were not at all likely to be understanding. The situation invited a risky strategy.

The desperate man didn't owe any money directly to Ike. However, he knew that, one way or another, everything that happened in the South Block was connected to the guy, and he decided to try to find a way to gain his favor.

Rick realized that it wouldn't be wise to approach Ike directly; thus, he opted to first raise the issue with Ike's right-hand man, Phil. He reasoned that if he could convince Phil to put in a good word, he might just have a chance with the notoriously unpredictable skinhead leader. Bearing that in mind, he now walked the yard, seeking an opportunity to speak one on one with Phil.

Luck was with him; he observed Phil, sitting alone, eyes closed, face to the sun, on the bleachers behind the ball diamond. Screwing up his courage, he walked over and introduced himself. "Excuse me. I don't want to bother you . . ."

"Then don't!" Phil shot back without opening his eyes. However, curiosity caused him to look as the dejected man began to turn away. The expression on the stranger's face amused him, and he was bored. "Wait a minute," he called out without really knowing why. "What's your name, and what do you want?"

The strangers face brightened. "My name's Rick, and I was wondering if I could talk to you for a minute?"

Phil looked him over in an impromptu attempt to determine if Rick's request would be a waste of time. He'd seen the guy around, and he seemed like a halfway intelligent individual. "What the fuck?" he asked himself before concluding, "It's not like I've got anything better to do!"

"Shoot!" Phil demanded, "What's up?"

"Well, trouble for me, I guess," Rick admitted right off the bat.

Phil was surprised by the admission, and it piqued his curiosity. "So why are you talking to me?

"Do you even know who I am?"

"Everyone knows who you are, Phil. I'm just hoping that maybe I can get you to help me out with Ike."

"You are, are you? Well I'm just hoping that I'll go back to my cell in an hour and find my unconditional release papers lying on my bunk!"

Rick accepted the rebuff like a slap in the face. "Sorry," he mumbled, "I should've known better than to bother you!"

Phil watched him turn away a second time and very nearly let him go. Then, inexplicably, he heard himself saying, "Wait a minute. You're here now. Why don't you tell me what the problem is? I mean, we're all in this boat together . . . we should at least listen to each other, right?"

A half hour of whining and sniveling later, Phil was convinced that he had the third member of his team lined up; he simply needed to reel him in slowly. "Okay," he interjected in a supportive tone of voice, "let me sum this up. You're a lifer. You're in debt up to your ears, and you've no way to pay."

Rick nodded silently.

Phil sensed that the time was right to bait the trap. "Well then, are you willing to work it off?" he asked with an inward smile, and he was rewarded with the answer that he wanted to hear.

"I'll do whatever I have to!" Rick promised.

Phil quickly donned his good guy hat. "No, brother, it's not like that! We don't wanna force anyone to do anything around here. This is on the up and up.

"Ike's not nearly as cold and mean as most people seem to think him to be. In fact, he can be downright friendly. More importantly, I know that he's working on something right now, and I know that he's looking for people to help him. I can't speak for Ike, but I'm pretty sure that if you help him, he's gonna wanna help you."

Rick's demeanor lit up like a slot machine that had just spun and displayed all cherries. He couldn't believe his good fortune. "I'd love to hear what Ike's workin' on," he declared without hesitation.

Phil wisely concealed his glee. "Now you're talkin'," he encouraged, "and I'd love to put a good word in for you with big guy. C'mon, he's around here somewhere. Let's go and find him."

Ike smiled at Phil and Rick's approach. He didn't know Rick, but he had little doubt as to what was on Phil's mind. The man was good at following orders, and Ike had been very pleased with Alex and Lefty. Both men were going to work out just fine. Now it appeared as though Phil had number three in tow. Ike happily anticipated the conversation that he felt certain was about to take place.

"How ya doin', Ike," Phil called out as they drew near. "I've got someone here that I'd like you to meet. This is Rick," he announced with a nod at his potential new recruit.

Ike grinned and held out his hand. "Hey! Good to meet ya! What's up with you guys?"

Phil eased into the subject. "We were just talkin'," he explained. "It seems that Rick has a bit of a problem—he owes quite a lot of money to some of those good ol' boys down on two and three. I told him that you were sometimes willing to give a lifer a chance to work his way out of a tough situation, if he felt like he could handle it."

He gave Rick a meaningful look. "How about I leave the two of you to talk things over . . . these old legs of mine could use a few trips around the track."

"Good idea," Ike agreed. "C'mon back in about twenty minutes. I want a word with you before they close the yard."

"See you in twenty minutes then," Phil promised as he walked away.

Rick tried to relax. He failed. Though feeling cautiously optimistic, he couldn't escape Ike's intimidating energy; however, he put on a brave face while Ike blatantly sized him up.

The silence seemed to go on forever before Ike finally startled him with an unexpected question. "You ever gonna get out of jail?"

"I don't think so," Rick answered honestly. "I don't have much time in. I'm nearly thirty years old. If I do get out, it'll be so far down the road that I don't think there'll be much of me left to work with, if you know what I mean."

Ike reached over and patted him on the shoulder, "Yes, brother, I know exactly what you mean. That's why we have to take control . . . that's why we have to do what we can to make a life for ourselves in this place. This is pretty much it for the duration. It's all we've got, except for each other!

He let his last comment hang in the air for a moment before continuing, "The thing is, there's a guy livin' down on the third level that really ought not to be livin' with folks like us. Fact is, I'm thinkin' that he shouldn't be livin' at all. He's a skinner and a snitch. Some of the guys are planning to do something about him. If you're willing to help them, I can definitely make sure that all your money problems go away."

Rick took a deep breath. "If what you mean by 'do something about him' is what I think you mean, that's no small thing that you're talkin' about! We'll all be hurtin' *big time*, if we get caught . . . but I'm listening."

Ike assumed his very best "I'm in total control of everything" attitude. "My guys know what they're doin' . . . they won't be gettin' caught . . . not at this or anything else. We run a professional show around this place."

Rick believed him; he was under a lot of pressure, and he made a snap decision. "I'm in," he impulsively declared.

It was all that he needed to say. Ike threw his arm around the man as though greeting a long-lost sibling. The trap was sprung. There was no turning back. "All right then, my friend, why don't you go for a walk and blow off all that stress you've been feelin' this last while." So saying, he reached into his pocket, withdrew a small package and offered it to Rick, "Take these just before lockup. They'll help you get a good night's sleep . . . you look as though you need it!"

"Thanks, bro," Rick whispered as he gratefully accepted the barbiturates.

Ike watched Rick turn and walk away; he noted the spring in the man's step that hadn't been there when he'd arrived, and he chuckled, calling out, "Send Phil back this way, if you see him!

"Oh ya . . . and don't you worry about those good ol' boys—I'll have a word with them before the night is out. I promise you, as of today, you can forget all about your money problems. You're one of us, now, and we take good care of our own!"

"Thanks, Ike," Phil hollered over his shoulder, "this is a big break . . . you call on me whenever you're ready!"

Phil kept an eye out, watching and waiting for Rick and Ike to finish talking. Observing that the conversation had ended, he made his way back to see how it'd gone between the two and to find out what Ike wanted.

"Okay, my man," Ike greeted Phil happily. "Here's what I'm thinkin' . . . and here's what I want to see happen.

"Rick's perfect for this, and I want you to be the fourth man." Then, without further preamble, he laid out his entire plan. Twenty minutes later, Phil came away convinced that he was the lead in something that was going to save the world from the evil of a man that he had yet to meet, and he felt really good about it.

CHAPTER 31

INSANITY?

Vivian's enthusiasm over the idea of spending the next two weeks with Sylvester rendered him befuddled and temporarily speechless. Several seconds passed before he finally broke the awkward silence. "Would you like to come inside and meet my grandmother?" he asked brightly.

Of all the things that he might have said, nothing could have surprised her more. "Your grandmother!" she exclaimed in astonishment. "What's your grandmother doing here?"

"Making lunch, I would expect," he happily announced, "and believe me, Ma's lunch is something that you don't wanna miss out on!"

Vivian couldn't help but laugh. "If this is a dream," she thought to herself, "we're definitely not headed for the hot, steamy love scene that I'm used to." Nevertheless, she suddenly became aware of hunger pangs. Lunch seemed like a terrific idea. "Lead the way, mister," she agreed. "I'm starving, and I truly can't wait to meet your grandmother."

Ma had been watching through the window as the two conversed. She couldn't hear the conversation but was being a wise old soul, and she immediately began to set a third place at the table.

"Hey, Ma, guess what?" Sylvester blurted with childlike excitement as he and Vivian entered the house, continuing without waiting for an answer. "I've got someone for you to meet."

"Oh, and who's that?"

"It's the woman I told you about . . . the one from down by the pond," he announced excitedly.

"You mean the woman you were spying on . . . the one that you went chasing after on horseback?" she teased.

"C'mon, Ma, it wasn't like that . . ."

Vivian couldn't help but cut into the conversation. "You actually came chasing after me on horseback?"

"No," Sylvester insisted, "the horses didn't even show up until the next day . . . but yes, I did go looking for you."

"What do you mean, the horses didn't show up until the next day?"

"That's the way things happen around here," he explained. "Stuff, animals, things—in this case, horses—sometimes they just show up . . . usually right when you need them. I don't know, it's hard to explain. It's kinda like magic. Lucky says it's got something to do with the power of the tree."

Vivian found herself increasingly confused, and questions began to pile up in her mind. "Lucky? Who's that? And what do you mean the power of the tree?"

"It's complicated," Sly admitted. "Lucky—the squirrel—is my friend. I saved his life, and now he's saving mine . . ."

"ALL RIGHT! All right, that's enough, stop right there," Vivian demanded in exasperation. "This isn't making any sense at all!"

Ma wisely interrupted Sly's poorly thought out explanation. "Lunch is nearly ready. We've got fresh garden salad, warm homemade bread with our own cheese and butter, plus I've got some pan-fried fish that Sylvester caught this morning." She hesitated. "However, if you don't like fish, I'll be happy to make you something else."

"I love eating fish," Vivian assured the kind woman, "where can I wash up?"

The small group sat around the table, dining in a relaxed, comfortable atmosphere. Vivian ate slowly while she reflected on three central truths. "I've never felt so at ease," she silently admitted. "No meal that I've ever prepared for myself tasted anywhere near this delicious, and I've never experienced such a vivid dream!"

She recalled her arrival, and the image of Sly conversing with a squirrel atop a fence post surfaced in her mind. "I am dreaming," she reminded herself a second time, "anything is possible. So why should I doubt the things that he's telling me?

"If Sylvester believes that he's indebted to a squirrel for saving his life—and vice versa—then why worry about it? This is more fun and adventure than I'm ever likely to have in the real world . . . why not simply suspend disbelief and enjoy it?"

With both her hunger and her immediate concerns alleviated, Vivian finally initiated further conversation. "What were you doing when I arrived?" she asked of Sly.

Given her obvious difficulty with previous conversation, he thought it best to omit further reference to Lucky, at least for time being. So he simply stated the obvious. "I was building a fence. The farm animals are making a smorgasbord of our garden, and we need the fence to keep them out."

Never one to fear a challenge, Vivian immediately responded to their need. "Well, do you mind if I lend a hand?"

Ma was surprised but favorably impressed by the offer. "What a terrific idea!" she chimed in. "Why don't the two of you work together . . . and see if you can get that fence up by the end of the day?"

Unlike his grandmother, Sylvester felt rather perplexed by Vivian's offer. He hesitated, scratching his head, appearing somewhat foolish. "Is this really how I want to spend the first day with the woman of my dreams?" he wondered. "It doesn't seem to be particularly romantic!

"On the other hand, there is a certain honest quality about the prospect of working side by side . . . and it's definitely a good way to get to know someone—not to mention the fact that I do need to get that fence built!

"Sure," he finally agreed, sliding his chair back from the table. "It'll be fun!"

He smiled broadly at Vivian. "I'll check the shed for a pair of gloves . . . why don't you meet me out by the garden?"

Sylvester and Vivian worked all afternoon on the fence. She worked with efficiency and the practical perspective of a nurse. He worked with the diligence and intensity of the farm boy that he'd once been. They were never in each other's way, but they were always in the right place at the right time. It was a naturally synchronized relationship that good workers on any job site readily recognize, and it engendered in each a healthy respect for the other's abilities.

The job was completed before sunset. Both had truly enjoyed the afternoon. Vivian offered an appreciative smile as they packed the tools, gloves, and leftover material into the shed. "I don't know about you, but I could use a swim before dinner," she suggested.

"Terrific idea!" he enthusiastically agreed. "No need for showers or bathtubs in this place . . . I love that pond." Then he paused, a look of concern descending over his face.

Vivian noted the change in his demeanor. "What's the matter?" she worriedly inquired.

Embarrassment caused him to hesitate a moment before blurting, "We don't have any bathing suits!"

The astonished woman exploded in laughter. "What's the matter, tough guy," she teased, "are you a little shy?" Then she lightly kissed his cheek, turned, and walked in the direction of the pond. "You can wait until I'm finished, if you want," she called out over her shoulder, "but you're welcome to join me!"

Sly felt incredibly foolish. Nevertheless, it took him a couple of minutes to find the courage to follow her lead. Vivian was already swimming by the time he reached the shore. Not yet ready to set modesty aside, he quickly stripped down and dove into the water before she had the chance to see him naked.

Immersed in the soothing comfort of the pond, the two swimmers reverently beheld the wonder and the beauty of their new world. The sun was now low on the horizon, though not quite low enough to fade the rainbow above, and the splashing waterfall played like the soundtrack to a love scene in a movie. The effect was magical.

Vivian dove deep, exploding to the surface and gasping for air some fifty feet closer to the cascading flow. "I could never have imagined anything so beautiful!" she breathlessly declared.

"I never get tired of it either," he assured her. "It's almost as though the pond and the tree are one—I never get tired of the pond, and I never get tired of eating the fruit of the tree.

"What kind of tree is that?" Vivian inquired. "I've sampled the fruit, and I have to agree with you . . . it's incredibly delicious!"

"You ate from the tree?"

"Yes, why? Is there something wrong with it?"

"No, not exactly," Sylvester cautiously explained. "Let's just say that soon you can expect some very strange things to start happening.

"Lucky says that the tree is the source of power for this place. However, all I know for certain is that, once you eat from it, the energy is both in you and flowing through you, and nothing is quite the same— seemingly impossible things simply happen."

"Will it hurt me?"

"No," Sly quickly promised, "not at all . . . no harm can ever come to you here. This is a safe world where you can grow—a place to realize your potential to create . . . to create in many different ways. Be patient, and you'll soon see what I mean."

Vivian considered his words for a moment, then changed the subject. "Well, be that as it may, I think I'm just about ready to see what your ma's created for dinner—I'm starving!"

"You go ahead," he encouraged, "I'll be along shortly. There's something that I need to do on my own. Ma'll keep you company until I get there." So saying, he returned to his leisurely swim, granting Vivian the privacy that she'd allowed him.

Vivian took no offense to Sylvester's claim that he needed to attend to a personal matter. She viewed the claim as a ploy and simply assumed that his shyness necessitated that she be the first to leave the pond.

Displaying no evidence of shyness or modesty, she rose from the water, casually wringing out her hair before wriggling into her clothes. Her thoughts were focused entirely on Sylvester. "Can this guy be for real?" she wondered. "Have I finally found someone that I can respect?"

CHAPTER 32

REALITY?

Wilfred was a rapist. The media record of his behavior was extensive. His entire twenty-four years of existence were now summed up in that one label. No one was ever going to let him forget what he had done, not even Pastor Paul.

To his credit, unlike the others, Pastor Paul attempted to be gentle and helpful. "I'm not here to judge you," he'd said to Wil during their last counseling session, "I just want you to understand why you've done the things that you've done.

"It seems to me that the best you can do, at this point in time, is to make the effort to think about why shaming and humiliating another human being continues to appeal to you in the way that is has in the past."

It was good advice. Unfortunately, it was coming from the wrong person. The well-meaning, self-identified counselor had no real understanding of Wil's behavior, and Wil knew it. Wil was well aware that, on this issue, Brother Paul was way out of his professional depth. It was clear to him that the clergyman lacked the ability to assist in opening up and exploring areas of insight; thus, Wil believed that when it came to his recovery, he was completely on his own—Pastor Paul would have been wise to simply teach the Bible and the healing power of Jesus Christ!

Nevertheless, Wil accepted the pastor's point of view, and Wil was actually engaged in the process of analyzing his own thought patterns, feelings, and behaviors while he mopped the floor of South Block's third tier. However, his introspection was disrupted by the sound of approaching footsteps.

Tim walked by. He stopped a few feet beyond, coughed up some phlegm and then deliberately spat on the floor where Wil had just mopped; he further challenged him with an intimidating look. "Do something about it, *bitch*!" he hissed.

Wil ignored the challenge. Unable to provoke a reaction, Tim sneered, turned, and confidently strode away. In those few seconds, the Spirit Tree of Abaddon worked its magic. The question on Wil's mind was transformed from "Why would I want to shame, humiliate, and degrade anyone?" to "What is it about shaming, humiliating, and degrading me that appeals so much to people like that?"

Sadly, Wil lacked the insight necessary to connect the two similar but different questions. Pastor Paul had not been able to provide him with the wisdom or the skills that he needed to strip away the layers of self-deception and illusion in order see things for what they really are, and he chose, instead, to feel sorry for himself.

Wil knew Tim well enough, and he knew why the man was serving time—Tim'd murdered two teenage girls. To Wil's utter astonishment, he'd actually overheard Tim brag that the murders were the result of a drug debt, as though the debt justified what he'd done. Now, overwhelmed with self-pity and in full victim mode, Wil silently questioned Tim's motives. "What makes that son of a bitch think that he's any better than me?" he wondered before raging out loud, "At least all my victims are still fuckin' breathin'!"

His chaotic emotions caused his thoughts to swirl in an ever tighter negative spiral, and his thinking drew him further into his own personal hell, which was now so much worse than it'd been only minutes earlier.

Wil did attempt to change his thinking and thereby escaped his feelings—his thoughts briefly turned to pleasant memories. Not all of Wil's past life had been a disgrace. He loved animals. He'd worked as a veterinarian's assistant, often spending his spare time as a volunteer at the animal shelter, and the workers had been very supportive of each other. Yet even these memories became painfully reframed within the present negative context.

"Who cares if I've ever done anything decent?" he asked himself. "Everyone loves to hate me, even the people who run this place . . . no one is interested in anything other than the crimes that I've committed! Why? What do they hope to accomplish with their single-minded hatred?

"Surely they don't believe that they're achieving anything positive or that they're assisting anyone to become a better human being—even the workers at the animal shelter had more sense than to attempt to correct the behavior of a vicious dog by subjecting to violence and abuse. So why would society apply such methods to a human being? It doesn't make any sense!"

His line of thinking presupposed that the purpose of Abaddon was to create better human beings, a mistake which only served to further underscored his lack of insight. However, he was instinctively correct on one point: he wasn't going to become a better human being as a direct result of anything that he experienced at Abaddon. What he didn't know—what his present state of mind prevented him from considering— was the fact that, through supreme effort and determination, he could become a better human being in spite of that experience.

CHAPTER 33

INSANITY?

Sylvester emerged from the pond, shook the water from his head and reached for his clothing. He didn't even bother to glance over to where Lucky enjoyed to sit and soak up the sun; he simply knew that the squirrel would be there, and he couldn't help but smile as he turned, proving himself correct. "Man, I'm so glad to see you!" he admitted to his friend. "This has been an amazing day . . . I'm exhausted!"

Lucky nodded empathetically. "I don't doubt it for a minute," the little creature consoled. "I've been watching from a distance. You've been through a lot, and your day is not yet finished!

"However, before we get into that, let me first say that you're doing extremely well. Everything appears to be as it should, given Vivian's arrival. I'm confident that you're going to be okay," he assured the tired man, "but we've still got work to do, and time remains an issue.

"Now, first things first, did you think about your experience at Abaddon, in the way that I asked you to?"

"Yes, I did," Sylvester answered quickly, "but I'm sorry to say that I really didn't get very far, in terms of figuring things out. In fact, all I managed to do was to confuse myself. I tried to imagine all of the different ways in which my actions, or nonactions, have affected people and events, but no matter which event I thought about, my behavior always resulted in both good and bad consequences. Usually more of one than the other, to be sure . . . but always both, and the outcome was never predictable. Even more confusing, sometimes, for no particular reason, I took the exact opposite decision in very similar situations, and the result was the still the same . . . both good and bad consequences. I really don't see how anyone can be sure of making the correct decision in any circumstance!

"The only thing that I am certain of is that my decision-making process has been almost entirely dependent upon how I was feeling at the time, and I know that's not good—that's why the shrinks labeled me amoral."

Lucky liked what he was hearing, and he couldn't help but compliment Sly for his efforts. "Believe me, my friend, you're doing very well. You've figured out a whole lot more about yourself than you realize.

"What you're beginning to discover is that you need something more . . . a value system . . . a way of defining yourself . . . something to both guide your decisions and to help you to evaluate the consequences. Plenty of people live out their entire lives and never come to understand as much about themselves as you now do."

The squirrel hesitated, allowing Sylvester time to absorb his words, then he proceeded to the heart of the matter. "A successful life isn't as much about what you want to do in the world as it is about who you want to be. That may sound simple, but for some strange reason, most people never figure it out, and it's definitely not a process that they consciously engage. The vast majority of the population actually invests more thought and effort into the things they want in life than they do into the development of their own personalities. Jobs, cars, houses, etc., become more important to them than who—or what—they ultimately become; and, more often than not, the result is misery!"

Lucky looked up at the setting sun; it reminded him that time was short. He hurried on, "The reason I'm saying all of this right now is that, from this point forward, Vivian is going to look for ways to get to know you better. If the relationship is to achieve its full potential, you must develop your identity; and you need a concrete way of making decisions—of transcending your feelings, deciding right from wrong, and evaluating the consequences."

"Just how am I supposed to do that?" Sylvester demanded.

"You can start by developing a credo—"

"What's that?" he interrupted.

"It's a word that means *I literally believe* and a practical way of defining yourself. I want you to come up with six to twelve core beliefs. Think hard! Decide on the most important principles upon which you desire to base the remainder of your life—principles upon which to focus and guide your creative energy. Stay away from frivolous, temporary, and conditional stuff. Concentrate on the things that you wish to remain constant until the day that you die, and understand that this is, by far, the most important thing that you're ever going to do . . . far more important than owning a car, a house, or anything else!

"As for Vivian, just remember to put her needs ahead of your own. Don't be afraid to allow her to take the lead. She's much further down the spiritual path than you are, and it will be of great benefit to you if you allow her to help you figure out your credo—that's part of why she was drawn here."

Sylvester laughed. "No problem there. I never seem to know what to do or say when I'm around her anyway!"

"That's okay," Lucky reassured, "as I said before, everything is as it should be. Don't worry about anything! Now go home and enjoy dinner with Ma and your new friend!"

Vivian grew ever more concerned for Sylvester as the evening progressed. Both he and Ma had been excellent company. However, she'd sensed that Sylvester had something serious on his mind, and she worried what it might be. However, with the evening drawing to a close, her thoughts now turned to the topic of sleeping arrangements.

Vivian caught Ma's attention with her eyes. "If you've got an extra sheet and blanket, I think I'll be comfortable on the couch," she suggested.

"No way," Sylvester interjected, without giving Ma a chance to respond, "you take my bed. I'm gonna sleep in the cave tonight."

"In the cave!" Vivian blurted out in disbelief. "What cave? You can't be serious!"

"Oh sure I am, and it's not like what you're thinking. I slept there the night that I arrived. It's a special kind of cave—it almost seems to take care of me . . . it's clean, very comfortable, and I assure you, spending the night there is no hardship!"

Vivian laughed. "I've often thought that every man ought have his own cave. I just never imagined that I'd meet someone who actually has one. Still, if it pleases you to sleep there, I'm sure that I'll be much more comfortable in a real bed . . . so thank you very much!"

Ma listened to the conversation, wisely opting not to raise the possibility of Vivian or Sylvester sleeping in his father's room. She felt reasonably certain that Sly's feelings around his father had been put to rest, but why take the chance? "If Vivian's happy sleeping in Sylvester's bed and if he's happy sleeping in the cave," she reasoned, "then let them be happy!"

Sylvester rose to leave. "I think I'll check on the animals before I call it a night. You two sleep well, and I'll see you both in the morning."

"Hey!" Vivian called out after him. "What're the chances of going horseback riding tomorrow?"

Sly poked his head back around the doorway. "One hundred percent. We can go right after breakfast, if you like."

"I'd like it very much!" she declared enthusiastically.

Vivian lay awake, examining the strange, compelling dream within which she presently found herself when she was suddenly struck by an amusing thought. "I'm dreaming!" she reminded herself. "I'm dreaming that I'm lying awake, examining a dream! How crazy is that?"

Nevertheless, four questions emerged as a result of her efforts—who is Sylvester, really? Why was he so preoccupied this evening? What role does Lucky play in this adventure? And is there anything real about the overall experience? However, the answers to her questions remained elusive.

"Tomorrow!" she promised herself. "Tomorrow I'll ask Sylvester directly about his thoughts . . . as well as the matter of Lucky's role in our lives. One way or another, I will find out what's on his mind and I will figure out what's going on with that talking squirrel."

Then she hit upon a plan that would allow her to test the reality of her dream itself. Sylvester's middle name had not been on his medical chart; the chart only recorded his middle initial, and she felt certain that one of the officers from Abaddon would be willing to reveal this information.

"Tomorrow I'll ask Sylvester what his middle name is," she decided, "and when I awake to my regular life, I'll compare it with the answer that the officer gives me. If the names match, then I'll know for certain that this experience is more than just a dream."

Pleased with her idea and satisfied with the plan, she closed her eyes and slept peacefully within her dream.

CHAPTER 34

REALITY?

Steve paused his morning routine to think about his friend; he was becoming increasingly worried about Al. The young man seemed unusually withdrawn; he wasn't talking much, and he was sleeping a lot during what were normally his waking hours. However, the most perplexing thing that Steve'd noticed was the appearance of a large teddy bear, which Al now kept stuffed under his pillow.

A teddy bear was certainly not something that one would typically find in a prisoner's cell, to say the least! He'd asked Al about it, and Al explained that he'd gotten the bear from the guy down on South 1, who made them as a hobby. Al claimed to be thinking about taking up the hobby and that the bear was both an inspiration and an extra pillow.

Al's explanation seemed reasonable, but Steve feared that there was more to it than that. Part of his fear was based on the frequency with which Al called out in his sleep at night. This was not something that he'd done in the past, and Steve now faced the fact that Al was deeply troubled. However, he quickly arrived at the conclusion that he'd have to wait for Al to decide if—or when—he wanted to talk and that all he could really do was hope that Al would reach out to him soon.

With that final thought on the subject, Steve tossed back his last swig of coffee, butted his cigarette, and headed off to work. Whatever the issues at hand, he still had to earn his modest day's pay.

It was midmorning coffee break when the newest addition to the canvas shop stopped by Steve's work area to introduce himself. "You look like you're set up pretty good back here," the stranger offered with a smile. Then he held out his hand. "My name's Pete. Have you got a smoke?"

Steve chuckled. "Hello, Pete, and yes, I do." He passed him a pouch of tobacco and papers and then watched while Pete expertly began to produce a cigarette.

Pete talked as rolled the tobacco. "I used to work in the kitchen. That is, until two weeks ago. They caught me stealin' eggs and cheese for Ike. Had a good thing goin' there . . . Ike paid me well!" He tucked the newly made cigarette between his lips, held a lit match to the end, and took a long drag, then exhaled before continuing, "All good things come to an end, I guess. Now I have to go back to livin' on prison wages!"

Steve bristled inwardly at the mention of Ike's name. Holding his emotions in check, he spoke in rapid-fire fashion, attempting to keep conversation going. "I've been working here six months now. Been in the joint about eight months. I'm livin' up on West 3, double-bunked with Al McFarlan."

Pete visibly reacted to the mention of Al's name, "Little Al!" he exclaimed in delight. "I haven't talked to him in ages. Me, him, and Ike used to party together a lot . . . we were all livin' up on South 4. It was a good time! Then we both got out. I've been back for about two months. I didn't know that he was back as well. I guess he blew his parole. Strange that Ike didn't mention him. Al must be keepin' a very low profile." He stopped and thought for a moment. "Come to think of it, I can't say I blame him. As I recall, he owed Ike a lot of money when he got out. I wonder if Ike even knows that he's back."

Steve felt his legs go weak. The room seemed to spin. Waves of nausea radiated from the pit of his stomach, and he had to place his hand on the table in an effort to keep from collapsing.

"Hey, man, are you okay?" Pete asked. "You don't look good!"

"I'm all right," Steve whispered. "This kind of thing happens to me once in a while—low blood sugar—I just need a minute to get my strength back. Do you mind if we put this conversation off until later?"

"No problem, big guy! You take good care of yourself, and make sure that you say hi to little Al for me," Pete called over his shoulder while returning to his own work area.

That's all it took for Steve to be certain that Al had set him up from the beginning. His heart broke. He wanted to cry. Then he started to get angry. All afternoon he thought about what had nearly happened as a result of Al's duplicity, and he considered all that might yet happen. His thoughts fueled the anger which grew into rage. "How could he do this to me?" Steve screamed inwardly. "I trusted him. I loved him like a brother. And all the while that no-good son of a bitch was setting me up! He's made a complete fool out of me!"

By the end of the workday, Steve's thoughts had become murderous—he walked determinedly back their cell, removed his homemade weapon from its hiding place, slipped it under the waistband in back of his pants, and waited for Al to return from school.

Al returned from school and immediately found himself in a life-threatening situation. Steve didn't even give him a chance to speak; he stood up and rushed the man as he entered the door, pushing Al back against the wall, ramming his left forearm against Al's throat while positioning the blade under his chin. Steve's words betrayed the rage that had been building all afternoon. "I should kill you right now, you fuckin' punk!" he hissed.

Al's face paled and his voice trembled with fear as he attempted to speak. "H-h-hey, Steve, c'mon, man, what are you doin'?"

"What am I doin'? WHAT AM I DOIN'?" Steve echoed, "YOU FUCK! WHAT DID YOU DO TO ME?"

"Nothin', man. Nothin', I swear! Please don't . . . ," Al begged.

Steve ignored Al's pleading. "You're a fuckin' liar!" he raged. "You set me up! I met your old buddy, Pete, today. He told me all about how he and Ike and you are friends from way back . . . how the three of you used to party together up on South 4. So don't fuckin' lie to me anymore!"

A change came over Al. He slowly exhaled, appearing to physically deflate. His eyes glazed over, and the fear seemed to dissipate. "Just fuckin' kill me then," he urged. "I don't even care anymore!"

Steve's act of aggression relieved some of his pent-up anger, allowing room for other emotions. The ammonia-like, acrid smell of urine reached his nostrils. He glanced down at the pool of liquid spreading around Al's feet. "Fuck," he cursed in a much more subdued tone of voice while releasing the traumatized man. "I don't want this . . . just tell me why you did it?"

Al was beyond explanations. "It doesn't matter why I did it," he countered defiantly. "I just did it. So let's figure out how this is gonna go down and move on."

Steve's anger resurfaced, resulting in a snap decision. "You're moving. I want you out of this cell and off the West Block . . . *tonight*! You go talk to the *man*, right now! I don't care what you tell him—you tell him whatever you have to in order to make it happen. I'm not spending one more night with you in this cell."

Al knew how to get it done on short notice—he suggested to the watch commander that he ought to be given a break, on account of the fact that he hadn't officially reported the sexual assault. "I really need help," he pleaded. "I need to move to a different cell. Please make this easy for me!" The watch commander silently considered the possibility that Al's cellmate had been responsible for Al's suffering, and he agreed to Al's request without asking a lot of questions. It was the closest that he dare come to what he felt to be an act of compassion.

Unfortunately for Al, the only cell open at that particular point in time was number 3 on the fourth level of the South Block—less than an hour later, Al was living at the opposite end of the same tier as Ike.

CHAPTER 35

INSANITY?

Vivian awoke to the most profound sense of well-being that she'd ever experienced. Feeling utterly contented, she pulled the warm quilt tight around her body, gradually becoming conscious of the fact that she'd never felt so safe, secure, and happy.

Casting her eyes around the room, she happened to glance at the dresser against the far wall, and something strange caught her attention. She gave her head a gentle shake before looking a second time. There was no doubt about it—the dresser now had a double set of drawers, whereas the night before, there'd only been a single set. "Strange!" she murmured while climbing out of bed to investigate.

What at first had been slight confusion and a sense of strangeness quickly blossomed into full-blown astonishment. There, atop the dresser, lay all of the usual hygiene and toiletry items that she was normally accustomed to using on a daily basis, and there was more. Examining the contents of the second set of drawers, she further discovered a variety of clothing, which included everything that she could possibly imagine she might require in the near future.

Vivian paused a moment, trying to take it all in. Then she laughed, closed the drawers, picked up her toothbrush and toothpaste, and made her way out to the kitchen. "This is certainly a very detailed dream," she silently acknowledged.

On entering the kitchen, her senses were immediately bathed in the aroma of percolating coffee—Sylvester and his ma sat at the table, enjoying their first cup of the day. "Good morning!" Vivian chirped pleasantly, her bare feet padding softly across the warm floor.

"Good morning to you, sleepyhead!" Ma teasingly replied. "The sun's been up for half an hour. The day's nearly over. I was beginning to think that you'd given up on this morning's adventure!" She rose from the table and walked over to the wood stove, which was already radiating heat.

"What would you like for breakfast?" she inquired. "How about pancakes and eggs? You ought to eat well if you're going to spend the morning on horseback."

"One pancake and two eggs, please," Vivian mumbled enthusiastically with her mouthful of toothpaste while gazing excitedly through the window above the sink at the horses frolicking in the field. There was no doubt in her mind that this was going to be a fantastic day.

"Did you sleep well?" Sylvester asked.

Vivian spat her mouthful of toothpaste into the sink and rinsed from a glass of water before answering. "The best sleep that I've ever experienced in my entire life, and I awoke to a surprise. That double dresser—which last night was a single dresser—contains all the clothing I need . . . not to mention all the toiletries that I normally use on a daily basis. Can you explain that to me?"

"I warned you," he reminded her with a laugh and an emphatic nod of his head. "Strange things happen once you eat from the tree.

"I know exactly how you feel. I assure you, I was no less surprised. I don't really understand what's going on, but somehow we're able to channel the power of the tree in order to create certain things in this world . . . things that we really need. It just happens. You may as well get used to the idea. You'll see a lot more of this type of thing as time goes on.

"For example, I'm willing to bet that when we go looking for riding equipment, we'll find everything that you need, right alongside the riding equipment that appeared when I needed it."

He paused thoughtfully before echoing Lucky's explanation. "There seems to be only one rule here—we must work and do what we can for ourselves. I built the barn, planted the garden, and we both built the fence. However, the materials and the rest of it . . . the seeds, the chickens, the milk cow, and the horses, etc., were all gifts by the power of the tree. To quote Lucky, 'The tree provides for us the things that we cannot in order that we may have the opportunity to provide for ourselves—from each, according to our ability, to each, according to our need.' That appears to be the guiding principle in this wondrous realm."

Vivian picked up on Sly's reference to his friend, seizing the opportunity to find out more about the little creature. "Who—or what—exactly is Lucky?

"I know that you've already said that he's a squirrel, and I even *imagined* that I that saw you talking to one, shortly after I first arrived—but really? A talking squirrel? It does seem to be a bit far-fetched, to say the least . . . even for a dream!"

Sylvester sighed heavily. "Believe me, Vivian, I've many times questioned my sanity on this issue.

"Lucky says that I can think of him as being my spirit guide, and at this point in time, I tend to believe him. His kitchen-sink wisdom, knowledge, and insight have me convinced that I'm sane and that both he and this place are as real as anything can possibly be.

"You just wait until you meet him. I'm sure you'll understand exactly what I'm talking about.

"He's helped me to understand so many things, and just yesterday he got me to begin developing a credo, which he promises will help to both guide and focus my creative energy . . ."

"A credo!" Vivian interrupted in surprise. "Is that what you were thinking about last night?"

"You noticed?"

"Yes, I did, and let me add, that's a very good thing to think about!"

"I'm glad you feel that way because Lucky says that you're the ideal person to help me with it. He even claims that it's part of the reason that you've been drawn here."

Vivian took a few minutes to ponder that thought while Ma placed eggs and a pancake on the table in front of her. "I'd like to be much more to you than a spirit guide's assistant," she silently admitted to herself with a hint of a smile, and she seemed to hear a voice reply, "United in spirit for a single purpose, the two of you will be all that you need of each other, from this day forward."

CHAPTER 36

REALITY?

Ike wasn't all that surprised to see Al move into cell 3. He was disappointed, to be sure. He'd held out hope for as long as possible that Steve would become his newest drug mule, and it was hard for a man like Ike to give up on that kind of thing. However, he presently accepted the simple fact that Al had failed—that Steve had gotten away on them.

Ike now faced two decisions. First of all, given that he'd allowed his name to be used—and in that sense, put his reputation on the line—what should he do about Steve? Second, what should he do about Al?

Ike opted to deal with the last question first. Although it was true that Al still owed him money, that Al had let him down, and that he'd already told Al what he intended to do if he failed to get Steve to pack drugs, there seemed to be little or no value in actually following through on specific threats. Especially when there were other, more profitable ways to handle the situation—Al'd made Ike a lot of money in the past, and Ike could see no reason why he shouldn't continue to do so in the future. With that in mind, he searched his cell until he found all necessary items, placed them in a paper bag, and strode purposefully down the tier to talk to the young man.

Ike entered Al's cell, greeting the young man with the usual put down: "Welcome home, ice queen. How're you settlin' in?"

Al looked up from his seat on the edge of the bed, shuddering inwardly as he faced his ongoing nightmare. "Hello, Ike, how're you?"

"I'm all right," the big man responded in a voice that conveyed a strong sense of evil, "just a bit disappointed that you weren't able to make things work out for us. But here we are, and you owe me money . . ."

"C'mon, Ike, you don't have to hurt me," he interrupted fearfully.

Al's fear caused Ike to warm to the game. "Ah! You're remembering my earlier threats . . . don't be silly! I'm not gonna follow through with that. You're one of us. No one wants to hurt you! You're home . . . and you'll be safe here.

"Don't get me wrong, you will have to work off what you owe, but that's no big deal. You take good care of me and the boys, and me and the boys'll take good care of you. Forget about all that stuff I said about protective custody and burying you in a hole in the yard—I was just lettin' off steam."

Ike reached into his pocket, withdrew a small packet containing a couple of rocks of crystal meth. "Here," he offered, tossing the drugs over to Al, "it's on the house. Make yourself a pipe." He began to turn away, then feigning an afterthought, he turned back, smiled, and added, "Oh ya, you'll need this, as well." So saying, he casually placed the paper bag with its contents on the bed. Clearly enjoying himself at this point, Ike paused once more for effect before concluding the tortuous interlude. "Like I said, Al, welcome home!" Then he exited Al's cell, striding arrogantly back down the tier, stopping at several cells along the way. At each stop, he advised those within that Al was back—that he was ready, willing, and able to take care of their needs and that they were all entitled to credit at the usual rates, payable to himself on canteen day.

Moments later, Al opened the paper bag and examined the contents; it contained lipstick, nylons, and flowered, pink panties. He closed the bag, placed it under his pillow, alongside the teddy bear. Next he took his woolen blanket, draped it across the front of the cell, attaching it to the bars at intervals with bits of wire, in the way that prisoners at Abaddon always did whenever they desired privacy. Lastly, he took an empty pop can and began to make himself a pipe, all the while hungrily eyeing the packet of crystal meth beside him on the bed. "I'm definitely going to need it!" he admitted sadly.

Back in his cell, Ike rolled a smoke, made himself a cup of coffee, and turned his thoughts to the secondary matter of Steve. "What am I going to do about you?" he wondered.

Ike realized that he didn't necessarily have to do anything; he hadn't interacted directly with Steve, and with Sly out of picture, his interest in pursuing the matter was marginal—it never even occurred to Ike that Steve might be contemplating retribution.

Oblivious to such a possibility, he decided that he could assess the damage to his reputation at a later date, and he resolved to leave the issue on the back burner while he dealt with what now seemed a more important matter—the stool pigeon rapist! "After all, a man ought to keep his priorities straight!" he silently reminded himself.

Ike impatiently began to put the fine details to his plan. "This needs to happen soon," he resolved. "Let's see, today is Thursday . . . maybe this Sunday? Ya, that works . . . weekend routine means that the cells will be open all day long, and a skinner Christian oughta die on a Sunday—that's perfect!"

He walked over to the door and hollered down the tier for Phil, then laughingly declared, "It's time to arrange a Saturday night premurder party!"

CHAPTER 37

INSANITY?

The horses were saddled, but things were not going well, or so it seemed. Sylvester'd made the decision that Shylow was best suited to Vivian's needs, and he'd readied the big roan stallion for himself. Vivian had been the first to attempt to mount up. However, Shylow would have no part of it. The agile creature nimbly evading each effort, in the same way that she'd previously evaded being saddled without a proper saddle blanket.

Shylow followed up each failed attempt with a look in Sylvester's direction that seemed to Vivian to be akin to hurt mixed with anger. Nevertheless, it wasn't until the roan softly whinnied and nuzzled Vivian's hair that the situation started to become clear.

Vivian's laugh drew Sylvester's attention to the interaction between herself and the big stallion. "He likes me," she pointed out. "In fact, I believe he's choosing me.

"Not only that, I think Shylow is quite displeased that you've abandoned her!"

Sylvester gazed thoughtfully at the mare, silently conceding that Vivian could be right; but he remained concerned that the stallion might be *too much for a woman*. "He's a big horse, are you sure that you wanna give him a try?"

Vivian swung easily into the saddle before confidently answering, "Yes, I'll be okay. I know how to ride.

"Not only that," she reminded him, "you did say that no harm could ever come to me in this place."

Seated atop the stallion, Vivian felt as though she'd just reached the summit of Mount Everest. Her heart pounded with excitement while the powerful horse waited patiently for guidance and direction.

Sylvester watched as the woman then did much the same as he'd done on his first ride—she walked the roan up near the entrance to the cave and then turned, galloping back to where he and Shylow awaited.

He was impressed with her riding skill; but more than that, a seemingly important thought began to form in his mind. Sly realized that he'd made certain assumptions about himself, Vivian, and the stallion that were obviously not realistic—he'd assumed that a man would automatically do better on the bigger, stronger horse than a woman, and he wondered why he'd made such an assumption. "Horseback riding isn't a wrestling match," he scolded himself. "It's about balance, coordination, and agility . . . and many women exceed men in these areas. It's obvious that she rides better than I do! So why did I assume an attitude of superiority?"

Exhilarated, excited, and breathing hard, Vivian nonetheless seemed able to interpret some of what he was thinking. "Don't feel bad," she soothed, "most men assume that they can handle pretty much everything better than a woman." Then, unable to resist teasing him just a little, she laughed and added, "It's a genetic flaw in men that many women have learned to live with."

"No!" he countered emphatically. "I don't feel bad. I'm thrilled to see how well you ride. I think that you and the big stallion—which you should probably find a name for—are going to get along just fine. It simply occurred to me that I don't want to always make the same mistake that, as you just pointed out, most men habitually make. In fact, one of the statements in my credo is going to be that men and women are equal in all that they do."

It was Vivian's turn to be impressed. "That's a very good statement," she responded sincerely, "and one that makes me happy to call you my friend. Now why don't you mount up and show me how well you can ride?"

Sylvester glanced at Shylow, who seemed to have forgiven his earlier transgression. He patted the sturdy horse's shoulder before leaping up into the saddle. "I'll race you to the pond," he hollered at Vivian before quickly reining his enthusiastic mount around and thundering off to a head start.

The head start was nearly enough, but not quite. Vivian caught and passed them near the exit between the rock bluffs. Seconds later, laughing and gasping for breath, both riders reined their horses to a stop at the edge of the water. There followed a moment of mutual appreciation, which was interrupted by Sylvester. "Let's go exploring!" he invited, beaming with admiration for his newfound companion.

The riders traveled in comfortable silence, following the trail that Sylvester had previously traversed. Vivian was the first to speak. "Tell me about prison."

Her request seemed awkwardly out of context. Sylvester wasn't at all emotionally prepared to respond. He hadn't thought about prison for quite some time, and he really didn't want to think or talk about it now. However, he reasoned that there was probably something in particular on Vivian's mind, and he recalled Lucky's words: "Remember to put her needs ahead of your own." Thus, he took a deep breath and asked, "What would you like to know?"

"What was it like in there? What was the worst thing about being locked up?"

"Prison is a hard place in a lot of ways," he admitted. "The stark conditions, the deprivation, and the loneliness can be difficult. Prisoners miss their families, miss their freedom, and they miss the things that they used to enjoy in life. That's all huge! However, the worst thing, by far, is the way that prisoners treat each other. Through one form of violence or another, they actually make their lives much harder than they would otherwise be."

Vivian gave the appearance of being genuinely confused. "Why do they do that?" she wondered out loud.

"Why indeed!" Sly spat out bitterly. He let the rhetorical question hang in the air for a moment before continuing, "You don't see a lot of well-adjusted, middle-class kids in prison. That's a fact! Prisoners all have serious issues, and they certainly bring those issues to the gathering, so to speak. However, it's about a lot more than that.

"The horror of Abaddon is clearly predicated on fear, pain, false perception, and self-deception. Although many will deny it, the vast majority of prisoners are afraid. They're hurting, and they're behaving in a way that they subconsciously believe they need to in order to survive. Sadly, most are not surviving—they're not surviving emotionally, they're not surviving spiritually, and all too often, they simply end up dead! That's because their false perception, in conjunction with their self-deception, prevents them from recognizing the true nature of their own behavior. I can't think of anyone back there who actually understands why he does the things he does—they're all guided by the lies that they tell to themselves and to each other.

"To paraphrase my wise little friend, evil seldom identifies itself as such. It's routinely disguised as something else. That is to say, it's extremely rare for anyone to simply admit or declare, 'I want to do this or that evil thing.' Instead, they first fool themselves into believing that they're decision is either correct or necessary, and then they attempt to convince others likewise.

"The methods of deception are infinite—self-identified righteous indignation, gang loyalty, revenge, self-preservation, or whatever. It doesn't matter. The end result is always the same—the behavior is then viewed as being both necessary and justified. Prisoners actually convince themselves that any combination of these things are central to their interests, and then they violently defend those interests. That's the heat that boils the pot. Very few ever realize that through their own willful blindness and brutal behavior, they actually create the conditions that often bring about their worst fears, and the tragic result is a culture in which individuals experience exponential suffering."

"Why doesn't someone do something about it?" Vivian asked.

"There are a few who try," Sly assured her, "but they invariably fail. It's simply too big to stop. The challenge for every prisoner is to truly survive—to become a better human being—in spite of Abaddon. That's a reality that will never be altered by the failure of the majority."

"What about you, Sylvester," Vivian asked worriedly, "now that you understand the problem, how will you cope with that kind of pressure when you return?"

Unhappy with the topic of conversation, Sly's thoughts were already drifting in a slightly different direction. "I have no intention of ever returning to Abaddon," he answered reflexively while a new idea began to surface in his mind—it was another potential statement in his credo; he was suddenly certain that he ought to take some sort of a stand against violence.

CHAPTER 38

REALITY?

Al patiently waited for his new cellmate, Stan, to leave. It was Friday morning, the first morning after what he knew would prove to be an unbearable repeating nightmare. He felt physically, psychologically, and emotionally exhausted. The paying customers had been hard on him—they'd all demanded full value for their money.

Hung over from the meth, the young man also felt dirty in ways and in places that no shower could cleanse. He gazed into the mirror above the sink, and for the first time in his short life, he hated what he saw. "Enough of the horror," he whispered to himself. "Enough of skinners talking about skinners. Enough of snitches talking about snitches. Enough of the brain-dead, homosexual jokes. Enough of the violence. Enough of the same old, never-ending pile of shit!"

Stan discreetly watched Al. He was well aware of what the kid had been through; and he hated it. However, there seemed little that he could do about the situation. The older man paused by the door before heading off to work. "Hang in there, lad," he kindly encouraged.

"It's all good," Al lied behind a forced smile.

Stan nodded, silently acknowledging the lie before sadly turning to make his way down the tier.

Minutes later, a uniformed officer arrived on his scheduled morning rounds. "Are you stayin' or leavin'?" he demanded to know before closing the cell door.

"I'm stayin'," Al responded weakly.

"You got a sick chit?"

"C'mon, boss, gimme a break," Al pleaded. "I really don't feel well enough to walk to the medical wing, the school, and back to my cell in order to get a piece of paper that says I need some rest! How about cuttin' me some slack?"

The officer chuckled. "I hear ya . . . I know, the system's fucked! Go back to bed," he urged before continuing his rounds.

Al watched him leave and then once again took up the gray woolen blanket, draping it across the bars as he'd done the previous evening. "Everyone will think I'm using the toilet," he calculated, "or that I want privacy.

"It's nine o'clock . . . the guard won't be around again for at least an hour—that should be more than enough time to get the job done!"

Al didn't bother to write a note. There was no one that he wanted to communicate with, and he doubted that there was anyone who wanted to hear from him. He tore a strip from his bedsheet, attaching it over the bolt and through the slot between the top bunk and the wall. Then he tied the other end around his neck. Next he took a deep breath, permitting himself to slowly relax, allowing just enough pressure to stop the flow of blood to his brain without cutting off his airway. He immediately passed out, sinking into the darkness of Abaddon's cold embrace, and then nothing. There was no panic. There was no pain. He never even knew that he was dead.

At 10:00 a.m., the officer once again began his rounds of the South Block. By ten twenty, he was in front of the third cell on level 4. He pushed the blanket aside, observed the scene, stepped back, and thumbed his microphone. "This is South 402 to 100, we've got a code blue on level 4"—the suicide protocol immediately kicked in. They'd seen this many times before. They all knew what to do.

A reasonable effort was made to resuscitate Al, but it was too late. South 4 was locked down while they took pictures and bagged the body. The whole process took less than an hour. Then everything returned to normal routine.

At 11:45 a.m., Stan returned to his cell to discover that his cellmate of one night had killed himself. "Bummer," he mumbled, pretending to be tough by feigning indifference, "the kid seemed all right to me." Then he looked around the cell to see what'd been left behind. He found Al's teddy bear under the bed. "Hey, guys," he hollered jovially in a further attempt to hide his pain from himself and the others, "check this out!"

One of Al's customers from the previous evening saw what Stan held in hand. His laughter disguised both his shock over Al's death and his own sadness over the realization that he'd probably helped push the kid over the edge. "Hey, give that to me!" he demanded, intent on contributing to the macabre charade.

Desperate to hide his emotions, the former customer took the bear back to his cell, scrounged up a four-foot piece of twine, and used it to fashion a hangman's noose. Next he secured the noose around the bear's neck, walked to the end of the tier, and taped the loose end of the twine to the wall, leaving the bear suspended at eye level. "That's in honor of Al," he declared with a forced snicker. "I'm really gonna miss that kid!"

No one really thought it was funny; however, everyone laughed.

Just then, Ike returned from cleaning the gym. "Al's dead," Stan bluntly declared. "He hanged himself this morning." Ike's face remained blank while his sluggish brain processed the information. Then he saw the teddy bear hanging from the wall at the end of the tier, recognized it as belonging to Al and also started to laugh. "I guess Al won't be leaving me hanging anymore," he joked in a futile attempt to sound clever.

Not a single person present expressed how he truly felt over Al's demise—they each pretended according to what they believed everyone else was feeling, and they were all wrong! It was a typical example of the deceptions and illusions that routinely empowered the Spirit Tree of Abaddon.

CHAPTER 39

INSANITY?

Sylvester often had difficulty in figuring out what Vivian was thinking—her mind seemed to simultaneously operate on a number of different levels. She was a complex woman, perfectly capable of thinking one thing, doing another, and all the while talking about something else. Such was the case today. Vivian was thinking about Lucky, she was enjoying the day's activities, and she was talking about herself, allowing Sylvester to get to know her in a more meaningful way.

They'd been riding and exploring for most of the day, stopping to investigate nooks and crannies while taking the time to pick berries and flowers. It was all punctuated by Vivian's periodic talk about herself and her life. She spoke casually, in her typical no-nonsense, matter-of-fact way that somehow caused Sylvester to feel as though he'd always been a part of it all; and he viewed her approach to life as a lesson in success.

Like Sylvester, Vivian had grown up dirt-poor—an only child. However, unlike Sylvester, she'd always been proud of her working-class parents who'd provide for her as best they could. Her mother had worked as a cleaning lady, cleaning homes for wealthy families. Her father had worked as a handyman, often hauling garbage with his old pickup truck and otherwise doing odd jobs wherever available. It'd been a financial struggle, but they'd managed, and they'd been happy.

Sylvester learned that somehow her parents had found the money to put her through grade school, after which, Vivian had worked her own way through nursing school. Now she earned enough money to see that her parents were well taken care of at the retirement home. She visited often. Their needs were few. They were still together, and they remained happy.

He listened intently while she talked about everything from her favorite color—purple—to the music that she liked to listen to—classical. She was actually recounting her first romantic love when she paused and then suddenly changed the subject. "I want to meet Lucky," she announced.

"I'm sure that he'd be pleased to meet you!" Sly agreed, somewhat psychologically whiplashed from the abrupt shift in the conversation. "We'll look for him near the pond when we get back—that's where he likes to hang out."

"I'd like to know your middle name as well," Vivian added quickly.

"Why is that?" Sylvester asked, for no other reason than to give himself a chance to once again adjust to what he wrongly identified as another abrupt shift in the conversation.

"For the same reason that I want to meet Lucky. I need to figure out for myself just how real this entire experience actually is."

"How will knowing my middle name help you with that?"

Vivian hesitated. She didn't want to ruin the ambiance of the day by bringing to mind the fact that, at some point in the near future, she'd have to withdraw from this world—wake up. However, she couldn't avoid answering. "When I get back to taking care of you in the hospital, I'll ask the same question of the duty officer that's supervising your stay. If the two answers match, I'll know that this is much more than just a dream."

"Well," he agreed, admiring her logic, "I can answer that question and more. My middle name is Bartholomew, and I can also tell you what Lucky is likely to say—he and I have been down this road already. He's going to tell you that you have the power to define your own reality. Inasmuch as you're free to choose how to respond to all that you see and experience in this place, it's as real, or not real, as you want it to be. Then he'll tell you that what is defined as being real, or not real, will always be real in its consequences; and, in that sense, nothing could be more real. In other words, you're either going to learn from this experience or you're not. And either way, the decision will have a lasting effect on your present and your future."

Vivian laughed. "That's about what I'd expect to hear from a spirit guide. But I'd like to talk to him anyway. Why should you be the only one to get to talk to a squirrel? If we're going to be crazy, let's be crazy together. And while we're on the subject, why don't you tell me how you came to meet Lucky in the first place?"

It was Sylvester's turn to talk, and he had quite a story to tell! Vivian listened intently as he told her all about that day—all about Steve, Ray, and Ray's unpleasant plan for a hapless squirrel, who'd nicknamed himself Lucky. "As I mentioned before," he concluded, first I saved Lucky, then Lucky saved me."

Sly's story raised more questions in Vivian's mind than it answered. She decided to began with his last statement. "I see how you saved Lucky, but how did Lucky save you?"

Sylvester felt safe enough to be completely honest. "I was dying in Abaddon—I was confused, blind, and lost in every sense of the word. Lucky guided me here. Then he helped to open my eyes. Together we examined my role in many things, and I was able to discover the true motives behind my own behavior. He assisted me to see and to understand the nature of evil—how we empower it through self-deception. Everything that I said earlier regarding the most difficult part of being in prison is an extension of his teaching. He's the reason that I understand it all in the way that I do. His insight restored my sanity. Equally important, he's still helping me. I think that this whole credo thing is really going someplace that I very much want to be, and as things now stand, I've never felt so alive or in love with life!"

Vivian liked what she was hearing, and she wanted to hear more, "What about your credo, how far along are you with that?"

Sly grinned. "It's funny that you should ask—I was considering another aspect of it just a few minutes ago.

"Listening to myself explain the worst thing about being in prison caused me to realize that I need to make a stand against violence, but I'm not sure just how to work it out. I feel I need to reserve the right to defend my life or the life of a loved one—that may or may not be a good thing—but beyond that, I'm definitely done with violence, and I want it out of my life!"

"Another excellent statement," Vivian cried out in delight. "I'm not sure what to say about wanting to reserve the right to use violence in certain situations. There does seem to be some sort of argument to be made there—it's pretty much the same logic that soldiers on the battlefield draw on—I'm afraid that I'll have to leave you to work it out to your own satisfaction.

"Now that I think about it, you really don't need me to help you with this at all . . ."

"On the contrary," Sylvester countered before she could finish, "I'd never have come up with either statement without you—you suggested the first one by way of your excellent riding skill, and it was through our conversation that I arrived at the second. Thanks to you, my credo is progressing very well!"

He pointed to the trail ahead, "We're near the pond. This is going to be a very unusual experience—you'd do well to decide in advance what you want to say to Lucky . . . I'm guessing that you may find yourself at a loss for words."

As Sylvester had anticipated, Lucky was waiting for them atop his favorite rock. "Salutations, happy people," his voice rang out rang out cheerfully. Vivian slid out of the saddle, leaving the roan—which she'd earlier named Prince—to satisfy his thirst. Sylvester dismounted a little slower, allowing Shylow to follow Prince's lead. Then he watched with intense amusement from a short distance away while Vivian endured her own face-to-face encounter with the impossible—a talking squirrel.

"I must apologize," Lucky confessed while Vivian stood before him with eyes as wide as saucers, "I really should have introduced myself sooner!"

Vivian said nothing; she merely stood there, mesmerized by the sight. Though not often at a loss for words and having rehearsed several questions, speech simply failed her. She'd thought that she'd been prepared, but the reality of the experience was so much more than she'd imagined.

Finally she began to giggle and laugh. Her mirth and laughter continued to increase until tears ran down her face, all the while attempting to apologize for her bad manners, which only made her laugh more.

"Well I'm glad to see that you have a sense of humor," Lucky announced, pretending to be miffed at not being taken seriously. However, he was happy to see her laugh—he knew that Vivian would take him seriously soon enough.

CHAPTER 40

REALITY?

It was Friday afternoon. The canvas shop was winding down for the week. Steve had just stopped for coffee when Pete wandered over. "Too bad about Al," Pete commented sadly, as he bummed yet another cigarette.

"What about Al?" Steve asked suspiciously.

"Didn't you hear? He's dead—he hanged himself in his cell this morning . . . up on South 4."

For the second time in two days the room seemed to spin; once again Steve's legs went weak, and he found it necessary to lean on the table, lest he collapse on the floor. Waves of nausea spread out from the center of his stomach—he literally felt sick with grief.

"Why would he do that?" Steve wondered out loud in a barely audible voice.

"I think it had a lot to do with Ike—I'm sure I mentioned it yesterday—he owed Ike tons of money. Word is that Ike decided to pimp him out to cover the debt. I guess Al wasn't up to it. What surprises me is the fact that Al moved over there in the first place . . . he should have known better! Didn't you tell me that the two of you were double-bunked on West 3? What the fuck happened?"

Steve was in no condition to answer questions. "I can't talk about that right now," he mumbled. "I'm really fucked up—I've gotta get out of here!"

He brushed past Pete, hurried out of the shop and back to his cell where he fell to his knees and heaved into the toilet until there was nothing left in his stomach. Then, trembling with emotional pain and physical weakness, he sat on the floor, allowing the tears to stream down his face.

At first Steve's pain and anguish caused him to see himself as Al's victim. "How could he do this to me?" he complained. "He should have known how much I'd be hurt!"

Then the pain became anger, and his thinking shifted accordingly, "That little fuck never cared about anyone except himself!" he vehemently declared.

Steve allowed the new thought to percolate in his mind for a few minutes before silently repeating the question that he'd already asked of Pete: "Why would Al do that?"

Pete's answer came to mind. "It had a lot to do with Ike. It was the answer that Steve needed to shield himself from the shame of his own failure.

Steve wasn't about to face the fact that he'd forced Al out of his cell and, in that sense, helped to push him over the edge or at least to put him in a very dangerous situation. Nor was he willing to consider the possibility that he'd allowed himself to be controlled by his rage—that he'd been too quick to lose his temper and that he'd acted inappropriately, without bothering to uncover the full truth. No! This was definitely all Ike's fault!

His willful blindness and self-deception continued until, in due course, he'd convinced himself that Ike was solely to blame for Al's death and that Ike was further responsible for everything that Al had done to Steve. His logic was simple. Al owed Ike money. Ike was the one who'd forced him to betray Steve's friendship. Ike was the one who decided to pimp him out. Thus, Ike was to blame for everything, and Ike was going to have to pay!

By concluding that Ike would have to pay, Steve was able redefine himself as well as his role in the entire matter—he was no longer Al's victim nor had he failed Al in any way. He became an avenging angel, seeking justice for his deceased friend, and he actually began planning Ike's demise.

The more he planned, the less pain and shame he felt—a process that promised victory for Abaddon!

CHAPTER 41

INSANITY?

Vivian lay snuggly nested beneath her quilt, counting the days since her arrival. She counted sixteen, and she realized that there was a good chance that she'd soon be gone—that she'd awake from her dream to find herself in alone in her own home. She had no way of knowing if or when she'd ever return, and she was beginning to find it difficult to imagine life without Sylvester. "So much for being between boyfriends," she happily criticized herself before an intrusive question stifled her silent laughter. "How wise is it to actually fall in love with this guy?" she suddenly wondered.

The uncharacteristically introspective woman recalled what the supervising officer had said about Sylvester: "He's gonna burn in hell, for sure!"

Vivian doubted that very much!

Obviously the officer viewed heaven and hell merely as an eventual destination at some future point in time; and it was a view that she disagreed with. To her way of thinking, heaven and hell began as states of being in the here and now, at opposite ends of a continuum. She was convinced that, through their thinking and behavior, people placed themselves somewhere on that continuum, creating and recreating a measure of one or the other on a day-to-day basis, until they arrived at their ultimate self-determined destination.

What she admired most about Sylvester was not the fact that he'd escaped the hell of Abaddon. That was largely Lucky's doing. Her admiration was based on the simple truth that, by changing his thinking and behavior, he'd actually become a much better person; and as a result of becoming a better person, he now experienced something of heaven. What she saw in the man reinforced her own belief that, through their choices, people are in every way largely responsible for their present and future well-being, and his happiness was proof enough to her that the officer had been completely wrong in his assessment of Sylvester's ultimate destination. Nevertheless, she still wondered, "What will happen if he ever returns to Abaddon?"

Though Sylvester'd clearly stated that he'd never return to prison, the question lingered.

He'd talked a lot about his life in Abaddon as well as his past, and he'd talked even more about the things that he was now learning. Vivian felt that she had a pretty good grasp of who—and what—he'd been in his youth, and she also felt that she had an equally good grasp of who— and what—he is now. The differences were easy for her to compare and contrast, and she very much appreciated what she was seeing. Yet the question reframed itself, surfacing in her mind a second time: "How much will his changes mean outside of what Lucky refers to as our little bit of extra space?"

Vivian thought about this for a long time. Being no fool, she understood the power and the effect of social, cultural, and psychological pressures. However, after careful consideration, she felt certain that Sylvester would continue to be who he is—the man that he'd become— no matter what the circumstance. She concluded that, from this day forward, whatever the context, she wanted the two of them to remain united in spirit, creating, recreating, and sharing their own small measure of heaven.

Satisfied with her decision, she closed her eyes and invited sleep; however, sleep remained elusive. Vivian lay tossing and turning until she could stand it no longer. Then, reminding herself that her stay in this wonderful place was likely about to come to an end and that she might never be able to return, she rose from her bed, dressed, and made her way to the cave.

Sylvester lay bundled comfortably within his familiar sleeping accommodations, silently observing the slightly hypnotic patterns cast upon the cavern walls by the dancing flames of his lively campfire, while he once again pondered the reality of Abaddon.

He meditated on the culture of hate that permanently anchored prisoners to their past transgressions.

Sly was willing to face the fact that, within the context of Abaddon, he was, is, and would always be considered nothing other than an arsonist and a murderer. He understood why the authorities maintained this stance—it remained necessary in order to justify their own agenda. However, even with his new understanding of Abaddon's culture—or perhaps because of it—he found it increasingly difficult to accept the way in which prisoners continued to treat each other.

He recalled Vivian's question: "Why doesn't someone do something about it?" and he felt unhappy with the answer that he'd given; it felt cowardly to simply give up without trying, no matter what the odds. So now he wondered, "Is there something—anything—that I can say or do about it? Is there any way to help prisoners peel back the layers of illusion and self-deception? Is it possible to help them to see and to understand what they're doing, why they're doing it, and the effect of their behavior on each other?

"Surely there are others willing—and wanting—to break their chains in order to free themselves," he assured himself. "I've been fortunate . . . I met Lucky. But what about those who perceive themselves as being alone? How can I help them?"

"Maybe you should write a book?" the same strangely familiar yet unidentifiable voice that'd once commanded him forward onto the path to Lucky's World now simultaneously asked, suggested, and encouraged.

The voice shocked Sylvester out of his meditative state, and his attention was immediately diverted by the sound of approaching footsteps. He glanced up in time to see Vivian enter the cave.

The surprised man watched wordlessly as Vivian paused near the fire, seductively turning to face him while slowly beginning to disrobe. Her eyes mirrored the flames, which also illuminated her satin skin. Time seemed to stand still. Her beauty and the intensity of the moment took his breath away. Sly hesitantly closed his eyes, desiring only to capture and preserve the mental image. However, when he looked again, she was gone.

CHAPTER 42

REALITY?

Vivian awoke to the sound of her alarm clock. "You've got to be kidding me!" she cried out in disappointment while stabbing her finger at the snooze button. "Oh Lord, not now . . . don't let me wake up now! Please, please let me go back to sleep!" However, it was already too late—she was awake, and there would be no immediate return to Lucky's World.

Reluctantly accepting the situation, she glanced again at the clock, noting that there remained a little over an hour before the start of her night shift at the hospital; and the thought of Sylvester resting unconscious in his bed roused her to action—Vivian very much desired to be the one attending to his needs.

Arriving at work ten minutes early, she began her nightly duties in an entirely professional manner. One by one, Vivian visited each patient on her list. Although she was anxious to see Sylvester, the well-trained nurse in her allowed no shortcuts. Each patient received due care and attention with her typical attentive bedside manner until she finally arrived at her much anticipated destination.

Vivian hesitated outside the door, unsure what to expect. Then she steeled herself and breezed into the room in her usual no-nonsense manner.

Sylvester remained in exactly the same state that he'd been during her previous shift. Her own heart pounded while she checked his vital signs, his medical chart, and then attended to his hygienic needs.

Completing her assorted tasks, Vivian casually glanced a second time at Sly's chart. "That's strange," she commented in a voice just loud enough to gain the attention of the sleepy, bored security officer, "someone failed to properly record this man's name . . . there's only an initial!

"You don't happen to know what his middle name is, do you?" she inquired in an offhand manner."

Happy to be helpful, the officer compliantly flipped through his paperwork. "Bartholomew," he responded, thinking nothing untoward of the request, "his middle name is Bartholomew."

"Thank you," Vivian softly replied, diligently jotting down the information while carefully concealing her emotional turmoil over the fact that it matched the name Sylvester'd given while they'd been together in Lucky's World. Her outward appearance suggested nothing other than efficiency. She replaced the chart and turned to leave. "Have yourself a fine evening!" she urged with a smile.

The astonished nurse reached the hallway before partially losing her composure, whereupon she gasped and sagged against the wall. "So it is all real!" she silently admitted in stunned disbelief. "I've actually shared an alternate reality with a catatonic patient! It seems impossible, but there's no other way that I could have known his name—it has to be genuine experience!

"So what do I do now?" Vivian wondered. "Should I laugh, cheer, or cry with happiness? Maybe I need to do all three?"

Feeling at a loss as to how to react, her thoughts refocused on her present responsibilities. "If I'm gonna flake out emotionally, it'll have to be later," she self-scolded, "I have a shift to complete!" Then, forcing all else from her mind, she straightened up, took a deep breath, and resumed her nightly duties.

Vivian waited until her meal break before allowing herself time to ponder the implications of the fact that what she'd first felt inclined to believe to be an unusually detailed dream had, indeed, turned out to be an alternate reality.

The discovery raised many questions. "What does it mean in terms of my life here in this world?" she wondered. "Will I ever return see Sylvester? Will he ever return to this world? What about his body . . . what happens to him in Lucky's World if he dies in this world?" The questions piled up until her head began to ache.

Vivian went to sleep early Saturday morning, wishing with all of her heart to surface, once again, in the pond beneath the rainbow. She awoke Saturday evening with no memory of anything in between. Although she tried to console herself with the thought "Sometimes a girl just has to get some sleep," it simply wasn't enough to set her mind at ease—she remained haunted by questions. "What if I can't return to his world? Is there some way that I can compel him to return to my world? Should I even try? Do I really want to see him in Abaddon? Would having him in prison truly bring him any closer? Isn't his happiness as important—if not more so—than my own? What would he want?"

The last question was the only question that she honestly felt able to answer. Certain that Sylvester would want to be with her, no matter what the circumstance and aware that she felt the same, she promised herself, "If I ever get back to his world, I won't waste the opportunity—Sylvester and I are going to have a very long talk, and we're going to figure out a way to be together."

CHAPTER 43

INSANITY?

Vivian's sudden departure left Sylvester feeling despondent for the first time since he'd followed Lucky, and his feelings of sadness had lingered in the back of his mind for the entire month that he'd been waiting, hoping for her to return. In an effort to stop feeling sorry for himself, he now focused on all that he had to be grateful for, compared to those that he'd left behind at Abaddon, and it wasn't long before Steve emerged foremost in his thoughts. "Here I am, safe and secure with unimaginable resources," he silently admitted, "and I left that guy alone, in a real tough spot. At the very least, I should be grateful for the opportunity to live without fear . . . with or without Vivian's company!"

Sly's efforts succeeded in alleviating his self-pity; however, they also resulted in an unintended consequence—recalling the nature of his conversation with Steve, he was unexpectedly struck by alternating waves of guilt and shame. "I pretty much promised the guy that I'd help him out," he further admitted. "Now he's on his own, and it's very likely that Ike'll tear him to pieces!"

He slowly shook his head, "That doesn't seem right . . . it doesn't seem right at all—a decent man would keep his word!"

Sylvester wondered again about Vivian's well-being. Although he'd dealt with his self-pity, he still felt lonely. He'd dreamed about her twice, each time sensing that she was somehow nearby; and each time he'd awakened, laughingly recalling how she'd teased him about such dreams. "I'll bet she's as lonely as I am," he assured himself. "I ought to be out there with her!"

Then the two thoughts fused into one—"I ought be out there with her and I ought to keep my word to Steve!"

The single thought resonated deep within his being while he casually walked the enclave surrounding the farmhouse, examining the many different types of fruit trees that'd recently appeared at the base of the rock bluff.

"Why so pensive, big guy?" came Lucky's cheerful voice from the lower branch of a nearby cherry tree. "What's on your mind?"

"Hey, Lucky, how're you doin'?"

"I'm well, but you look as though you need somebody to talk to . . . you wanna chat?"

Sylvester knew that there was no use in lying—the little guy had an uncanny way of knowing things. It was almost as though he could see right into Sylvester's soul. So he decided to come straight to the point. "I'm feeling like I have to go back to Abaddon in order to keep my promise to Steve and to be closer to Vivian," he blurted.

Lucky noted the strain in Sylvester's voice. As usual, he took his time before answering. "I hear what you're saying," he kindly consoled, "but I think that you need to try harder to listen to yourself. You say that you feel as though *you have to return*. That's something very different than saying that *you want to return*.

"Why do you feel this way? Your reasons for doing things are as important—if not more important—than the things that you do. Right thought must be paired with right action in order to produce the right result. Feeling that you have to do something, as opposed to feeling that you want to do something, usually signals that you're either doing the wrong thing or that you're doing the right thing for the wrong reasons. Guilt, shame, and loneliness are seldom good reasons for anything.

"I understand that you're lonely, and I know it's not good for anyone to be alone. However, staying here for a while longer may be the better option—for you and for them. I don't want to hurt your feelings, but I don't think that you're strong enough yet to survive emotionally or spiritually in Abaddon. I'm not sure that you could survive at all. Your commitment to nonviolence, admirable though it is, has yet to be paired with an alternate defense strategy. Other prisoners aren't going to stop being who—and what—they are just because you've decided that you don't want violence in your life. How do you imagine that you're going to be able to help Steve?"

Sylvester listened. He'd spent enough time in Abaddon to recognize the truth in Lucky's words, and he was surprised at himself for not considering things from the same perspective. He'd been so proud of the first two statements in his credo—and so busy patting himself on the back for pleasing Vivian—that he hadn't even thought about the practical application of either. It was one thing to adopt a commitment to nonviolence in a place where the commitment would never be challenged; it was something else entirely to attempt to live that commitment in a hostile environment where it would be challenged often. "You're absolutely right," he agreed. "I might not survive in Abaddon at this point in time, and I likely wouldn't be any help to Steve at all!"

"How'd you get to be so wise, my friend?"

Lucky laughed. "I'm not as wise as I often appear," he countered honestly. "I've been known to get into trouble from time to time. You might recall the situation that I was in when we first met, and I've encountered many more difficulties, but I've also been around what seems like forever. I've learned to listen to others and to try to learn from my mistakes. That's really the best that any of us can hope to do!"

Lucky pointedly surveyed their surroundings before summing up his opinion. "This is a beautiful, safe place. It's well suited to your learning needs. You're progressing nicely. I believe that you should stay until such time as you feel that you actually want to leave.

"If you choose to stay, you can take heart in the certainty that Vivian will be back . . ."

"Are you sure?" Sylvester interrupted excitedly. "Will she really be back? When?"

"The answer to the first question is yes. As to the last question, I cannot say!"

Sylvester looked hard at Lucky, wondering if he might pry more information out of him. "I've noticed that you often say, 'I cannot say,' rather than 'I do not know.' Why is that?"

Lucky felt delighted with Sylvester's insight but not at all inclined to enlighten his student any further. "Yes, indeed," he happily observed, "you're learning, and you're also getting to know me a bit too well. Let's just say that I like to be honest and leave it at that—at least for now."

Sylvester accepted the answer and nodded his agreement. "If Vivian's going to return and if I'm of no help to Steve, then I've everything to lose and nothing to gain by leaving," he reasoned out loud.

"In fact, I'd be crazy to leave!" he concluded, completely forgetting that he was talking to a squirrel.

CHAPTER 44

REALITY?

Phil, Rick, Lefty. and Alex arrived within minutes of each other at Ike's cell. It was eight thirty, Sunday morning. The premurder party had commenced after dinner the previous evening, and they'd been smoking crystal meth throughout the night. All four were very high and extremely tense with excitement.

Ike felt powerful and in complete control; he adopted the attitude and demeanor of an army general planning the invasion of enemy territory. "All right!" he spoke loudly in order to gain their attention. "You guys already know how I want the murder to go down. Let's review the preliminaries and the aftermath.

"First, you're all gonna go quietly back to your cells and wait until the guard completes his 9:00 a.m. rounds. As soon as he's finished, you'll individually head for level 3, meeting up at the front of the tier. Then you go straight into the skinner's cell—fast—and get it done.

"They won't find the body until noon, which gives you plenty of time to clean up the mess and get rid of your bloodied clothing. Once the evidence is dealt with, you go back to your cells, make a coffee, have a smoke, and relax.

Ike paused a moment to meet each man's gaze before pressing his final instruction. "Now remember, when they find that creep dead, the shit's gonna hit the fan. No matter what happens, be cool . . . we'll all be fine as long as we stick together—is everyone clear on that?"

"YA!" Phil exclaimed, high-fiving his coconspirators, "LET'S GET IT DONE!"

"YA!" the others enthusiastically agreed, following Phil's lead. Then the four set off to carry out the plan—judge, jury, executioner, and one who would turn out to be a witness for the prosecution.

There were many things on Wil's mind when he returned from breakfast, intent on grabbing his Bible before heading off to Sunday morning service. The possibility that he might be dead in less than fifteen minutes wasn't one of them.

Wil thought nothing of the four prisoners loitering near the entrance to the tier. He did become a little nervous when they followed close behind, and he definitely panicked when Alex locked him in a chokehold, covered his mouth, and pushed him inside the cell. However, by then, it was far too late.

Alex was very strong, and so was his hold. He could easily have broken Wil's neck, killing him right then and there. Nevertheless, that was not what Ike had instructed him to do, and Alex had no intention of disobeying. Thus, he stuck to the script. "If I hear any noise out of you," he malevolently hissed, "Phil's gonna slice your fuckin' eyes right out of your fuckin' head!"

Wil fearfully glanced in the direction of the assailant that he guessed to be Phil. He noted the threatening manner with which the man held a razor-embedded toothbrush in his right hand, and he rightly assumed the danger to be real. Terrified, he did exactly as he'd been told—he remained silent, not that it made a whole lot of difference. Alex continued to hold his hand over Wil's mouth, and Wil wouldn't have been able to scream anyway.

Satisfied that they'd established complete control over their victim, Phil turned to supervise Lefty and Rick while they draped Wil's blanket across the bars in order to conceal what was about to take place. "Hurry!" he urged, fearing that someone might witness the crime.

Lefty and Rick quickly finished their task, then silently turned their attention to Wil. First they ripped off his shirt. Next they stood on each side of the man, laying hold of his skinny arms and extending them straight out, as though he were nailed to a cross.

The preplanned horror show now called for Phil to act. He stepped up close to Wil and spat in his face. "Do you really think that Jesus loves a fuckin' rapist?" he laughingly taunted. "No! No one loves a sick fuck like you. You guys are all gonna burn in hell, but if it makes you feel any better, you can pretend that you're being crucified—like He was."

Seeing what Phil was about to do, Wil really did attempt to scream and struggle. However, his efforts proved futile. The sharp blade sliced deeply from elbow to wrist on a slight angle, easily severing his arteries and tendons. Alex managed to stifled Wil's screams, and Wil's struggles ceased significantly as soon as he lost the use of his arms.

The frothy crimson spray spurting from Wil's open wounds actually spurred on their homicidal frenzy.

"Ya!" Alex urged, "Cut him good!"

"HOLY SHIT!" Lefty exclaimed excitedly, "LOOK AT THAT FUCKIN' RAT BLEED!"

"What're you stoppin' for?" Rick demanded to know when Phil hesitated after slashing Wil's second arm to the bone. "Cut him some more!"

Phil answered with a question. "How long do you think that it'll take this fuckin' guy to bleed out?"

"Too long," Alex immediately calculated, "we can't hang around here!" Moving his left arm from around Wil's neck and holding both hands over Wil's mouth, he added, "We've gotta finish this—just cut his fuckin' throat and be done with it!"

Phil agreed. He frantically slashed Wil's throat several times, semidecapitating the unfortunate man and causing him to die within seconds. The lethal four then quickly stuffed the body under the bed before making their escape—they completely forgot about cleaning up and destroying the evidence.

As Wil's blood seeped slowly into the cement floor, the Spirit Tree of Abaddon was, once again, nourished by violence and death.

CHAPTER 45

INSANITY?

Sylvester stopped under the tree and stripped off his clothes, enthusiastically intent on an evening swim. Without further hesitation, he waded into the pond up to his waist, dove deep, surfacing seconds later, gasping for air and surprised to discover Vivian treading water twenty feet away.

Struck dumb by her sudden appearance and perceiving her to be even more beautiful than he'd remembered, Sylvester actually forgot to keep himself afloat. He sank, flailing his arms in a most undignified manner, barely managing to regain control in time to greet Vivian's approach. However, he remained too happy to feel embarrassed, and Vivian's laughter was genuine music to his ears.

Overwhelmed with joy, he hesitantly reached out, touching her face as she neared, "I'm so happy to see you again . . . it's been such a long time!"

Vivian silently wrapped her arms around his neck, kissed his lips softly, and hugged him tight. "I missed you too!" she whispered.

Sylvester forgot about his shyness—he and Vivian exited the pond, pausing under the tree to clothe themselves before impulsively sharing a piece of low-hanging fruit that once again seemed to invite their attention.

"How's your ma?" Vivian asked between bites.

"Happy as ever," Sylvester assured her, "but I know for a fact that she'll be especially happy, now that your back. She speaks of you often— Ma's convinced that you and I were meant for each other.

"I can't wait to see the look on her face when we arrive!"

"Well, my love," Vivian countered with a seductive smile, "that's going to have to wait." She glanced meaningfully in the direction of the cave, "You and I have unfinished business!"

Sylvester swallowed his last mouthful of fruit. "It's truly difficult to imagine a worse time to have been interrupted!" he agreed. "I closed my eyes for a split second, and when I looked again, you were gone . . ."

He was silenced by a soft, tender kiss.

Gazing through the kitchen window, Ma observed the two walking, hand in hand, toward the cave, and she smiled a knowing smile. "Everything is finally as it should be," she happily declared to Luther, the calico cat that now ruled the farmhouse. Humming an old love song, she placed a lid over the vegetable stew that she'd been preparing for dinner. "They're going to be very hungry in an hour or two!" she assured the regal feline.

Vivian and Sylvester lay exhausted, wrapped in each other's arms and nestled comfortably within their luxurious accommodations. The conversed in the intimate tones of lovers, and they talked about the things that only those truly committed to each other talk about.

"I believe in love," Sylvester declared blissfully.

Vivian laughed softly. "Of course you do—it's easy to be poetic, once the passions are satisfied."

"No. I really mean it. Now that I've experienced what it's like for a man and a woman to come together in both spiritual and physical unity, I can't imagine that anything less would ever do. I hate to sound crude, but the truth is, being here with you makes all past sexual experience seem as little more than assisted masturbation. I'm certain that this is what two people are meant to be to each other. I believe it, and I believe in it . . . I also believe that I ought to include some sort of statement about it in my credo!"

Vivian loved him too much to allow him to deceive himself on so important an issue, even at such an intimate moment. "I like what you're saying—I like it very much, as far as you've stated it, but love is much bigger than that.

"What we've just experienced is wonderful . . . magical! I too believe in it. However, if you're thinking about love as a third component of your credo, you need to appreciate and practice it as a way of seeing, being, and doing in the world. That is to say, love cannot simply apply to the subject of your affection—be it myself or otherwise—it must apply to everything and to everyone . . . even to your enemies."

"E-e-even my enemies?" he stuttered incredulously.

"Yes, even your enemies!" she affirmed.

Sylvester took a moment to consider the idea. "That's not an easy thing to for me to do—for anyone to do," he asserted sincerely. "I don't see how anyone can love their enemies!"

"It's not so hard," Vivian patiently assured him. "First, you start with respect and good manners. Second, you peel back the layers of illusion, in the way that Lucky taught you to do, until you come to a place of thorough understanding. And third, you apply a healthy dose of empathy."

She paused, holding him tight before whispering in his ear, "If all else fails, you can come and cuddle up with me."

"Now that I will always be able to do!" he promised.

They lay in silence a while longer before Sylvester again felt the need to speak. "I think that we should get married," he declared in a hopeful tone of voice.

Vivian laughed. "We are married! We're as married as married can be in Lucky's World—or in any world!"

"We are?"

"Of course we are!" she insisted.

"Don't tell me that you're one of those people who've convinced themselves—or allowed themselves to be convinced—that marriage is possible and valid only after the license is bought and paid for. I assure you, that is not the way that it all began, nor is it necessary . . . certainly not in this place! You've already told me that you sense our unity of spirit, and you were clear as to how you feel about the two of us together. Unity of spirit is marriage! We were married the last time that I was here—it was our honeymoon that was so unceremoniously interrupted."

Sylvester suddenly felt hungry. "Well," he announced, feigning authority, "if I'm your husband, then I declare it to be time for the wedding feast!

"How do you feel about that?"

Vivian became aware of her own hunger. "Good idea . . . great idea!" she heartily agreed. "Let's go see if Ma's got something hot on the stove . . . I can't wait to see her again."

They dressed and exited their honeymoon suite, walking hand in hand back down the path in the direction of the farmhouse, neither aware of the fact that the next time they entered the cave would be their last.

CHAPTER 46

REALITY?

The experienced prison guard had often bragged that, over the years, he'd "witnessed it all." He certainly had plenty of stories to back up his claim, but nothing prepared him for what he saw when he pushed aside the blanket that was draped across the bars of Wil's cell—it was literally the scene of a bloodbath! Fighting his gag reflex, he stepped back, thumbed his microphone and called for support, "This is South 302 to 100, we've got a code red on level 3!"

Code red meant murder, riot, or officer in distress. It always resulted in the quickest response. The emergency protocol kicked in. As Ike had predicted would be the case, all hell broke loose. The loudspeakers blared, "LOCKDOWN! ALL PRISONERS RETURN TO YOUR CELLS! LOCKDOWN!" Within minutes, the emergency response team converged on South 3; the watch commander followed close behind, and the civil authority arrived shortly thereafter in order to investigate the crime. Everyone agreed that they'd never seen anything like it.

"*Fucking animals!*" the watch commander blurted while conferring with the civil authority. "Only fucking animals would do something like that to another human being!"

The investigating officer agreed with a single caveat. "Very fucking stupid animals," he spat out in disgust. "A half-blind traffic cop with a migraine could solve this one!"

Although it certainly was one of the most brutal murders ever committed at Abaddon, it was nowhere near the most well-thought-out of such crimes. Bloody footprints actually led to the respective cells of each of the participants, who were still smoking crystal meth and celebrating. They were so high, they'd almost forgotten why they were celebrating, and when they were reminded, by way of their arrest, they all cursed and wondered out loud, "Who snitched?"

Ike was the only one who didn't get arrested, and at the end of the day, he was the only one pleased with the outcome. However, it wasn't enough—as a main branch of the Spirit Tree of Abaddon, he could never be completely satisfied. No amount of violence or drugs would ever sufficiently meet his dark emotional needs or permanently alleviate his pain. He would always require more. This was evidenced by the fact that he was still high and already considering additional violence—he was thinking about Steve and Sly.

Sly was foremost on Ike's mind, and the lockdown gave him time to remember why he hated the man so much—he recalled the night that they'd fought.

Neither man had been at Abaddon long; both were living on the East Block at the time, and as is so often the case, it began over a trivial issue. The issue was nothing more than whose turn to next use the shower. Sly had actually been in the process of stepping aside, allowing Ike to go first. Then he'd heard Ike mutter under his breath, "That's right, nigger, back of the fuckin' line." That was Ike's mistake!

Certain things trigger certain people—Sly never allowed anyone to get away with using that word. Emotionally and physically supercharged with rage, he administered a vicious beating to a shocked, surprised—and ultimately bruised, bleeding, and seemingly repentant—racist. However, it wasn't the beating that hurt Ike the most. He'd lost fights before, albeit not for a very long time. The matter might actually have ended there, had it not been for Sly's coup de grâce.

Sly wasn't satisfied to simply administer a beating—he wanted to humiliate, in the way that he'd felt humiliated by that word. With the entire tier as witness, he'd made Ike fetch a mop and bucket in order to clean up his own blood, thereby providing Sly a clean shower area. The real pain and suffering resulted not from the beating but from the shame and humiliation of all those pairs of eyes watching while Ike was forced to complete the task. It was the reason that he'd moved from the East Block to the South Block. It was the memory that he'd never completely let go of, and it was Sly's mistake!

Ike shook his head in an attempt to clear the memory, his thoughts returning to the present. "What's up with that black cocksucker?" he wondered. "So many rumors and so few answers! I need to find out what's going on.

"On the other hand, I could really piss him off by simply killing Steve!"

It was the abundance of rumors regarding Sly's circumstances that truly troubled Ike. Steve was almost an afterthought, primarily relevant in connection to the possibility that Sly might come back and lend "the fool" his support. With Al dead, the possibility seemed remote. However, Ike took pleasure in thinking and planning what he'd do to Sly, Steve, or both if things were to ultimately evolve in that direction.

Whichever way it went, he definitely wanted to see Sly dead. Nevertheless, he remained determined to proceed carefully. There would be no mistakes. He wouldn't allow Sly to humiliate him a second time!

With his mind made up on that score, Ike decided to complete the night's celebration—it was time to take the edge off the crystal meth. He dug into his stash for barbiturates. He knew what he liked, and he knew how to manage his drugs!

CHAPTER 47

INSANITY?

Vivian and Sylvester were building beehives. She'd mentioned over breakfast that it would be nice to have some honey. "Brilliant!" he'd exclaimed. "Let's build the bees a home. I bet we won't even need protective gear to keep from being stung—this place is bound to have the friendliest bees that you've ever met!"

Sly's assumption proved correct. No sooner had the first hive built than it became populated by large numbers of happy buzzing insects, while many more waited patiently for the construction of additional accommodations. Not only did the bees appear to understand what was happening, they actually seemed to anticipate the prospect of a new home.

The amateur carpenters were working on the second hive when Lucky emerged from the surrounding shrubbery, leaped atop the first hive, and greeted them brightly, "Good morning, good people!"

"Good morning to you!" they replied at once.

"To what do we owe the honor of your company, my friend?" Sylvester politely inquired.

"No emergencies," the squirrel assured them both. "I just want to make sure that everything's okay now that Vivian's returned?"

"Why?" Vivian asked in sudden concern. "Did something happen while I was away?" A split second later she realized the answer, looked at Sylvester, and changed the question. "How long was I away . . . that is to say, from your perspective?"

"Nearly three months," he answered in a voice that attempted to conceal his earlier unhappiness.

Vivian wasn't fooled—she quickly gauged the time difference in light of the distress that she'd experienced as a result of being away from Sylvester for a relatively short period of time. She realized how hard separation would have been for him. "From my perspective it was three days," she consoled, "and that seemed to me like an eternity . . . you must have been very lonely."

"Yes, I was," he admitted honestly, "but I did my best to stay positive . . . and to keep busy. It helped a lot when Lucky promised that you'd return—having that to look forward to seemed to change everything . . . I was able to spend my days preparing, rather than lamenting your absence.

"How about you? What'd you do while we were apart? Did you miss me too?"

Vivian gave him a chastising look that silently declared, "Didn't I just tell you that it seemed like an eternity?" before responding verbally, "I worked at the hospital—part of my job being to care of you," she added with smile.

"Beyond that, I followed through with the plan that we discussed involving your middle name . . . which proved to my satisfaction that this experience we're sharing is definitely much more than a dream. However, that raised more questions than it answered.

"As a matter of fact," she elaborated with a meaningful glance in Lucky's direction, "I promised myself that we'd discuss those questions at the earliest opportunity."

"Well, then, how fortunate I am to be here," the little squirrel offered. "What was of most concern to you?"

"First of all," Vivian began, "what happens to Sylvester or me in this world if something unthinkable happens to our bodies in the other world—what if we die?"

Lucky nodded his understanding of the problem—the nurse in Vivian was thinking practically regarding a subject that could not be evaluated in practical terms. Nevertheless, all he could do was reassure the woman. "As I've said before, no harm can come to you while you're here. There is nothing to fear. More than that, I cannot say."

Sylvester smiled at the familiar phrase. Then he shifted the conversation with an inexplicable piece of insight. "It doesn't matter if it's safe. Nor does it matter if I want to stay here forever. I will have to leave here eventually, won't I?"

"Yes and no," Lucky answered. "It's true that realization of your full potential will ultimately be dependent upon whether or not you choose to return to Abaddon. However, the decision will always be your own—no one is ever forced to realize his or her potential—we all must choose. You will only go back if, and when, you want to.

"Equally important—as we previously discussed—you must make the right choice, for the right reasons.

"Granted, there is a certain irony to that proposition. Very few men or women take the time to consider their own motives. Choosing the right course of action for the right reasons is seldom a priority. They're mostly success oriented, convinced that the ends justify the means in any given situation. Worshiping at the altar of competition, they perpetually struggle in the dark, subscribing to the myth that the last person standing is the winner.

"Curiously, these people almost always self-identify as being the 'good people' of the world. Few ever realize that the last person standing—if ultimately he, or she, stands alone—stands for nothing!

"You, on the other hand—though socially identified as a lesser human being—are learning to truly walk in the light. The spirit of cooperation guides your steps, and you're actually beginning to hold yourself to a higher standard than those who see themselves as your social superiors.

"Nevertheless, you could yet share their fate. If you stay here—if ultimately you stand alone—you will also stand for nothing. To achieve your potential, you must live your life in community with—and in contrast to—the 'good people' who choose to look down on you. That is to say, for their sake, as well as your own, you must put what you've learned into practice in that hostile and largely antithetical environment.

Sylvester understood. "It's like the issue of my commitment to nonviolence," he suggested.

"Exactly!" Lucky agreed. "It means much less to you in a world where violence is impossible, and it means nothing to those who've no idea that you've made it."

"That's not fair," Vivian interjected. "I know! I know how much he's accomplished, and I know how he's chosen to live his life. Surely that counts for something? Isn't that validation enough?"

"Of course it counts for something," Lucky admitted, "but let me put a question back to you—will either of you be fully satisfied to leave things the way that they are?

"Remember, the decision is yours, not mine." His eyes seemed to glow with wisdom as he added, "I'm betting that you'll both want to follow that Path of Life, no matter where it leads."

Sylvester and Vivian instinctively knew that Lucky was correct. "So what does that mean in terms of where we go from here?" Sylvester wondered out loud.

"It means that you continue to live, learn, and grow. Nothing's changed. Nothing will change until if, or when, you decide the time is right and you choose to change it.

"I recommend that you stay focused on your credo—a lot of really good things will flow from both the process and the result."

Sylvester smiled and nodded in agreement. "I've had that same thought. I've even said as much to Vivian, but can you be more specific? What can I expect to happen? How much will change?"

"As I've said before, first you'll be able to define yourself. This will, in turn, guide and focus your creative energy and skills. It will also help you to figure out where you belong in the world—where you best fit in.

"Once your credo is completed, you'll never again need to worry about your decision-making process falling victim to your own feelings—it will become a solid basis for every decision. Of equal importance, it'll make it much harder for you to deceive yourself in the ways that we've talked about in the past. It won't make you perfect, and it's no guarantee that you'll never make a mistake, but it will help you to organize your life, make sense of the world and participate in society in a much more meaningful way."

Sylvester sensed the truth in Lucky's words. However, the pieces of the puzzle weren't quite all in place. So he asked yet another question. "Why should I be concerned about where or how I fit into the world? I'm exiled to Abaddon. The world doesn't care about me, why should I care about the world?"

Lucky sensed that his next point would score a direct hit; his voice revealed his excitement as he continued, "Abaddon is your world!

"Where you fit into Abaddon is as important as where anyone fits into anywhere. The people that you come into contact with will be affected by you, and you will be affected by them. It's an interactive process. You'll either lift each other up or drag each other down.

"Recall what I told you when Vivian first entered this world—she's drawn to you because of the man that you're in the process of becoming. Like-minded people are always spiritually drawn to one another, no matter what, and the power of the relationship is in their spiritual unity.

"United in a healthy spirit, people become so much more—and accomplish so much more good—than they could ever hope to as individuals. The flip side of the coin is also true. When negative forces unite in spirit, they also become so much more—and accomplish so much more evil—than individuals would ever achieve.

"You should care about your world because there are those in Abaddon who need you as much as you need them . . ."

Sylvester took it upon himself to sum up Lucky's argument. "What you're saying is that, first, I figure out a basis for who I want to be. Second, I figure out where I fit in, and third, I get connected . . . thereby strengthening myself and my chosen community."

Lucky began to express his delight. "You've got it, my friend, and there's more . . ."

"Enough for now," Vivian quickly interrupted, foregoing the opportunity to pursue answers to her remaining questions. She looked at Sylvester. "I know who you are, and I know where you belong—you belong with me. As long as we stay together, we'll both be fine. Now I think that we should get back to building this beehive."

"Good idea!" Lucky happily agreed, satisfied that he'd already accomplished much more with Sylvester than he'd originally intended. "You two go right ahead and do something nice for those bees, and then those bees will do something nice for you—I love symbiotic relationships!" Without further comment, he leaped from atop the beehive, disappearing from whence he came.

"That was intense!" Vivian admitted while returning to the task at hand. "Interesting too!

"He tells you that you that it's important for you to figure out where to fit in, but he never actually suggests anything . . . such as Buddhism, Christianity, or whatever. He seems to be saying that everything is good."

"I didn't interpret his words quite that way," Sylvester thoughtfully replied. "The message that I get from him—the message that I've always received from him—is somewhat more nuanced and finely tuned. I hear him saying that it's my responsibility to find the truth, to discover where I belong, and that no one has a right to judge me for the path that I choose.

"However, I believe that you're mostly correct. He definitely intends that we should discover for ourselves what to believe and where we belong, and that, in itself, is truly a very nice break from a world where people so often feel free to impose their views on others!"

CHAPTER 48

REALITY?

Phil awoke Monday morning hung over from the meth, frightened and confused. The world looked very different from the perspective of his segregation cell, and he was desperately trying to understand just how he'd arrived at such a tragic point in his life.

He remembered being physically ill at the thought of the violence that Ike had first suggested. He clearly recalled his limited and reluctant acceptance of becoming a part of the conspiracy. "So how did I get from there to being the lead in such an ugly fuckin' murder?" he wondered. "It just doesn't make any sense!"

Mental images of blood squirting from severed arteries and a young man's pathetic struggle for his life now resurfaced. "Oh my god! What did we do that for?" he groaned out loud while trying to push the memory aside. "What were we thinking? What was I thinking? Holy shit, they're gonna have our asses for this!"

The despondent man slowly shook his head, silently calculating the consequences. "One thing is for certain: my days of serving life on the installment plan have come to an end—I'll be serving a life sentence for real now!

"At my age, I'll never see the street again," he fearfully admitted. "I'll have to spend years in maximum security. In fact, I may never even see another medium-security institution. This is a seriously bad situation—I need to find some way out of it!

"The question is, what can I do?" he desperately wondered. Then an idea flashed through his mind like lightning. "What about turning snitch?"

He smiled as the idea began to take root. "It'd look good on Ike!" he cynically continued. "This is definitely all his fault, and he's the only one that didn't get arrested. Why should that sick fuck get to sit back and laugh at the rest of us?"

Phil rose from his thin mattress and began to restlessly pace the cell. "The cops would likely be very interested in hearing about the guy that organized it all," he assured himself. "Still, serving a life sentence while labeled as an informant is a hard way to live—they'd have to make me a helluva good deal before I'd risk testifying!"

"Nevertheless, it's something to consider!" he thoughtfully concluded with a shrug of his shoulders. "But for now, I'm probably better off keeping my mouth shut—it's never a good idea to say too much, too soon . . . best to wait until the time is right."

The possibility of competition—one of his coaccused also turning snitch—never even occurred to him!

Phil's attention was drawn to the sound of a key in the lock—the door opened, revealing a prison guard and two homicide investigators. "Time for a walk and a talk," the guard curtly informed him while holding out a pair of handcuffs.

The trip to the interview room was silent and uneventful. Upon arrival, Phil seated himself and spoke without waiting for the first question. "I've got nothing to say," he announced as the bigger of the two—clearly the lead investigator—pressed the record button on the tape recorder which sat in the middle of the table.

"You don't have to talk," the investigator responded with a grin. "You just have to listen. First of all, there were traces of bloodied footprints all the way to the door of your cell. Second, we found the clothing that you were wearing at the time of the murder. Third, we have witnesses on level 3 that saw all four of you arrive, and we have others who saw all four of you leave. They'll testify that you were covered in blood. Better yet, we have the weapon—with your prints on it—which unequivocally points to you as the one who actually did the murder. In short, we've got the whole package wrapped up nice and tidy. Like I said, you don't have to say a word—*you're royally fucked!*"

The smaller of the two investigators spoke next. "You can give us a statement or not. We really don't care!"

"I've got nothing to say," Phil repeated in a subdued voice.

"Fine!" the first investigator spat out. "Then we'll just put you back in your cage. Take a good look around when you get there—it's the only view you're gonna have for a very long time!"

Alex was next to be interviewed. He'd been wishing all morning that he could go to the weight pit—he was used to pumping iron for at least two hours each day, and today's half hour for a shave and a shower simply didn't satisfy his physical needs. Not to mention the fact that he was anxious for the opportunity to brag to someone about what he'd done—to experience some of the respect that Phil had promised.

He was actually happy to see the investigators at his door. They cuffed and walked him down to the same interview room, laid out the general information that they'd laid out for Phil, and then asked Alex if he had anything to say.

"Am I gonna lose my job in the kitchen?" he inquired.

"Don't get smart with me, punk!" the lead investigator snapped. Then the room went silent while the authorities gaped at each other in utter astonishment—it was obvious from the expression on Alex's face that he'd truly asked a serious question.

"Tell me, Alex," the second investigator began after recovering from the shock, "do you have any idea what you've done? Do you know what kind of trouble you're in?"

"I didn't do nothin', and I ain't got nothin' to say," he assured them. "I just wanna go back to work in the kitchen."

"Well, you're not going back to work in the kitchen," The second investigator reacted angrily. "You're going to trial. When you're convicted—and you will be convicted—you'll be transferred directly to a supermaximum-security facility. There you'll live in an empty cell, with a light that never goes completely dim and with nothing to do but stare at the bare walls while you think about what you've done. You're going to be there for at least the next two years."

The first investigator now resumed the lead, "Are you sure that there's nothing more that you want to say to us?"

"Can I at least go work out in the weight pit?"

The session ended.

The interview with Lefty was even more inane. Aside from the fact that Robert William Goodwin insisted that they call him Lefty, there was the fact that the guy just wouldn't shut up—all he wanted to do was brag!

"You should've seen that fuckin' skinner bleed!" he exclaimed. "Man, I had no idea that there was so much blood in the human body. Fuck! It was totally cool! We did a hell of a good job on that fucker! I wish I could have had a video camera. I could sell that movie and make a fortune.

Sure! A lot of people would pay to see that! Fuck, I'd pay to see it again, myself! Of course, it probably wouldn't be so cool if I was straight— Lucky for me I was high on . . ."

At that point they cut him off, ignoring his last comment. They definitely didn't want to allow the issue of intoxication to be raised as any kind of a defense.

"Do you want to make a statement," the first investigator asked.

"No! I got nothin' to say to you fuckers!" Lefty sullenly declared, apparently oblivious to the fact that he'd just confessed everything.

He too was escorted back to his cell.

Lastly, the investigators turned their attention to Rick. Like the others, he was cuffed and escorted to the interview room, whereupon they laid out their evidence. "Do you want to make a statement?" the lead asked in a tone of voice that clearly revealed his boredom and fatigue.

Both investigators were immediately shocked into alertness by Rick's casual reply. "Not just now, boys—but maybe later. There might be more to this case than you realize. I need a couple of days to think . . . before I decide if I want to talk to you or not."

"Are you suggesting there's a fifth person involved?" the lead investigator anxiously demanded.

"There might be," Rick answered noncommittally. "Like I said, I need time to think about it."

It was a stunning turn of events. Was he lying? Given that, to this point, things seemed to be so nicely wrapped up, did they even want to know what he had to say? The investigators sadly concluded that it would be too hazardous to their careers to ignore potential new evidence, whatever it might be—the prosecutor would most certainly be interested in the involvement of a fifth person!

"Okay, Rick," the lead investigator agreed, "we're patient people. You take a couple of days and think about it. We'll come back for your statement. You can have until then to decide if you've got some sort of new information that you believe we might be interested in."

"This is actually gonna work!" Rick silently promised himself, smiling inwardly while being escorted back to his cell. "There's a deal to be made here, and I'm the one who's gonna make it!"

The issue of additional information and the possibility of a prolonged investigation lingered after the interviews had been completed. "I hope this doesn't drag out too long!" the first investigator vehemently declared to the second as they drove away from Abaddon. "I really don't give a fuck what those guys do to each other. So far as I'm concerned, that's just one less rapist for us to worry about—he'll definitely never reoffend, and the additional benefit is that four other creeps will never get out of jail. It's all good . . . so much the better if there's a fifth. Either way, we win—I just want to get it over with. I hate dealing with these dirtbags!"

CHAPTER 49

INSANITY?

They'd completed four beehives—at least two more than required for a steady supply of honey. "Enough already!" Vivian exhaustedly exclaimed after hammering home the final nail. Plopping down on the grass and surveying their handiwork, she added, "I think we might have gotten a little carried away in our enthusiasm for the project."

Sylvester laughed. "It was fun though, wasn't it?"

"Is anyone hungry or thirsty," Ma cheerfully called out, approaching with a tray of sweet tea and biscuits.

Sylvester allowed his tool belt to fall to the ground before hurrying to meet her. "Am I ever!" he admitted, while accepting the carefully prepared meal. "You're the best!"

Ma smiled. "Enjoy yourselves," she encouraged while turning to make her way back to the farmhouse.

Sylvester placed the tray on the grass and sat beside Vivian. The two dined in relaxed silence for several minutes, delighting in the hot drinks and delicious treat.

Vivian took the opportunity to reflect on the day's earlier conversation, wondering what Sylvester would think about her own spiritual beliefs. She decided to explore the issue in a roundabout way. "Tell me more about love," she softly asked of him.

Sylvester swallowed the last of his biscuit, washed it down with a gulp of tea and attempted to please her in a semihumorous manner by quoting the age-old line, "My love for you is higher than the highest mountains, wider than the widest sea . . ."

"No," she laughingly interrupted. "I'm serious. What's your opinion of love? What are its attributes? When you examine your own heart, what does it tell you about love?"

"Well," he answered thoughtfully, "first of all, I think that it endures, no matter what. It's patient and kind. It's ready to believe the best about the other person. It sets aside its own needs, and I think that it always forgives.

"Perhaps it's just as easily understood by identifying what it's not. I can't imagine that it would ever be selfish or self-seeking. It's not arrogant or conceited. It never rejoices at injustice, and though it learns and grows, it keeps no record of wrong."

Sylvester stopped and thought for several seconds about what he'd just said before concluding, "And I have no idea where all of that just came from!"

Vivian burst out laughing—partly from happiness, but mostly from relief. It was obvious to her that there was no significant difference between their beliefs. "I know where it comes from," she assured him. "I also think that the time is right for you to work a statement about love into your credo!"

"Well, thank you very much," Sylvester replied, feeling genuinely pleased and not thinking to ask as to the source or her insight. "I believe you're correct, and that's exactly what I'm going to do."

Satisfied and ready to put the issue to rest, Vivian's thoughts turned to the future. "What would it look like for the two of us if you were to return to Abaddon?" she wondered out loud. "How would we live? What do you think our lives would be like?"

Sylvester opted for a painfully honest answer. "That kind of life presents many difficult challenges!" he assured her. "Nothing associated with Abaddon is easily managed. It takes weeks to simply get regular visits approved. We'd have to be legally married in order to qualify for conjugal visits, and that would take another six months. Until then, we'd have to live with the loneliness of severely limited access to each other. It wouldn't be easy to support one another, emotionally or otherwise—certainly not to the extent that we're used to.

"On the flip side—the positive side—it is possible to maintain a healthy relationship. Visits, conjugal visits, phone calls, and letters all make it possible for two people to grow together, rather than apart. It's something that we would definitely have to work hard at, but it can be done."

"What about the violence?" she asked. "How would you reconcile your commitment to nonviolence with the realities of survival under such conditions?"

Sylvester's answer was unequivocal. "I will defend myself—I'm just not a turn-the-other-cheek kind of guy. However, I won't provoke violence, and given the opportunity, I will walk away." He paused for a minute, seeking words to further alleviate her fears. Then he hesitantly added, "I think my previous reputation will help to protect me a little—at least in certain circles. However, for the most part, I'm going to have to earn respect in different ways—nonviolent ways—perhaps by showing more respect to others. A splash of humility never hurts. As you so wisely pointed out, respect and good manners can carry a person a good distance in a healthy direction.

"Over the long term, I'll need to follow through with Lucky's teaching and advice, thereby establishing a nonviolent identity and way of life. First, I'll finish my credo. Second, I'll pay close attention to the dangerous traps of illusion and self-deception, always seeking the underlying truth in my motives and in the motives of others. Third, I'll support—and cultivate the support of—a strong spiritual community, most likely a Christian community."

"Why a Christian community?" Vivian asked in an attempt to encourage him to define his reasons and cement his choice.

"I don't know. I mean, I am baptized—I was baptized as a child. I remember my father reading his Bible, though he didn't read it to me . . . probably because it was hard for him to read.

"He didn't have much education. I recall watching him silently struggle, trying to sound out some of the words . . . so I imagine that he would have been very uncomfortable reading aloud. Plus the fact that he and I were never very close. Still, a Christian community seems the natural place for me to be. That is to say, I can't imagine where else I would go."

Sylvester grew tired of talking about himself. He decided to shift the focus of conversation. "What about you? How will you manage if I return to Abaddon?"

It was Vivian's turn to be painfully honest. "I imagine that much of my life would remain the same. Nursing is important to me—I enjoy my job, and I'm good at it!

"Beyond that, I'm fortunate to have a close circle of friends. With the exception of one or two, I'm sure that they'd support my decision to be with you, as would my parents.

"I'd love for my mom and dad to be able to meet you. They're such kind and generous people—very much like your ma . . . real salt-of-the-earth types. They'd love you, and I'm sure that you'd love them.

"Life with you serving time in Abaddon would be a bit strange, at least at first. However, everyone would adjust. If you do decide to go back, I'm sure that I'll have all of the love and support that I need to walk hand in hand with you on this journey that we've undertaken."

Having concluded her initial thought, Vivian surprised herself with a further comment. "Equally important," she assured Sylvester, "you need not worry about your decision to join a Christian community. That's the way I was raised. It's all I've ever known. Nothing would make me happier!"

CHAPTER 50

REALITY?

Steve stalked Ike, albeit very carefully. He had to be careful. With Al dead, there was no telling what Ike might be thinking in regard to Steve! However, having arrived at a decision to kill the man, Steve needed to familiarize himself with Ike's habits and behavior patterns in order to formulate an effective plan—it was essential that he choose the right time and place to act.

There appeared to Steve to be two major problems.

The first problem was the fact that Ike was almost never alone. He was nearly always surrounded by his skinhead brothers, who would be more than happy to earn his favor by blocking Steve's attempt on his life. Steve needed to find a time and a place where Ike would be alone and vulnerable.

The second problem rested in the fact that Ike was a big tough guy. Steve accepted the fact that he was overmatched, and he decided that it would be foolish to risk a face-to-face encounter. Ike being perfectly capable of taking Steve's weapon away and turning the tables, Steve sought to find a time when Ike would be physically compromised—at the very least, giving himself the element of surprise!

Nevertheless, Steve now felt elated—he believed that he worked out both problems.

Ike lifted weights in the gym six days a week. Afterward, he always enjoyed a long, hot shower in the gymnasium shower room. Most everyone gave him lots of privacy. Once or twice a week, Ike would also eat a handful of pills after his workout, then sit around and bullshit for an hour. That's where Steve sensed Ike to be most vulnerable—alone in the shower, naked and high on drugs.

The act itself would be risky and difficult—Steve needed to slip into the shower room without being noticed, sneak up on Ike, and strike quickly. If he missed, Ike would probably kill him. If he was observed coming or leaving, Ike's goons would probably kill him. However, if he got it right—if everything went perfect—he might actually succeed; and with luck, maybe even get away with it!

Steve walked the track, mentally rehearsing his plan—he reasoned that the ice-pick-like weapon that he'd fashioned earlier would draw little blood, and it would draw almost none at all if he simply left it in Ike's heart. He'd wear the latex gloves that they sometimes issued to the cleaners on the tier. If he managed to exit the shower area successfully—without being seen—he would discreetly bury the gloves in the yard. Then he'd simply walk laps until the body was discovered, which wouldn't take very long at all. There was no doubt in his mind that, if he made it that far without getting caught, he'd be home free. The more that he thought about it, the more he convinced himself that it'd work.

Confident of success, Steve's thoughts inexplicably turned to Sly—it was now six days since they'd taken him away in an ambulance, and Steve felt emotionally shaken to realize how much things had changed in such a short period of time. He recalled the sense of relief that he'd felt after first talking to Sly, and he momentarily tried to recapture the feeling. He failed. "It doesn't matter," he consoled to himself, "I can handle this on my own!"

Refocusing on the issue at hand, he imagined how good it would feel to be walking laps with the knowledge that Ike was indeed dead. "That would be sweet!" he whispered into the breeze, adding softly, "This is for you, Al!"

Steve felt energized. Everything seemed to be moving in the right direction—he was in perfect harmony with the Spirit Tree of Abaddon.

CHAPTER 51

INSANITY?

It was nearly dawn. Vivian and Sylvester lay entwined in bed, silently contemplating the future. Two weeks had passed since they'd finished building the beehives, and they were both conscious of the fact that, if the pattern remained constant, their happy union was soon to be interrupted a second time. However, neither felt inclined to speak such thoughts. So Sly simply offered up the first question to come to mind. "What church do you belong to?"

It was a question that Vivian had often been asked in the past. Her answer was automatic. "We don't like labels. We believe that the differences that serve to separate Christians are a consequence of man's illusions, which serve no useful purpose. I suppose some would try to label us as a protestant sect, but we just see ourselves as followers of the teachings of Jesus Christ—we're guided by the gospels."

Her answer piqued Sylvester's curiosity regarding other aspects of her faith. He asked a second question. "You're a nurse. You have at least some background in science. How do you come to terms with the more scientifically disputed aspects of the Bible? Do you really believe that there is a god who created the world in six days, some six thousand years ago?"

Vivian answered without hesitation, "Yes, I definitely believe in God!" Then she squeezed his hand before further answering, "I come to terms with the scientifically disputed elements of the Bible in the same way the you first came to terms with all that you found in this place.

"I don't want to belittle Lucky, but think about it. The doctors in the hospital where I work believe that you're insane, and here you are, taking lessons in life and spirituality from a talking squirrel. How crazy is that? Nevertheless, think what you would have missed if you had simply written it all off on that basis! Think of how you've grown and changed because of your willingness to discern the truth in the seemingly impossible. You are not the man that you were when you arrived because you chose to open your mind to the seemingly impossible!

"I treat all that I find in the Bible in the same manner that you wisely choose to treat all that you find in this place. Do you remember what you told me when you quoted Lucky? You said, 'We all must decide what is real. We have to define our own reality, and we need to remember that what we define as being real, or not real, will always be real in its consequences.' Well, I'm in complete agreement with both of you!

"People read from the Bible. They either learn from the lessons that they find there or they don't. Either way, there are practical consequences in their everyday lives. In that sense, the Bible is as real as anything can possibly be. We all have to choose! We all experience the consequences of our choices!

"To write any of it off—to ignore the valuable lessons—simply because some of it seems to be impossible . . . that, to me, is a terrible waste and a huge mistake!

"Not that I'm a big Old Testament person. To be honest, I'm not. I always urge Christians to be less concerned about how many days it took God to create the world and more concerned with the teachings of Jesus Christ. After all, our relationship with Jesus Christ is what it means to be Christian! However, I don't throw any of it out. I never dispute with people, and I refused to criticize anyone's choice to believe . . . whether they believe literally or otherwise. I always focus on the things that I have in common with other Christians."

Sylvester listened intently. He'd developed quite an ear for the truth, and he knew that he was hearing it now. He made his choice. "I'm with you, beautiful lady! On some level, I've always believed in God. Now seems a very good time to open my mind—I choose to learn and to grow from all that God has provided."

Vivian felt momentarily elated; however, her positive emotions were quickly overpowered by the return of her earlier thoughts. Sensing that it was foolish to continue avoiding the subject, she spoke the words they dreaded to hear. "I'm going to have to leave soon," she whispered.

"I know."

"I don't want to go back alone. It just doesn't feel right!"

"I don't want to stay here without you!" he answered honestly.

"Lucky doesn't think that you're ready yet, but it could take years for you to fully develop your credo . . . it could take the rest of your life! Now that I think about it, it might be good if you continued to work on it for the rest of your life, and how could you ever be more fully prepared to go back to a place like Abaddon? It seems to me that you're as ready now as you'll ever be. If we're going to walk the Path of Life together, we may as well start now."

Sylvester considered her words carefully. Then he thought again about Steve. "There's also someone out there that I promised to help . . . who probably needs my help," he speculated.

"Who?"

"Steve . . . he's one of the people that I told you about when you asked me how I first met Lucky. He's likely still in trouble . . . maybe even more so than ever!"

"Yes, I remember," she said thoughtfully. "And you're right. If you promised to help him, then you really should keep your word!"

"The question is, what do you actually want to do?"

Sylvester nodded. "That's kinda what Lucky said too. He said, 'Feeling that you have to do something, as opposed to feeling that you want to do something, usually signals that you're either doing the wrong thing or that you're doing the right thing for the wrong reasons.'

"I guess it's a good sign that I actually want to go back and be with you, and I really do desire to keep my word to Steve."

For the second time in nearly as many minutes, Sylvester made an easy choice. "I'm with you, Vivian. We'll go back after breakfast . . . after we've said goodbye to Ma and Lucky."

Breakfast was earlier than usual and a solemn affair. Ma sensed what was coming. She didn't wait for them to break the news. "Don't you worry about your old Ma, now, ya hear? There's more to all of this than you yet know. I'll miss you kids, for sure. But we'll meet again, and old folks like me are well taken care of in this place. You just clear your consciences and be the people that you were meant to be!"

Sylvester found it difficult to speak. "I know you'll be well taken care of. I don't really understand how . . . there's a lot of mystery in this place that I can't begin to explain . . . but I know you'll be fine.

"What I do understand is your love," he whispered as he hugged her tight, "and I thank you for being here when I needed you most."

Realizing there was nothing more that needed to be said, Vivian silently expressed her own love, holding the old woman and squeezing her tight in the way that she would've her own mother. Then, by unspoken agreement, all three walked outside to view one last magical sunrise.

Ma waited until the golden rays of sunshine spread their first fingers of light across the enclave. Then, wordlessly kissing each on the cheek, she returned to the farmhouse.

Turning to survey all that they'd built, Sylvester and Vivian noticed Lucky atop a garden fence post. "I must admit," he greeted their approach, "it's all good work. I've truly enjoyed watching you two create for yourselves and for each other in this place!"

"You also know that we're leaving, then?" Vivian exclaimed in amazement.

"Yes, my dear friends, I know."

"How?" Sylvester asked, completely exasperated by Lucky's perpetual display of knowledge and insight. "How do you know so much about everything?"

Lucky laughed. "I know what I know . . . as to how, I cannot say."

"Even now?" Sylvester pressed.

"Especially now!" he assured without elaboration. "Besides, there are other things that you need to think about."

The statement caught Sylvester by surprise. "What, good spirit guide, would you have me think about?"

"Tell me why you're leaving," Lucky urged.

"If you know so much, surely you already know that, as well?"

"True enough, but I'd like you to hear yourself say it. As always, I need you to understand why you do the things that you do!"

Sylvester paused for a moment to collect his reasons. Then he presented them, in the order of priority. "First, I want to be a full partner to Vivian. She needs more than an imaginary husband. Second, wherever possible, I want to help prisoners to break their chains and find freedom . . . I want to teach them about their own power to create and show them how to create for their own good as well as for the good of others. Third, I want to keep my implied promise to Steve, whom I suspect is in a bad way right now—I allowed him to believe that I'd help him, and I don't want to let him down . . . it's not guilt . . . it's just the right thing to do. In other words, I want to step back into the world and realize my full potential as a human being."

Lucky permitted himself a few moments of silence in order to enjoy the sweet taste of success. He was so pleased with Sylvester, and he finally said as much: "It's only been two weeks since we last had this conversation—you've grown fast, and there's no doubt about it, those are all very good reasons. In fact, I'd have to say that you're doing the right thing for the right reasons! True, you've chosen to leave much sooner than I would have wished . . . much sooner than I thought you would. You haven't really had enough time to put your knowledge into practice—there's a great danger that you'll forget at least part of what you know . . ."

"I won't allow that to happen!" Vivian cut in.

Lucky and Sylvester both laughed, and they both believed her.

Recalling to mind her arrival, the squirrel chuckled while echoing his own words, "Sure enough, there's always a reason for everything." Looking directly at Vivian, he added, "I can see that I'm no longer needed, and it's nice to know that Sylvester will be in good hands."

"Sylvester and I are both in good hands," Vivian responded matter-of-factly. "We'll take good care of each other, and God will take good care of us!"

"I've no doubt about that at all," the wise little creature admitted.

"Now how do we get back?" Sylvester inquired.

Lucky looked in the direction of the cave and then back at Sylvester. "The same way that you arrived, of course!"

The expression on Sylvester's face revealed his surprise. "I should have guessed that such a seemingly complicated thing would turn out to be so simple—it pretty much sums up my entire experience of this place!"

"It most definitely does," Lucky agreed. "No one ever went wrong keeping things simple and honest!"

Sylvester nodded. "Goodbye then, my friend. Thank you for everything!" He gazed around one last time before whispering, "There's no point in putting this off any longer." So saying, he and Vivian linked arms and turned to leave.

The lovers entered the cave and found themselves upon the same softly lit, grassy, serpentine path that had first revealed itself to Sylvester, and their eyes were treated to the same wide array of beautiful multicolored flowers. However, the far end was obscured in shadow, and the foreboding darkness caused them to hesitate.

"Hurry!" the unrecognizable yet somehow familiar voice again commanded. In response to the command, they journeyed the length of the walkway and into the shadows.

CHAPTER 52

BACK TO REALITY

Vivian's eyes blinked open wide. She was instantly awake. Glancing at the alarm clock, she saw that she didn't need to be at work for another two hours—she'd awakened a full hour before the alarm was due to go off. "That's because I came back early," she acknowledged thoughtfully. Then, reminding herself that she hadn't come back alone, she rose quickly from her bed, intent on arriving at the hospital even earlier than usual.

Thus, began Vivian's daily routine. She brushed her teeth, showered, and pinned up her hair before donning her uniform. Next came breakfast—poached eggs on toast, orange juice, and a multivitamin for good health. Afterward, she took a few minutes to apply a small amount of makeup, choosing to forego perfume and lipstick. As excited as she was about seeing Sylvester in this world, the nurse in her remained conscious of the fact that she was going to work, not out on a date. Thus, she carefully maintained her professional appearance.

Glancing once again at the clock on the wall, she noted that she was still more than an hour ahead of schedule. Sighing with impatience, she retrieved the newspaper from in front of her door and forced herself to spend fifteen minutes going over stories of minor interest. Finally, feeling as though she could wait no longer, she grabbed her lunch, purse, and jacket. Taking one last look around the apartment to assure herself that all was in order, she headed out the door and off to work.

Sylvester's eyes blinked open wide. He was instantly awake. The memory of Lucky's World and his time with Vivian quickly flooded his mind. However, lacking Vivian's experience—not having tested the reality of his memories—doubt and fear rapidly began to set in. "Please, God," he silently prayed, "don't let it all be just a dream!"

His attention then focused on the uniformed officer watching television on the far side of the room. "How long have I been gone?" Sly's stiff vocal cords croaked.

The officer's head snapped to attention at the barely audible sound. "Welcome back!" he exclaimed, his face revealing his surprise. "I wasn't expecting to hear from you . . . In fact, I was betting that you were gone for good!"

"How long was I gone?" Sylvester repeated in a smoother, slightly louder voice.

"This is day 8, almost to the hour, since they found you unconscious in the yard—do you remember anything? Do you have any idea as to why you were unconscious?"

Sylvester didn't want to lie, nor did he wish to reveal anything. He opted for the literal truth. "All I have are memories . . . mostly of a beautiful woman and a talking squirrel."

The officer laughed. "Well, whatever happened to you—wherever you were—at least you were thoroughly entertained." Rising from his chair, he added, "I guess it's time to buzz the medical staff and let them know that you're back among the land of the living!" Then, without further comment, he strode over to the call button beside Sylvester's bed and signaled the nursing station.

The duty nurse responded immediately to the call. The doctor arrived soon thereafter. The doctor began with the same question that the officer had asked. "Do you remember anything? Do you have any idea as to why you were unconscious?"

Sylvester gave the same answer he'd given the officer: "Memories, mostly of a beautiful woman and a talking squirrel . . ." which elicited the same response—they all laughed heartily. Then came several more rapid-fire questions, to which Sylvester responded with equally rapid-fire answers.

"Do you know what year it is?"

"1998."

"Do you know what month it is?"

"August."

"Do you know what day of the week it is?"

Sylvester had to pause to think about the question. Then he reasoned out loud, "The officer said that I was gone for eight days, nearly to the hour. I believe that it was either Monday or Tuesday that I lost consciousness, but I'm not sure . . . to be honest, I can't be positive what day of the week it is."

"That's okay," the doctor assured him, "a small amount of confusion is to be expected. You were close. You arrived on a Monday. Today is Tuesday.

"Let's continue. What about your name? Can you tell me your full name?"

"Sylvester Bartholomew Alexander."

"Do you know how old you are?"

"Fifty-four."

"Do you feel any pain anywhere?"

"My throat and my vocal cords seem stiff and sore. So do most of the muscles in my body, but no serious pain."

The doctor nodded knowingly. "That's due to vocal inactivity and a lack of physical exercise. it'll all pass in a day or two."

He picked up Sylvester's chart and began to look through it thoughtfully. He decided to be blunt. "We weren't able to find anything physically wrong with you. You were diagnosed with a psychiatric condition—catatonic schizophrenia—which appears to me to have remitted itself."

He glanced meaningfully at the nurse. "Your feeding tubes will be immediately removed. Then we'll find something for you to eat. If that goes well and you're also able to eat breakfast in the morning—pending consultation with the psychiatrist—I'm of a mind to discharge you back to Abaddon by noon tomorrow."

Sylvester didn't bother to respond. He certainly wasn't looking forward to his return to Abaddon, and there was nothing more to say. The doctor exited the room, leaving the nurse to efficiently carry out the instructions that she'd been given.

An incoming tide of depression now threatened Sly's emotional well-being. The doctors explanation of his mental and his physical condition caused the distressed man to begin to believe Lucky's World, Vivian, and all that they'd experienced to be nothing more than a dream—a beautiful dream.

He'd nearly given himself over to the depths of despair when Vivian breezed into the room.

"Good evening!" she called out to the guard while walking around the edge of Sly's bed, strategically positioning herself between the two, thereby blocking the officer's view. Taking a moment to read Sly's chart, she continued, "It appears as though you'll be leaving soon, now that our patient is awake."

"Not soon enough for me!" the officer declared in a bored tone of voice.

"All's well that ends well," Vivian consoled the disgruntled man while nonchalantly placing the fingers of her right hand against Sylvester's wrist, as though checking his pulse.

Sly's eyes revealed both surprise and relief when she discreetly caressed his hand. "I know what you're thinking," Vivian whispered, "but it wasn't a dream. I'm going out to Abaddon in the morning—as soon as I get off work—to pick up visiting forms. I've got all of the information that I require to apply for visits. I'll have the forms properly filled out and delivered to the prison before the day is out.

"This pretense won't have to continue much longer—I'll be out to visit as soon as I'm cleared. I love you!" she assured him before gently squeezing his hand and stepping away.

"Your pulse and vital signs are all good, Mr. Bartholomew," Vivian announced in a clear voice, loud enough for the officer to hear. "Congratulations, it looks as though you're going to make a full recovery! All you that have to do is get your strength back.

"I'll bring you a snack a little bit later. Is there anything else that you need?"

"It'd be nice to go for a swim," Sly answered honestly, his aching muscles craving the uniquely soothing, warm water found only in Lucky's World.

Vivian forced a small laugh. "I'm sorry sir, we've no swimming facilities here, and I doubt that nice officer over there would be willing to allow such a thing. But it's good to see that you're getting your sense of humor back—it's all part of your recovery! Now if you'll excuse me, I've got other patients to attend to."

Vivian stepped into the hallway and nearly collapsed. It had taken all of her energy to control her emotions and to present herself in a way that wouldn't jeopardize her job. However, she knew what she had to do. She gathered her strength and her wits about her, then set out to finish her shift.

CHAPTER 53

BACK IN ABADDON

Sylvester arrived at Abaddon at 1:00 p.m., quickly making his way to East 4 in order to enjoy a long, hot shower. Twenty minutes of steaming water soothed his stiff, aching muscles until his body began to feel somewhat more comfortable. However, not yet satisfied with the overall effect, he returned to his cell and followed it up with ten minutes of crunches as well as a half hour of gentle stretching, which both alleviated the remainder of the pain and restored his flexibility.

The tier was quiet—most of the prisoners were at their job assignments, and Sly felt grateful for a little time alone to make the emotional and psychological adjustment to the Pit—there was much that he needed to do and little time to prepare.

"What to do first?" Sly silently wondered, before the thought was interrupted by the sound of Ray's voice.

"Hey, old man! How are you, buddy?" Ray asked, appearing directly in front of Sly's cell like an actor entering stage left. "Are you okay?" he continued in a tone of voice that revealed genuine concern. "I sure do hope you're feeling better and that you're back to stay . . . I mean, back with the people who care about you . . . you know what I'm sayin'?"

Sly wrestled with his emotions over the heartfelt greeting, all the while struggling for words. "I know exactly what you're sayin' . . . and I am feeling better. Now why don't you come on in here—come sit and talk with me for spell!"

"Can't think of anything I'd enjoy more!" Ray assured his friend. "I got tons of things to tell you about . . . and you're not gonna believe some of the shit that's been goin' on around this place!"

Ray entered, greeting his friend with a hug before flopping down in his usual spot at the foot of the bed. Then he watched curiously while Sylvester began to pace the floor. "What's goin' on Sly? Why don't you relax and give your feet a rest?"

Sylvester continued pacing, searching for an easy way to say what was on his mind. He failed. So he stopped and simply blurted, "I'm really sorry, Ray. There's no excuse for the way that I talked to you the other day. You were right. You are my friend, and you deserve much better than that from me. I will never speak to you that way again!"

Ray sat in stunned silence for several seconds, utterly dumbfounded by what he'd just heard. He couldn't recall Sly ever apologizing for anything, and this was so much more than just an apology—although they'd known each other for years, the strangeness of Sly's words suggested the presence of someone that Ray'd actually yet to meet.

Ray laughed nervously, further taken aback by the depth and evident sincerity of the apology. "Who are you, and what have you done with my friend, Sly?" he demanded jokingly, but the laughter quickly faded. Ray slowly rose from his seat, walked over, and gave Sylvester a second hug. "It's long forgotten, old man. We've been neighbors and friends for years. It'll take a lot more than a few words to change that!"

Not quite in full control of his emotions, Ray cleared his throat and continued in a gruff voice, "The guards'll be around any minute to lock up. I'd best get back to my cell—let's have dinner together and finish this conversation."

Dinner made Sly long for his ma's cooking. Nevertheless, he forced himself to eat sausages, instant potatoes, and cream corn. However, with Ma's apple pie in mind, he did pass his lemon tart over to Ray, who was more than happy to accept it.

"So tell me," Ray inquired, with a mouth half full of tart, "what the hell happened to you in the yard? You were fine when I left, and the next thing I know, they're taking you out of the joint in an ambulance. What's up with that?"

Sylvester looked around as though he wanted to be certain that they weren't being overheard, but what he really wanted was an extra moment to decide how much of his experience to reveal to Ray. It took less than a second for him to realize that Ray would never believe a word about Lucky's World. So he opted for the simplest explanation.

"They tell me that I lost my marbles for a while—some kind of catatonic schizophrenic thing."

"No shit?"

Sylvester laughed. "It's true, I swear. However, to be honest with you, I think I just needed a break from this place."

"Ya," Ray agreed, "I need a break from time to time, myself . . . not that way though."

Then he presented a question as though he were a doctor, prescribing medication to a patient: "How often have I suggested that you should smoke a little dope once in a while? The human brain is a fragile thing. It wasn't meant to be cooped up in a cage like a gerbil"

"Come to think of it, I'm not sure that a gerbil does a whole lot better under these conditions." He started to laugh as he extended the thought. "Maybe I should get out and start some sort of compassionate movement to supply pot to gerbils? Now there's a worthwhile mission in life!"

Sylvester shook his head slightly, trying to clear it of Ray's typical nonsense. He loved the guy, but in his opinion, Ray smoked way too much pot. It resulted in weird thinking, and it was probably what'd led to Lucky's near demise.

He shook his head a second time in an attempt to clear it of the image of Lucky's bones at the bottom of a fish tank. "I hear you," he acknowledged, "but drugs really aren't my thing! I prefer to deal with stress in other ways!"

"Ya . . . and look what it got you!"

Sylvester decided that it was time to change the subject. "I think there might have been other reasons for that. Now why don't you tell me what's been going on around this place over the last nine days?"

Ray made a sour face. "It's been fuckin' crazy, man!" he exclaimed. "First we had a suicide up on South 4—a buddy of Ike's, Al McFarlan. He was just a short timer—only a couple of years left to go. Young too . . . twenty-three years old. Fuckin' tragic, man! People are sayin' that it had something to do with Ike pimpin' him out to cover debts. It probably did, but I don't know for sure what was goin' on.

"A couple of days later, there was a murder on South 3—some guy named Wilfred Arbuckle. Rumor has it that he was a rapist and a snitch. Whatever their reasons were for killing him, I'm told that it was seriously ugly—they carved him up like a fuckin' turkey . . . blood all over the cell! He had seven years left on his sentence. Another one that died young . . . twenty-six years old.

"I'm thinkin' that Ike was in on that too—four of his crew are in segregation, supposedly about to be charged with murder. That fuckin' guy seems to be everywhere and into just about everything—he's become a rabid dog . . . someone should put him down!"

Ray sighed heavily. "I don't know, buddy. Maybe I'm gettin' old. I'm thinkin' that I don't care anymore why anyone is here—that's between them and whoever. As far as I'm concerned, there's just too many people dying in this fuckin' Pit!"

Sylvester listened to it all, noting Al's name and wondering what Al's death meant in relation to Ike and Steve—was there still a problem to be dealt with?

Taking advantage of a break in the monologue, Sylvester picked up on Ray's last point, relating it to his comment about "putting Ike down." "The problem can't be the solution, my friend. Put Ike down—whatever the reason—it's just another murder in the Pit. You might think that you've got a good reason, but I assure you, everyone else is of the same opinion over the things that they choose to do. In the end, it's just an excuse for more violence, and violence cannot possibly be the solution to violence!"

For the second time that day, Ray stared at Sylvester in slack-jawed silence while he tried to figure out who he was talking to—these were not the words of the Sly that he knew so well!

The moment was interrupted by the approach of one of the officers. "C'mon, guys, time's nearly up. Finish your meals and clear the area!"

The two prisoners obediently rose from the table. Ray was the first to speak as they exited the dining area, "Are you going for exercise?"

Sly shook his head. "Not tonight. I'm gonna kick back in my cell, watch some television, and relax. I need a day or two to recover my energy."

"Ya, that's a good idea," Ray agreed. "I'll see you when I get back—catch you later, buddy!" With that, he veered off and followed some of the crowd out to the yard.

Back in his cell, Sylvester took time to reflect on his dinner conversation with Ray. He felt happy with himself for his stand on violence and for the way in which he'd been able to express his thoughts on the subject. Inspired by his success, he dug out a pen and paper and began to write—he completed his credo in less than an hour.

He sat for a long time, reading and rereading the six simple statements that would henceforth guide his life:

1) I believe in God,
2) I believe in love,
3) I believe that violence is always a problem and never a solution to anything,
4) I believe in gender equality,
5) I believe in racial equality,
6) I believe in freedom of religion and the intrinsic validity and value of each person's chosen path.

The satisfied man could find no fault with what he'd written. There was nothing abstract. He had a very good grasp and understanding of each and every statement, and he intended to live by them all— everything felt exactly as it should!

CHAPTER 54

A NEW BEGINNING

Sylvester awoke Wednesday morning to sunshine and a strong sense that something new and interesting was about to happen in his life. He felt physically much improved, ready to act on his reasons for returning to Abaddon, and he was anxious to speak to Steve. Thus, he hurried about his usual routine, quickly heading off for breakfast, hoping to get a chance to talk to the man before the workday began. His hopes were rewarded—he entered the dining room to find Steve sitting alone at his usual table.

Sly smiled at the look of surprise on Steve's face as he took a seat opposite. "How's it going, friend?" he inquired.

"How are you?" Steve countered. "I was worried that something serious had happened!"

"Thanks for your concern, but it was really nothing much . . . a minor problem that's now resolved."

Sylvester hesitated a moment, gazing thoughtfully at Steve, then he continued, "I heard about Al. What was he doing up on South 4? I thought the two of you were cellmates? What happened?"

Steve felt reluctant to discuss the subject. However, he realized that he'd been the one to invite Sly's interest; thus, he couldn't very well refuse to answer. He opted for blunt honesty. "Al set me up from the start," he stated matter-of-factly. "When I found out about it, he and I had a major blowout. As a result, he moved up to South 4."

Sylvester wasn't surprised to hear it—it was as he'd first suspected. He decided to explore a little further. "What's the situation now between you and the rest of the South Block crew?"

"They haven't said anything to me. I have no idea what Ike is thinking or what he intends to do . . . but I know what I'm gonna to do!"

"Oh, and what's that?"

Steve felt compelled to be honest with the semistranger who'd been willing to help him out. He looked directly at Sylvester, declaring, "I'm gonna kill that no-good fuck!"

Many years of prison experience had taught Sylvester to discern an idle threat from real intent. He could tell that Steve meant what he was saying. He also sensed that Steve was saying it because, deep down, he wanted to be stopped, and he correctly guessed that if he was going to stop him from acting out his threat, he needed to say or do something right now!

"You can't imagine how disappointed I am to hear that," Sly remarked sadly. "I remember the first time I saw you in V&C. My heart ached as I watched you with your wife and daughter. I was reminded of a woman that I once knew and a daughter that has long been lost to me. Watching the three of you there, so happy together, I would have given anything to be you.

"That's part of what made me to want to help you in the first place—I couldn't ignore your desperation to protect and preserve your family. It's so hard for me to understand how you're suddenly willing to throw that all away over a racist piece of work like Ike!"

Sylvester pause for a minute, giving his words a chance to sink in. Then he continued, "Years from now, when you think back on this period of your life—when you wonder how you could have been so stupid—remember the burned-out old black man who warned you that you'd regret it . . . because, I promise you, you will regret it for the rest of your life!

"When another man has taken your place in your wife's heart, when you can no longer even remember what your daughter looks like or how it felt to hear her laugh and call you Daddy, you'll curse the day that you gave yourself over to this evil thing that you're planning to do."

Steve was visibly shaken by Sylvester's words. The reality of his intent began to overtake and challenge the depth of his anger and his shame. "It isn't all of the sudden," he admitted as he began to pour out his heart. Then he described everything that had happened between him and Al and how he felt about it.

Sylvester listened to it all. He understood and appreciated every word—he knew very well what it was like to be motivated by feelings, rather than guided by principles. He listened patiently until Steve asked, "What am I supposed to do? How can I live with this? How can I let Ike get away with what he's done?"

"Those three questions are closely related, my friend," Sylvester answered gently, "but not in the way that you think that they are. What you're supposed to do is figure out how you can live with what has happened. Once you figure out how you can live with it, the last question will begin to take care of itself. In other words, deal with your pain and your anger, and the desire for revenge will start to disappear."

Steve weighed Sylvester's words. He thought about his wife and daughter. Finally he asked, "What about justice? Does Ike simply get to walk away?"

"Absolutely not! Sooner or later, everything that he's done will catch up to him. I've witnessed similar situations play themselves out dozens times over the years . . . it always catches up to them in the end. I can't say for sure where, when, or how, but Ike will pay for all that he's done. That I can promise you!"

Steve sensed the truth in Sylvester's words. "You're a wise man, Sly," he commented while rising from the table. "I need to get my priorities straight—it's time for me to put my family first. It might take a while, but I'll figure out how to deal with the pain—let's talk again sometime."

Sylvester spoke quickly before Steve had a chance to turn and walk away, "What's your last name, brother?"

Surprised by the question, he answered, "McMasterson . . . my name is Steve McMasterson. Why do you ask?"

"How about we go for a walk in the yard this evening, Steve? I'm thinking that the sooner you and I talk again, the better off we're both gonna be, and I'd like to be your friend!"

Steve nodded agreeably. "I'd like that too." He extended his hand, "I'd like that very much. I'll meet you out there after dinner. Now I've got to get to work.

"You have yourself a fine day!" he urged as he turned and headed off to the canvas shop.

Sylvester returned from breakfast to discover that he'd lost his job as tier cleaner—it'd been given to Les during his nine-day absence. The anxious man awaited Sly by the entrance, fearful and more than willing to give the job back. However, Sylvester declined the offer. "I'm due for a change anyway," he assured him. "Don't worry about it!"

"You've got that right," a voice seemed to say, "something much more interesting and challenging awaits!"

Sylvester froze. It was the third time that he'd heard the heretofore unrecognizable yet somehow familiar voice, and he slowly smiled as he realized that it'd become familiar—it was a voice that he knew he'd hear often in the years to come!

"Hey, man, are you okay?" Les nervously inquired.

"I've never been better!" Sly happily declared before turning and continuing down the tier.

Approaching his cell, Sly's attention was drawn to a letter resting between the bars on his door. He grabbed it and immediately saw that it was from Vivian. There was no postal stamp. That meant that she'd driven out to the prison and dropped it off by hand. His heart skipped a beat as he thought of her so close and yet so far away. He quickly entered the cell, flopped down on his bed with his back against the pillow, opened the letter, and began to read.

I was a short note, dropped off with the visitor's application forms—a declaration of love, a phone number, and a request that he call soon—the sooner, the better. It was everything that he needed to hear!

"Talk about the perfect start to a perfect day," he thought to himself while rereading the letter. Then, carefully folding and placing it back into the envelope, he concluded, "Now if I can just figure out where it is that I'm supposed to be employed, I won't have anything at all to complain about!"

Sylvester glanced at his watch. He could see that he had at least fifteen minutes before lockup to go down and check the job postings on the board beside the central control—he wasted no time.

The first posting on the job-board seemed to leap out at him. It simply read "Clerk/cleaner wanted in the chapel." He stared at it for several seconds. "Why not?" he softly asked himself. "It's definitely something new!"

"Hurry!" the voice urged.

Sly glanced at his watch a second time, attempting to gauge if he could make it to the chapel and back to his cell before lockup. Realizing the it would have to be one destination or the other, he opted to obey to the voice, rationalizing to himself, "If I want the job, then I'd better get my name into the hat!"

CHAPTER 55

IKE AND HIS BOYS

Ike was in another of his foul moods. Someone had started a rumor that one of his four good ol' boys might testify against the other three. He'd been unable to track down the source of the rumor, but he suspected that it might be true.

Not that he was concerned about the possibility of any of the four—or all of them—being convicted of the crime. Not at all—he didn't care about any of them! His only concern was that a snitch might finger him as the one who'd developed the plan and put it into motion. That would definitely result in a major headache!

He felt reasonably confident that he could beat any criminal prosecution in court, but it would mean many months in segregation, as well as numerous hours of courtroom bullshit and legal wrangling.

"Fuck!" he cursed aloud while wondering how any of them could be so inconsiderate and selfish as to drag him into their mess. After all, it wasn't his fault that they'd been too fucking sloppy to get away with it!

Ike's day was made even worse by last night's revelation that Sly was back in the joint. "I thought I'd seen the last of that black son of a bitch!" he snarled as, once again, his mind filled with memories. He recalled prisoners hiding their faces, trying not to be seen as they laughed while he mopped up his own blood. It never even occurred to him that most—if not all—had long forgotten the event and that it lived on only in his mind. Self-generated shame and hate inflamed his rage. He slammed the weights in frustration while attending his daily cleaning routine of the weight pit. "I can't put up with this much longer," he assured himself, "that fucker has gotta die!"

This time Ike began to make serious plans. The skinner was dealt with, and he saw no good reason to put off dealing with Sly in a similar manner.

It was, of course, profoundly ironic that he began to refocus his evil intent toward Sly on the very morning that Sly had convinced Steve to abandon his plans for Ike. Not that knowing this fact would have mattered to Ike—not at all! He'd have simply considered Sly stupid for having done so. The irony would not have dissuaded him. However, had he known what was happening at that very moment in the interview room adjoined to the segregation unit, he'd have most certainly been thinking along different lines.

The two homicide investigators were back to talk to Rick and Phil a second time. On this occasion, they opted to wait while the Abaddon officer escorted the prisoners individually, back and forth. Rick was the first to be interviewed.

Rick entered the room, seated himself at the table, directly across from the lead investigator, who pointedly turned on the recording equipment. "It is now 10:00 a.m. on Wednesday, August 17, 1998. Your name is Richard William Bellows, is that correct?"

"Yes."

"Do you understand that you're being interviewed in connection to the murder of Wilfred Michael Arbuckle?"

"Yes."

"Are you, at this time, waiving your right to remain silent and your right to have an attorney present?"

"Yes."

"Then tell us, if you will, everything that you know about the murder."

"What I know is a matter of life and death," he joked with a smile.

"How so?"

He actually laughed while springing punch line. "The skinner is dead, and there's one more person who's gonna get life."

"You'd do well to forego the humor," the second investigator coldly advised. "Just tell us what happened, clearly describing the role of each person involved."

Rick sighed his disappointment at their lack of humor before relating the entire story to the two investigators, emphasizing Ike's role in planning and organizing the murder. "It was Ike's idea from the start," he insisted, "all I was trying to do was get out of debt. Now I'm in more trouble than ever!"

"Will you testify as to Ike's role in the murder in open court?" the first investigator asked.

Rick knew that this was the moment—this was the only power card that he had. He played it. "That depends on what's in it for me!" he stated matter-of-factly.

The investigators exchanged knowing looks. The second one then spoke up. "There may be something that can be worked out. However, that will be between you and the prosecutor. We'll pass this information along. Someone will get back to you very soon!"

"Put him back in his cell," the first investigator directed the prison guard. Rick rose from the table, feeling his knees go weak as the second investigator requested, "Bring us the other one, please."

It was then that Rick realized that he had competition—someone else was talking. He guessed that it was Phil, and he cursed inwardly as he further realized that the market value of his testimony was now half what it otherwise would have been!

The interview with Phil echoed the interview with Rick. Of primary importance to the investigators was the fact that Phil supported Rick's account of Ike's role in the whole affair. This caused them to have confidence in Rick's account of the facts of the case.

As they'd done with Rick, the two investigators assured Phil that any deal would have to be worked out between himself and the prosecutor and that someone would be out to see him soon. However, privately, they were not nearly as optimistic—as they'd been about Rick—that something might be worked out in exchange for Phil's testimony.

There were two reasons for their doubt. The first reason was the fact that Phil had been the one who'd actually committed the murder. The second reason was the fact that they would have Rick's testimony; and they felt confident that this, alone, would be enough to convict Ike.

Shortly after Phil was returned to his cell, the investigators requested of Abaddon's internal security officer that Ike be arrested and placed in segregation for his role in the murder of Wilfred Michael Arbuckle.

Ike had just returned from lunch when the inmate extraction unit appeared in front of his cell. He heard the lead member of the team bark the usual commands. "Get down on your knees, and place your hands behind your head!"

He knew better than to refuse, and he kneeled before asking, "What the fuck is this about?"

"You're being placed in segregation, pending completion of the investigation into the murder of Wilfred Michael Arbuckle," the officer replied as he cuffed Ike's hands behind his back.

"Wilfred fucking who?" Ike spat out. "Never fucking heard of him!"

There was no response. There was nothing more to say. He was escorted to the segregation unit, processed, and placed in a cell.

Though it had been a long morning, the two investigators decided to give Ike an hour alone in his cell to cool off before bringing him out for questioning. They need not have bothered. Ultimately, Ike had only one thing to say: "I want a lawyer!" He was arrested, but he was a long way from being convicted of the crime.

CHAPTER 56

A PLACE TO FIT IN

Pastor Paul was sitting in his office, feeling somewhat despondent over Wil's death. As a Christian, he truly believed that all things work for good for those who love and serve God. However, he remained at a loss to see any good in what had happened to the young man. Security staff had given him some idea of the horror that'd transpired in Wil's cell, and the religious overtones to the murder were particularly hard for the pastor to come to spiritual terms with. After thirteen years at Abaddon, he began to question whether or not he was the right person for the job.

Struggling with his thoughts and feelings, he bowed his head and took a moment to pray. "Please, Lord," he asked, "if I'm the man for this job, help me to find a way to teach prisoners that the violence they do to each other is ultimately violence that they do to themselves." He allowed his mind to go quiet for a moment, seeking intimacy with God, then made a second request, "Lord, if it's not too much to ask, show me someone in this place—just one prisoner—who is truly open to Christ's message of peace and love."

The knock came before he had a chance to say amen. He looked up in surprise, remembered to say "Amen," and then loudly invited the visitor. "C'mon in, the door's open!"

Sylvester entered, looking just a little bit like a fish out of water. He nervously cleared his throat, then bravely proceeded, "Good morning, Pastor! I noticed a posting on the job board, and I'm wondering if the job is still open?"

"Well, yes, it is," he answered with a chuckle. "Do you have a name?"

"I'm sorry, my name is Sylvester Bartholomew."

Pastor Paul believed passionately in the power of prayer. Acutely conscious of the timing of the knock on his door, he was instantly and deeply interested in Sylvester. "Why do you want to work in the chapel?" he inquired.

Sylvester hadn't anticipated a job interview. He wasn't at all prepared for the question. That was a good thing—all he could do was be honest and sincere. "Well, for starters, I've been doing a lot of soul searching this last while . . . working on some things and trying to make some changes in my life."

"What kind of things have you been working on?"

Sylvester hesitated a moment. He didn't want to sound foolish. However, he'd started down this path, and he was pretty much committed. He took a deep breath, then continued, "I've been working on a credo. In fact, I only just completed it this morning . . ."

"A credo," Pastor Paul interrupted, not quite believing what he was hearing—it was the first time in his thirteen years of prison ministry that he'd heard a prisoner even mention the term. "What kind of credo have you come up with?"

Fearing that his efforts might appear inadequate in the eyes of the pastor, Sylvester began to feel very uncomfortable. "It's nothing much," he answered softly before forcing himself to recite the six statements: "I believe in God. I believe in love. I believe that violence is always a problem and never a solution to anything. I believe in gender equality. I believe in racial equality. I believe in freedom of religion and the intrinsic validity and value of each person's chosen path." Then he waited anxiously for chaplain's reaction.

Pastor Paul was literally rendered speechless for several seconds. Partially overcoming his astonishment, he managed to blurt out, "Are you a Christian?"

"I believe so," Sylvester responded honestly, "although I can't say for certain at this point in time. Now that I've nailed down some basics in terms of what I believe in, I have to figure out where I fit in. My father was a Christian. The woman that I love is a Christian, and she's confident that I am too. However, I need to study and learn more before I make such a commitment. That's part of why I want to work here.

"A friend of mine taught me that a healthy spiritual journey is a three-stage process. First, you figure out what you believe, second, you figure out where you fit in, and third, you get connected. I guess I'm somewhere between the second and third stages. However, Christianity does seem to be the natural place for me to be—it's certainly going to be my starting point."

Sylvester thought for a moment, then asked a question of his own. "Why, is being a Christian a job requirement?"

"No, it's not," Pastor Paul replied emphatically. "I'm just trying to get to know you, and I've heard enough," he concluded while reaching into his desk drawer for the paperwork that he needed to fill out in order to hire Sylvester. "You're exactly the kind of man that I need in this place."

It only took ten minutes to fill out the paperwork. Then came the tour and the list of required duties. "This is a position of trust," the chaplain explained. "You'll be spending a lot of time here alone. You'll need to get used to that. I'm often called away. The chapel is closed when I'm not here, but you'll be allowed to remain to perform your duties, and I suspect that you'll welcome the opportunity to get away from all the prison hubbub. Now you go ahead and take a look around on your own while I walk this paperwork over to administration for approval."

"I've got the job then?" Sylvester asked in surprise.

"You will have, before the day is out," Pastor Paul confidently promised. "I've got quite a lot of pull around here on this issue. Your official start date will be tomorrow morning, 9:00 a.m. sharp. However, I'd appreciate it if you'd make yourself a cup of coffee and relax . . . I'd like to talk some more with you when I get back."

Sylvester watched the pastor leave. He noted the urn of coffee on the table in the corner, walked over, and poured himself a cup. Then he pulled a Bible off the nearest shelf, sat back in a comfortably cushioned chair, and—for the first time in his life—began to read.

It was by pure accident that he began to read from 1 Corinthians chapter 13, and he recalled Vivian's words, "Tell me more about love." He also remembered how surprised he'd been at the clarity of his answer. He'd really meant it when he'd admitted, "I have no idea where all of that just came from!"

Reading the chapter a second time, he continued to be astonished by what he found there, only this time he recalled Vivian's answer: "I know where it comes from."

A smile of understanding lit up his face. "She really did know!" he exclaimed in wonder. "The proof is right in front of me!" Then he read the chapter yet a third time in order to confirm the revelation. Sure enough, 1 Corinthians, chapter 13, contained his exact definition of love—it was the first of many occasions that he'd find himself on the pages of the Bible.

CHAPTER 57

VIVIAN'S TRUTH

It was Saturday—a little more than two weeks after Vivian and Sylvester's decision to leave Lucky's World. Vivian finally had security clearance to visit Sylvester, and she was scheduled for Sunday afternoon. However, this evening she faced a related—but different—challenge. She was on her way to have dinner with her parents and to tell them all about the man that she loved.

Vivian drove carefully, silently reviewing the basis for her decision. "I've put this off long enough," she admitted while fighting off a wave of anxiety, "maybe too long!

"One thing is for certain: I can't attend tomorrow's visit without telling Mom and Dad what's going on. It wouldn't be fair to them, nor would it be fair to Sylvester. They'd wonder why I'd hid the fact, and he might believe that I'm ashamed of him. Only Sylvester would believe the truth—that I'm at a loss to explain how we met and fell in love!"

Vivian sighed heavily. "There's no time like the present to do what needs to be done," she assured herself. "I'll figure something out!"

She glanced at her watch without taking her hands off the steering wheel. It read 4:48 p.m. "Looks like I'll be a little early," she silently acknowledged. "I'd best hurry and figure out what I'm going to say!"

She practiced a line aloud. "Guess what, Mom, Dad . . . I'm in love with a man who's serving life for arson and murder." Then she quickly nixed it, "No, that's not wise!

"How about, 'I'll bet you didn't know that squirrels could talk?'"

Vivian shook her head in exasperation. "No, that's not going to work, either.

"Too late . . . no time left to figure it out!" she exclaimed as she entered the parking lot. "I'm in so much trouble. I've no choice but to take this one step at a time . . . and be as honest as possible."

She parked the car but her mind remained in overdrive.

Henry and Maggie Southerman loved their daughter more than anything in the world. Not a day went by that one, the other, or both didn't find cause to thank God for providing them with such a wonderful, dependable, stable child. Their only unfulfilled wish for her—and themselves—was that she'd find a suitable husband—something that, in their opinion, she'd evaded for much too long.

They watched as Vivian emerged from her car, and they exchanged questioning looks—there seemed to be something different about her! Henry spoke what they were both thinking. "She's met someone!"

"Maybe!" Maggie thoughtfully agreed before warning her husband, "Now don't you go saying anything. If she's got some sort of surprise for us, don't you dare ruin it. You just wait and allow her get around to it on her own good time!"

Vivian entered without knocking. She gave them both a big hug and then passed some fresh-cut wildflowers to her mother. Maggie knew to expect them—Vivian had been bringing her fresh-cut wildflowers since she was a little girl. She wordlessly and appreciatively nested them in the vase that she'd already placed on the dining room table.

"How are you, Mom? How are you, Dad?" Vivian asked brightly while removing her jacket and slipping out of her shoes. "What's for dinner? I'm starving!"

"Dinner is a surprise," her mother answered. "You'll just have to wait for another half hour . . ."

"Mom, really now?" Vivian laughingly interrupted. "I could smell that stuffed chicken cooking from a mile down the road! I'm just wondering what you've got to go with it?"

Dinner turned out to be the usual comfortable affair. Her parents chitchatted between bites, revealing gossip and the activities around the retirement home. Vivian talked about some of her week at the hospital, without mentioning Sylvester. Dessert was more of a delight than the surprise Maggie'd intended—She'd baked Vivian's favorite, a delicious peach pie.

Vivian took a small bite, allowing the tender flakes and sweet fruit to rest for a moment on her tongue before swallowing. "What is it about elderly people and pie?" she wondered. "How do they always seem to get it so perfect? Between my mother and Sly's Ma, I think I'm in pie heaven!"

The memory of Ma's apple pie reminded her of the evening's objective, and she decided that now was as good a time as any to ease into the subject. "I'm surprised that neither of you have asked if I'm seeing anyone these days," she casually commented. "It's usually one of your first questions . . . aren't you curious?"

Henry blamed his wife. "It's your mother's fault!" he assured Vivian, pretending to be grumpy about it. "She told me that I wasn't allowed to ask you any questions this evening."

"That's not exactly true," Maggie countered. "I just didn't want him to spoil any surprise that you might have for us."

"What made you think that I might have a surprise?"

"You just seem different, dear," Maggie answered sweetly. "Parents pick up on these things quite easily. We both noticed that there seems to be something different about you this evening."

Vivian hesitated while trying one last time to think of an easy way to say what needed to be said. Failing, she simply blurted it out, "I have met someone—I'm in love. I'm more than just in love. I've met the man that I know that God wants me to be with."

The last statement got their attention—they'd never before heard her say such a thing. "Who is he?" Henry asked. "Is he a doctor? When do we get to meet this fine young man?"

Fearful of her parents' reaction, Vivian sighed and answered sadly, "It'll take a while, Dad, if it turns out that you want to meet him at all. He's serving life in prison."

Silence filled the room for full minute while her parents attempted to process the information—it was somewhat more of a surprise than they'd been looking for, to say the least. Maggie finally broke the silence with a question, "How did you meet him?"

The words that had previously eluded Vivian now flowed easily, "At first he was a patient at the hospital, but he became much more than that." She paused and looked directly at her father, "Daddy, I'll never tell another human being what I'm about to tell you and Mom. Please listen and try not to think that I'm crazy. You've told me many times that there are things in this world that cannot be explained, and this most certainly one of those things." Then Vivian bravely revealed the complete truth, exactly as she'd experienced it.

She left nothing out. First she talked about Lucky's World and the basis for her belief that this was a God-given experience. Then she explained how she'd used Sylvester's middle name to test the reality of the experience. By the end of the evening, they knew why Sylvester was in prison, Vivian's impression of the man that he'd been, her confidence in the man that he'd become, and even that he was now employed as the prison chapel clerk. However, of all that she revealed, what mattered most to her parents were the words: "He's the only man that I've ever felt completely happy with."

"I won't lie to you," Maggie stated matter-of-factly, "this is going to take some getting used to. However, I know that I can speak for your father, as well as myself, when I say that your happiness is what matters most. If this is what you truly want, we will support you. We just ask that you go slow and be sure of what you're doing."

"Yes!" Her father agreed. "And we are going to want to meet him. The sooner, the better!"

Tears of relief filled Vivian's eyes. "I'm so glad to hear that, Daddy!"

"You'll love him. I know you will. I'll tell him what you said and how you feel when I see him tomorrow. He'll be scared . . . but he'll want to meet you too.

"I'm so happy that you and mom are going to be okay with this. I should have told you sooner . . . I just didn't know how."

"Hush now, child," her mother comforted. "We've always worked through things together, and we always will. If this is part of God's plan for our family, I'm sure that it'll be a wonderful blessing in our lives!"

CHAPTER 58

YARD TIME

Sylvester and Steve walked the yard, as they'd done each night for the last two weeks, discussing various things of mutual interest in their lives. Steve was particularly curious about Sly's decision to work in the prison chapel, a recurring theme that surfaced, once again, as the topic of conversation.

"I have to be honest with you," Steve admitted, "that's the last place I'd have guessed that you'd find a job. You don't actually believe all that Bible stuff, do you?"

Sylvester had already read the Bible from cover to cover. Now he was slowly working his way through it a second time, reading much more thoughtfully. This dovetailed with his many telephone conversations with Vivian, workplace conversations with Pastor Paul, the insights that he'd gained in Lucky's World, and especially his own conscience. A lot of things were beginning to make sense. He was ready and willing to share them with Steve, "Can I answer in a roundabout way?"

Steve laughed. "Answer it any way you like, my friend . . . I'm all ears!"

"I think I understand why you're asking the question. To a certain extent, you're looking to me to help you to decide what to believe, and that makes it a very dangerous question.

"It saddens me to have to admit it, but the majority of time, the answer that you receive from other Christians on this subject will be more reflective of the agenda of the person answering the question than it will be of the truth. You put yourself at risk by looking for the right answer in the wrong place . . . you're looking outside yourself for something that must be found within.

"Too many Christians play at divisive politics on every level. For example, there's the issue of the authority of the Bible. On this issue, they separate, primarily, into two camps—fundamentalist and liberal.

"The fundamentalists claim that the Bible's authority emanates from its authorship, that the Holy Spirit inspired each and every word, and that God essentially wrote the Bible. This point of view leaves very little room for interpretation or critical thought. It demands blind faith in—and complete acceptance of—every word in the Bible, even when the Bible seems to be at odds with what some believe in their hearts to be true.

"Liberals, on the other hand, claim that the authority of the Bible emanates from its content, not its authorship. They maintain that the Bible is the work of human effort—that sometimes people got it right, and sometimes people got it wrong. This point of view leaves plenty of room for interpretation and critical thought. However, it also facilitates a tendency among some liberals to ignore the more inconvenient teachings of the Bible and simply do as they please . . ."

"Which camp do you fall into, then?" Steve interrupted.

"Both and neither—it's a false divide," Sylvester declared. "The lessons are in the Bible, and it's up to each of us to learn from them or not. We all have the right to choose. No one has the right to impose his or her views.

"The problem is that people tend to invite such imposition—as I pointed out, it's a consequence of people looking outside themselves for the answers that lie within . . . which brings me full circle. I'm drawing your attention to this now in the hope that you'll avoid making the same mistake and to prevent you from being duped into participating in this or any of the other foolish arguments that distract people from the teachings of Jesus Christ!

"When it comes to deciding what to believe, a very good friend of mine encouraged me to first examine my own heart, which happens to be biblically supported advice. Hebrews 8, verses 10 and 11 speak clearly about the supremacy of an individual's conscience—heart and mind—as the primary Spirit-inspired source of spiritual knowledge. I'm thoroughly convinced that Jesus brought us something new—the New Covenant. However, I'm also convinced that the truth of this covenant is written on our hearts and minds, and that it was written there long before the constituent parts of the New Testament were ever assembled. The logical consequence of this is spiritual unity, and any deliberate focus on spiritual divergence usually reflects an alternate agenda—more often than not, a political agenda!"

Sylvester hesitated for a moment to catch his breath and collect his thoughts. He desperately wanted Steve to understand his next point. He stopped walking and looked directly into his eyes. "There are plenty of people who will tell you that you must believe exactly as they do or you'll burn in hell. However, I'm not one of them. I don't participate in arguments that facilitate division. I'm not interested in politics. I have no personal agenda, and I'm very reluctant to influence your learning by telling you what I believe. I would prefer that you study with an open heart and an open mind in order to arrive at your own conclusions!

Steve was genuinely surprised to hear this and he said so. "I thought you guys were always on the lookout for converts. Aren't you supposed to be spreading the word, wherever you go? I'm asking for answers, and you're telling me to study. What's up with that?"

Sylvester attempted a slightly modified explanation. "What you choose to believe is the most important decision that you'll ever make," he answered patiently. "It's not a choice that should ever be made blindly or on the advice of another human being. You should always know exactly why you believe. For example, I believe, in part, because I find myself in the New Testament. I find how to love, I find the kind of husband that I want to be, I find the kind of worker that I want to be, I find the kind of citizen that I want to be, and I even find the kind of friend that I want to be. However, my journey of self-discovery is, by definition, a personal thing. I cannot take your journey for you. If your experience is going to be real, you must study, search, and find the truth for yourself—study the Bible and search your heart. If you do, I believe that the answers you seek will be found in both places.

"I do spread the word. I spread it in the best possible way. The best way to spread the word is to live it. You wouldn't be walking with me now or thinking along these lines if you didn't see something in my life that is of interest to you, and that's far more powerful than anything else that I can possibly do or say!"

Steve thought about this for a while before asking, "What about the flip side of the coin? How do you handle some of the criticisms of organized religion? How do you respond to accusations that the Bible has been used in hurtful ways?"

"I'm no apologist for historical wrongs," Sylvester answered without hesitation. "I'm responsible only for my own behavior. I say, let those who are responsible for bad behavior answer for what they have done.

"The accusation is often true—historically, the Bible has been misused by many people to support all manner of evil . . . war, torture, slavery, and a multiplicity of injustices. To my way of thinking, this says everything about the people involved—their agenda—and nothing at all about God or the Bible. I'm certain that, in each and every case, they failed to listen to—and obey—the truth that is written on their hearts and minds."

Steve liked what he was hearing, and he wanted to hear more. "Do you mind if I join you in church tomorrow morning?" he asked.

"Nothing would make me happier!" Sly exclaimed. "Vivian will be out tomorrow afternoon for our first visit. I'd love to be able to tell her that you and I spent the morning in church . . . she'll be so pleased!"

"Fantastic! We'll make a day of it then—my wife and Taba will be out tomorrow afternoon, as well. It'll be the best day that we've ever had in this place!"

Just then, the loudspeaker blasted the usual command: "Clear the yard! All prisoners return to their blocks!" Wordlessly, Steve and Sylvester turned and began to walk in the direction of the main building. It was a short, comfortable walk, and Steve offered a parting comment upon entering the main building, "I love you, brother. You have a good night. I'll see you in the morning."

Back in his cell, Steve couldn't help but be amazed at how different his world had become, compared to only a couple of weeks ago. "Sylvester saved my life!" he admitted out loud before silently reflecting on just how close he'd come to disaster.

"That dumb-ass plan of mine would never have worked. Had it not been for Sly, I'd have thrown everything away for sure and quite possibly have gotten myself killed! Now we're on the verge of a whole new experience—I'm actually looking forward to tomorrow!

"How cool is that?" he whispered in surprise.

On entering his cell, Sylvester also took a moment to reflect. He recalled what Lucky had taught him about his participation in the ongoing creation process. He thoughtfully charted his own progress— first he'd created according to however he felt at the time. Then he'd learned to create according to his needs, rather than his wants. Next he'd managed to put the needs of others before his own, and to this was added the additional insights that he'd gained in Lucky's World. Finally, he'd developed a credo, which further guided his actions. All of this had definitely produced good results. However, now he felt that there was something else going on—something even deeper and more powerful. He resolved to talk to Vivian about it.

CHAPTER 59

FREE TO BELIEVE AND
THE POWER OF PRAYER

Pastor Paul was preaching hellfire and brimstone. He was on a fundamentalist roll—the world was created in six days, it was no more than six thousand years old, and anyone who taught—or believed—otherwise was definitely destined for the fires of hell. It wasn't intended to be a political or divisive sermon—he taught what he'd been taught, and he taught what he believed. However, his insistence that everyone adhere to his beliefs proved difficult for some in the audience.

Steve leaned over and whispered to Sylvester. "This isn't what I expected. It's hard for me to listen . . . I simply don't believe some of the things that he's saying. I feel as though I'm being pushed away."

Sylvester nodded understandingly before asking, "Who told you that you have to believe everything that someone—anyone—says to you? Nothing could be further from the truth. As I said last night, you need to test everything that you hear against what you feel in your heart. Listen carefully to all that he says, accept what feels right and reject what feels wrong, but don't allow yourself to miss out on the one on account of the other.

"Intolerance cannot be defeated by intolerance, and his desire to make you believe exactly as he does cannot be defeated by an attitude that he should believe exactly as you do. Intolerance can only be defeated by respect and tolerance. You must allow him to be true to himself while you remain true to who you are. The way forward is to focus on the things he says that you do agree with—the points of convergence, rather than divergence—and let the rest fall by the wayside, at least for the time being.

"What harm can possibly come to you if you simply obey your own conscience and allow other people the freedom to do the same?

"Jesus gave us an eleventh commandment, 'Love one another as I have loved you.' The greatest gift—and act of love—that God bestowed upon us is free will, and that is what we must also grant to each other. Take the initiative! If you desire freedom for yourself, then first extend it to others. Start right now!"

Steve listened to the remainder of Pastor Paul's sermon from Sylvester's perspective. He was surprised at how much he heard that he did agree with, and he was also surprised at how much he learned. Of equal importance, he didn't feel at all pushed away.

The service ended. Sylvester gave his friend a look of concern as some of the other prisoners got up to leave. "Well, what do you think? Did you get anything out of it?"

"Yes, I did," Steve admitted. "I got a lot more out of it than I thought I would and a lot more than I would have, without your advice. Had you not spoken, I probably wouldn't have even stayed for the entire sermon. Now I'm thinking that maybe I'll come back next Sunday. What else can I say? You've something going for yourself, Sly. I don't know what happened to you in that hospital, but it sure does seem to have changed you, and all for the better!"

Sylvester contemplated Steve's words while on his way back to his cell—Steve's positive response to Sly's counseling felt good. However, Sly also felt curious as to why spiritual issues now so thoroughly permeated his own life. "Why am I so often faced with these types of questions when, prior to my stay in Lucky's World, the subject never arose?" he wondered.

It only took a moment to reason it out. "The questions must be a consequence of the life that I'm now living. I work in the chapel, so people ask me about the chapel. I spend time in church, so people talk to me about church. That ought not to come as a huge surprise." The simplicity of the obvious explanation made him smile.

"Whatcha smilin' about?" Ray asked as Sylvester walked onto the tier. "Where ya bin? Musta bin someplace special to put dat grin on your face!"

"Church. You should come with me sometime . . . it'll put a grin on your face too!"

"Na! I tried that prayin' stuff once. It didn't work," Ray said sadly. "I was eleven years old when my gramps died. I prayed to God, 'Please keep him alive just a little while longer.' But he died just the same. Ever since then, I knew that there was no point in prayin'."

"Here I go again!" Sylvester thought to himself, still amazed at how often these conversations were occurring. He looked at Ray; and it was easy to see that he was quite serious. The need was real, and Steve chose to respond. He had no idea what he was about to say—he simply let the words flow.

"Maybe your gramps was praying that night too?" he suggested. "Maybe he was in serious pain? Maybe he was feeling old and tired and asking God to bring him home? I have no way of knowing, but if that was the case, whose prayer was God supposed to answer?"

Ray fell silent for several seconds, clearly thinking about something. "Gramps died of cancer," he answered reflectively. "You might be right. I've never thought of it that way!"

"Not many people do, Ray. Imagine two armies on the battlefield—plenty of Christians on both sides, most of whom would likely be praying for personal security and victory. Which prayers does God answer? The truth is, God gives us free will. Governments make decisions to go to war, and everyone has to deal with the consequences."

"So why pray at all? If prayer doesn't change the outcome, why bother?"

"First of all, I didn't say that prayer doesn't change the outcome or that God never answers prayer. On the contrary, I'm certain that he always answers prayer! What I don't know—what none of us can know—is God's mind and God's reasoning in the way that he answers—prayer is answered according to God's infinite wisdom. All I'm trying to point out to you is that there's always so much more going on than any of us can possibly be aware of, and we ought not to grow cynical about prayer simply because God doesn't do as he's told! We should accept our limitations, appreciate God's wisdom, and continue to pray . . . for our own benefit and especially the benefit of each other!"

Ray seemed to chew this over in his mind for an unusually long period of time. Sylvester was starting to wonder if Ray'd been smoking pot when he finally spoke up. "I think I get it—it ain't all that different than a healthy relationship between parents and their children. Children don't often get to tell their parents what to do, and parents don't give their children everything that they ask for whenever they want it. Parents act out of love, in the best interest of their children. However, children don't always see it that way! Ya, it makes sense!"

"That's exactly right!" Sylvester burst out excitedly. Then, encouraged by his success, he decided to press ahead.

"Though I can't tell you God's reasoning for the way in which prayer is answered, I can tell you that prayer is about much more than simply asking for things—it's about relationships . . . it's about our relationship with each other, and it's about our relationship with God.

"When people gather in prayer—for any reason, be it sad or happy—in that single act, we become to each other everything that God wants us to be. We share the joy, we share the sorrow, we give each other strength, and we are always so much stronger than we could ever hope to be on our own. It's the exact relationship that God wants us to have with each other, and it's the exact relationship that God wants us to have with him . . ."

"You sure do talk funny these days," Ray interrupted. "You don't seem to be yourself since you came back from that ol' hospital! Are you sure that you're okay?"

"I pushed it too far, and I lost him!" Sylvester chided himself, feeling instantly discouraged.

Ray's next words seemed to prove Sly's conclusion. "Why don't you come and have a toke? A little bit of pot will help you clear your head of all that nonsense!"

Sylvester declined and then sadly watched as Ray wandered off to get high.

Had he known how much Ray would benefit from the conversation in the years to come, he would have felt neither discouraged nor sad. However, Sylvester was new at this, and he still had a lot to learn!

CHAPTER 60

VISITS FOR TWO

Sylvester smiled as he heard the page, "Sylvester Alexander to V&C," the speaker system blared. Exploding with excitement, he could have listened to the speaker system echo the announcement a thousand times throughout the jail—Vivian was here at last, and he'd long forgotten how much he used to hate the sound of his own name.

The officer at the central control desk asked the usual question: "What do you want?"

"I was just paged to V&C."

"Let me phone and check," came the automatic reply. Minutes later, the officer handed him the pass.

The floor in the hall along the way to V&C was as he remembered it—smooth, polished, and bright, and it felt even better under his feet. The transition from the noise and filth of the main building to the quiet and clean of the V&C area enhanced his sense of excitement and anticipation.

He arrived at the doorway to V&C. The guard at the front entrance nodded a silent greeting before examining his pass and giving him a quick pat down. Satisfied that all was in order, the officer spoke into his radio. "This is 111 to 113, one more at your door."

The response was immediate. "Roger that, send him in." There followed the familiar metallic click as the electronic lock that released the door was again triggered from within V&C. Sylvester promptly stepped through the door and into Vivian's arms.

Vivian had dressed to impress; and she'd spared no effort, applying perfect makeup to her face, which was now quickly ruined by her tears. "I don't know why I'm crying," she tried to explain while wiping at the tears with the back of her hand. "I'm so happy to see you! It's been so long!" Then, noticing the mascara stains on the back of her hands, she sniffed and added, "I shouldn't have put on so much makeup!"

Sylvester silently held her for several seconds, not speaking for fear that he'd start crying himself. It didn't help. Tears of joy began to flow down his face as well. Then he found his voice. "So many tears," came his hoarse reply. "God only knows what it might mean if something bad were to happen!" They both laughed.

Vivian was about to choose a table on the far side of the room from where Steve and his wife were playing with their daughter. Sylvester urged her a little closer to the happy family. "Steve's someone special, and I'd like you to meet him," he explained, "but not just yet . . . first we've got some catching up to do!" They chose a table that was close to Steve and his family, but not too close. Then they began to talk.

The conversation quickly turned to serious matters. Sylvester was especially anxious to tell Vivian about his experience with Steve in the chapel that morning and his later talk with Ray. He linked both conversations to what Lucky had taught him regarding his role—and responsibility—in the ongoing creation process, and then he expressed his confusion. "I understand what Lucky said about being an active participant in this process—I can see the different ways in which I've contributed to a shared experience, and the consequences are obvious. However, there seems to be something more going on now, something I find difficult to understand."

"Like what?" Vivian asked.

"I often seem to experience an inexplicable level of understanding on certain issues. Sometimes answers come to me—as with Ray this morning—and the words don't seem to be quite my own."

Vivian caressed his face gently. "Maybe there was always a little more going on than you realized? Maybe Lucky's World and everything that's happened from the start is the work of the Holy Spirit?"

She carefully watched his reaction to her words, and seeing that he was receptive to her suggestion, she continued with a question, "Is it possible that the final step in accepting and taking responsibility for your role in the ongoing creation process is to allow the Holy Spirit to work in you— and through you—in such a way as to facilitate God's will for all of us?"

Sylvester was stunned by the idea—by both the simplicity and the implication of it!

He needed time to process what she'd said in his own way. So he acknowledged her point and then shifted the subject. "You may very well be right," he admitted thoughtfully, "but let's talk about you for a while . . . how did things go at dinner last night?"

Vivian became very serious. "My parents are going to want to meet you soon . . . the sooner, the better." Then she gave him a hard look. "I anticipate your wedding proposal on the same day that daddy gives you permission to marry me!"

"Do you intend to say yes?"

"I don't know . . . you'll have to wait and see!" she teased.

"Well, if you do happen to say yes and we set a date, I'm in an excellent position to make sure that things go smoothly—everything happens through the chapel!

"That is good . . . that's very good!" Vivian agreed.

"Now tell me more about Steve and his family—why do you want me to meet him?"

Sylvester took Vivian's hand in both of his. "I'm hoping that we might be able to help him a little bit . . . him and his family."

"How so?"

"They don't get to see each other much. He sends his wife the money that he makes here in the institution. She saves what she can from her welfare check. It's enough for them to afford to make the trip from the city once a month. I know you're going to come out to visit me more often than that . . ."

"You can be sure of it!" Vivian interrupted.

"Well, then maybe you'd consider giving them a ride once in a while? Perhaps one extra visit a month? Just a little help to assist them to keep their family together?"

Vivian liked the idea. "Go ahead and make the introductions," she encouraged. "When it's time to leave, I'll offer his wife a ride back to the city. She and I can get to know each other along the way, and if I'm comfortable with her, we'll work something out. However, don't say anything until I have a chance to get to know her—let the two of us handle it. If things go well, it'll be a nice surprise for Steve!"

Vivian withdrew her hand and caressed his cheek. "As for you," she promised, "you can count on seeing me every Sunday!"

"You're the kindest and most beautiful woman in the world," he whispered in her ear as he hugged her close. "How did I ever live without you?"

"You're not sorry that we left Lucky's World?" she asked.

"Only in the sense that I can't be as close to you as I want to be right now," he assured her. "I'd love to go skinny-dipping in the pond and then carry you off to my cave!"

"Oh my . . ."

They were interrupted by the approach of Steve and his wife. "Hey, Sly, I'd like you to my family—this is my wife, Shelly, and this is my daughter, Taba."

"Hello, Shelly, hello, Taba, it's so nice to meet you," Vivian and Sylvester responded in near unison.

"Why don't you all sit with Vivian and me for a while?" Sly suggested.

Taba walked over and put her hand on Vivian's knee before asking, "Would you like to color in my book with me?"

"I'd like that very much," Vivian assured the girl while lifting her up onto her lap. "Why don't you show me your best picture?"

It was the beginning of a potentially long and enduring friendship between all five of them.

CHAPTER 61

TRIALS AND ERRORS

The prosecutor was in full agreement with the investigating homicide detectives—he felt that it would be unjust and inappropriate to make a deal with Phil Sanders, who'd been the lead in the murder of Wilfred Arbuckle. He was confident that, in addition to the evidence, the testimony of Richard Bellows—Rick—would be enough to convict all of them, including Ike Bisbane—that was his first mistake.

As a result of a plea agreement, Richard Bellows was the first to be sentenced. In exchange for his future testimony, he was allowed to plead guilty to second-degree murder, with a guarantee that, after he'd testified, for his own protection, he'd be transferred to another medium-security prison facility. There he'd serve out the remainder of his sentence— potentially the rest of his life—in protective custody. He'd hoped for a better deal; however, with a competing snitch waiting in the wings— Phil—it was the best that he could do.

Phil Sanders, Robert Goodwin—Lefty—and Alexander Burrows were the next to be put on trial. Confronted by overwhelming evidence and Rick's testimony, they angrily pled guilty to first-degree murder in the hope that, by doing so, they would appear cooperative and serve less time in a supermaximum-security prison facility.

Phil hadn't wanted to plead out. Unbeknownst to the others, he was especially angry on account of the fact that the prosecutor had refused to allow him a deal in exchange for his testimony against Ike. However, in the end, he decided that pleading out, along with the others would be in his best interest—it would ensure that his offer to turn snitch would remain secret and he wouldn't have to serve the rest of his life in protective custody.

All three were immediately transferred to a supermaximum-security prison facility. Within the bare walls, beneath the perpetual light of his prison cell, Phil's anger toward the prosecutor intensified. He resolved that, no matter what, if asked to, he would not assist in the prosecution of Ike Bisbane.

Convicting, sentencing, and moving Phil prior to the prosecution of Ike Bisbane, proved to be the prosecutor's second mistake.

Ike Bisbane was the last of the five to go on trial. From the outset, his court-appointed lawyer sensed a potential victory, and that was a rare opportunity under these circumstances. He decided to go for it.

There was no evidence. There was only the testimony of a twice-convicted murderer, who wasn't hard to discredit—he'd made a deal in order to escape the consequences of this actions. How far was he willing to go? Was he willing to lie? The jury thought so. In fact, they thought that he might be willing to do or say anything to help his cause.

The prosecutor perceived that he was losing the case. He realized that he'd needed Phil's testimony, and he reluctantly approached the angry man. However, it was too late—the prosecutor had nothing to offer that Phil was even remotely interested in. On the other hand, refusing the prosecutor's request was the only opportunity that Phil would ever have for revenge, and he gleefully took it!

Ultimately, the prosecutor's two mistakes were superfluous—either one would have been enough, and he was forced to watch helplessly while his case against Ike completely collapsed. Four months, nearly to the day, after Ike had been arrested and charged, the jury returned a verdict of not guilty.

Abaddon's warden stalled for time. Nevertheless, he was soon advised that, in the face of the "not guilty" verdict, he had no choice, and a little over four months after his arrest, six days before Christmas, Ike Bisbane was released into the general population of the prison. He was placed in the third cell of the first level of the South Block.

CHAPTER 62

KING OF THE SOUTH BLOCK?

Ike sat on the edge of his bunk, ruminating over the strange reception that he'd received from the other prisoners. He'd expected to be greeted as the returning king of the South Block; however, he was greatly disappointed. A few prisoners said hello, then quickly moved on. Others nodded from a distance before doing the same. Most nervously avoided his gaze and stayed as far away from him as possible. "What the fuck's going on around here?" he asked himself.

What simple-minded Ike failed to realize is that there's no such thing as a power-vacuum in prison—as fast as one king gets knocked down, another steps up to take his place. Others now controlled all of the things that Ike once controlled. Moreover, they enjoyed their privilege and their authority over the other prisoners. They had no intention of stepping aside for him!

The political change was something that the other prisoners were very much aware of, and they were most anxious to avoid being caught in a power struggle, which explained their behavior. However, all that Ike was aware of was the fact that he wasn't getting the recognition and the respect that he felt he deserved, and he was very unhappy about it!

He was also very unhappy about his cell location. The third cell down the tier on the first level was pretty much the worst possible place to live—there was practically no difference between the first, second, or third cell in terms of privacy and noise. "This won't do at all," he silently declared while tossing his belongings onto the bed. "I need to go and have a chat with whoever is living in my cell!" With this in mind, he made his way up to the fourth level.

Irish Micky White—Mick—had heard the news that was rapidly spreading throughout the prison—Ike was back on the South Block! He quickly reasoned that the man would attempt to reclaim his former cell, and he felt sure that pride—as well as a desire for privacy—would compel him to attempt to do this very soon, maybe even first thing! Mick had other ideas about where Ike should reside. He enjoyed living in his present location, and he rather liked running the South Block. Thus, he removed his shank from its hiding place, slipped it down the back of his pants, and then chuckled a little as he thought to himself, "Ike's going to have to get used to some changes around here! Either that or get dead!" Then he rolled a smoke, flipped on his television and settled down to wait.

Mick didn't have to wait long. Fifteen minutes later, some big guy with crazy green eyes and an ugly bald head appeared at his door. He correctly assumed that it was Ike.

Mick stood, leaned against the wall, and spoke casually, "What's up, big guy?"

Ike looked around as though surveying his kingdom. "I see that you've been taking good care of my cell for me. Nice! We can trade tomorrow . . . you can move down to level 1."

"Well, now," Mick replied in a tone of voice that usually froze people in their tracks, "you must be Ike." He then deliberately turned his head and spat a piece of tobacco from the tip of his tongue into the toilet, which was followed by the remainder of his cigarette butt. "The thing is, Ike, I kinda like where I'm livin', and I'm thinkin' that maybe I don't like you at all! I'm definitely sure that I don't like your attitude!"

Ike was anything but frozen in his tracks. His rage was clearly building. Mick could see that he was going to respond to the challenge. He gave Ike the opportunity to take one step, then revealed his weapon. That did stop Ike cold! Mick spoke again in a tone of voice and with an air about him that left no doubt as to the fact that he'd love to use his weapon. "What's the matter, tough guy? Are all your balls up your ass?"

"Bad odds!" Ike answered matter-of-factly, his cold green eyes burrowing into Mick's psyche. "I'll have to do something about that!"

Mick felt his blood run cold. He'd miscalculated—Ike wasn't going to be intimidated, and he realized that this was a seriously dangerous situation!

Ike's animal instincts detected the change in Mick, and he sensed his fear. "I should drag this out a little," he thought while realizing how much he was enjoying himself. "Ya! That's a real good idea!"

"I'll tell you what," he began, intent on extending the game. "I'm a reasonable man. I'll give you until Christmas—you've got six days to either trade cells with me, check into protective custody, or die. It's your call! Now if you'll excuse me, I've got to go and say hello to my mules . . . it's been way too long since I've been high!"

Mick simply stood there in silence.

Ike gave him another hard look, turned in disgust, and walked down the tier. He shook his head at the thought of the two cardinal rules that Mick seemed to have just broken—first, he'd pulled a weapon and not used it, and second, he'd given Ike the upper hand by allowing him to choose the time and the place for the next confrontation to occur. "What's this fuckin' jail come to?" he blurted contemptuously to himself as he neared his mule's cell. "I leave for four months, and suddenly the place is being run by fuckin' punks—fuckin' shameful is what it is!"

Had Ike's brain been as sharp as his instincts, he would have been less certain regarding Mick having broken that second rule—Mick was thinking to himself that this was the precise mistake that Ike had made and that he had six days to catch Ike by surprise!

The mule had also anticipated Ike's arrival, and his planned response was the opposite of Mick's. He jumped up and gave Ike a big hug, "Hey, brother, how was your holiday? I'll bet you're lookin' for something special . . . and I've got just what you need." With those words, he gave up his entire personal stash of drugs. He wanted no trouble with Ike!

Ike swallowed a good portion of the stash right then and there. He chased it with a cup of water and then slapped his mule on the back. "FINALLY!" he verbally exploded with satisfaction. "Someone's showing some common sense around this fuckin' place. I was beginning to think that everyone had lost their fuckin' marbles!"

"Not me, Ike," the mule assured the big man. "I know what's what, and I know you—I know that you're gonna put things back in order real soon, and I'm with you!"

Ike gave the mule's shoulders a brotherly squeeze. "I'll talk to you again tomorrow," he promised. "And don't worry, I'm gonna take good care of you too!" Then he turned and made his way back to his cell on level 1.

The mule quickly collected up his usual delivery and hurried off to see Mick; whichever way this went, he intended to be on the winning side.

CHAPTER 63

AN EVENING IN THE CHAPEL

It was 6:45 p.m. Pastor Paul was working late. Earlier that day he'd asked Sylvester to help him to decorate the chapel and the small Christmas tree. Anticipating that the two of them could handle the job, his initial plan had been to bring in some doughnuts, hot chocolate, and make an evening of it with Sylvester. However, Sylvester had surprised him by asking if he could call on Steve and Ray to lend a hand, a request to which the chaplain had quickly agreed. He now observed the men engaged in their tasks and felt very pleased with his decision.

He watched while Ray hung the last bulb on the tree and then stepped back to admire his handiwork, all the while chewing contently on a third doughnut. The pastor didn't know it, but Ray was seriously high and having a blast—he hadn't done anything like this in seven years!

Steve chose that moment to plug the last string of lights into the wall, lighting up the entire tree. "Wow!" Ray exclaimed as his eyes bugged out a little. "That's amazing!"

Pastor Paul's laughter drew everyone's attention. "I want to thank you all for coming down to lend a hand." He chuckled. "I've really enjoyed the last couple of hours!"

"Absolutely!" Ray agreed through a slurp of hot chocolate, accompanied by smacking lips as he declared, "Best night ever in Abaddon! Thanks a lot, man!"

"That being the case, Ray, why don't you join us next Sunday?" the chaplain suggested. "I'd love to have you here with us, and I'm sure that Steve and Sylvester would enjoy your company as well! You can come and admire all your hard work."

"You know, I might just do that," Ray further agreed. "You guys are all right! Yes, sir, that seems like not too bad of an idea," he repeated while eyeing the box of doughnuts. "Sly, here . . . he's always been the smart one. I was a little worried about his thinkin', ever since he got out of the hospital, but now I'm thinkin' maybe he's got somethin good goin' on. Yup! Sure, I'll be here!" he promised while reaching for another sweet treat.

There was a moment of communal laughter, after which, Sylvester walked to the table, poured himself a final cup of hot chocolate, changed the music on the stereo to a different mix of soft Christmas tunes. and then seated himself in order to relax and admire the tree. The others joined him.

Realizing that their time together was coming to a close, Steve took the opportunity to speak what'd been on his mind throughout much of the evening, "I don't want to ruin the atmosphere by being the bearer of bad news . . . but I need to tell you guys that Ike moved back onto the South Block this afternoon."

The hard edge to Pastor Paul's voice caught everyone by surprise. "Ya, I read in the newspaper that he'd been found not guilty."

"You know him?" Sylvester asked.

"I know of him—I was just starting to work with Wil, the young man who was murdered. I know that Ike was accused of arranging the whole thing, and I have some very strong feelings about the murder itself. Why? Do you guys have a problem with him as well?"

"Nothing that I can talk to you about, Pastor," Steve answered honestly. "I just want everyone to be aware of the fact that he's back."

Sylvester spoke quickly to alleviate any fears that the good chaplain might have for their safety. "You don't need to be worried, Pastor. Rumor has it that Ike's got plenty of issues to deal with for the moment . . . I doubt that he's looking for more trouble . . . at least, not just now."

The chaplain was no fool. He could see that there was something going on below the surface. However, he trusted Sylvester's opinion on the matter. He decided to let it be. The last thing that he wanted to do was to create problems for these boys! Still, he needed them to know that they had his support. "I'm here if you ever want to talk," he assured them sincerely. "I'm here for all of you!"

"We're okay," Steve countered. "It was different with Wil—his issues were different, and he was different . . . he was weak and he walked alone."

The last statement caused Sylvester to once again recall something that Lucky had said: "United in a healthy spirit, people become so much more—and accomplish so much more good—than they could ever hope to as individuals." To which he mentally added, "They're a whole lot safer as well. Too bad Wil had so much difficulty connecting with people."

This caused him to begin to reflect on his own life and the manner in which he was now connecting with people. Like a newly arrived prisoner, he'd carved out an entire new space for himself, a much different space, and he was astonished at the contrast between the way in which he continued to create within this new space and the way in which he'd created, prior to his experience in Lucky's World.

His creative influence on others was obvious—Steve was doing much better. He hadn't self-destructed as he'd been on the verge of doing. Steve's wife and daughter were overjoyed—and their lives were much enhanced—to be able to visit with Steve each weekend, as arranged by Vivian. With a wedding date set, Vivian's spirit was soaring, and her parents shared in her joy. Ray was stoned but he was here tonight in the chapel and definitely beginning to think along different lines. Even Pastor Paul seemed to be deeply affected in a positive way by Sylvester's behavior and companionship. It was evident that everyone was much more comfortable now than they'd been in the past, and all of it, in turn, impacted, in one way or another, on Sylvester's own life.

He could see that Lucky had been absolutely correct—the creative process was powerful, interactive, and interconnected, be it for good or for evil.

The thought of evil refocused Sly's attention on what had happened to Wil. "Why do you think that Wil had to die?" he asked Pastor Paul.

The chaplain looked at each of them, taking a full minute before responding to the question. "I have to admit to you boys, I'm deeply troubled and somewhat confused by what happened to Wil."

He paused again, sighing heavily before continuing, "I know it sounds cliché . . . but the truth is, God's sun and rain shines and falls on everyone—it doesn't discriminate between the good and the evil. Bad things sometimes happen to good people, and good things sometimes happen to bad people.

"Consider all the Christians in ancient Rome that were fed to the lions, and even the apostles are said to have been martyred in brutal ways.

"This may be hard for you to understand, but God's justice begins in the here and now. It's not justice in the way that most people tend to think of it, at least not at this stage—that's mostly about revenge and retribution. God's justice begins with an extended hand. He extends His hand of love and forgiveness to anyone who will reach out and take it. It's a hand that's as readily available to the worst sinner as it is to the most devout and courageous of His children. However, if we want it, we have to choose it . . . we have to reach out and take hold of it! God doesn't impose His love and forgiveness on anyone.

"Being free to choose means that we're free to make good or bad choices. Wil didn't have to die—he died because many people made a lot of bad choices, and they have to live with the consequences of that. Yet even now, God's justice, His hand of love and forgiveness, remains extended to each of them.

"God loves us all equally. There's no good thing that you can ever do that will make God love you more than He already does, and there's no evil thing that you've ever done that will cause Him love you less. The only thing that is at issue is whether or not you accept His justice— whether or not you reach out and accept the hand of love and forgiveness that He offers to everyone."

"Wow, that's heavy," Ray murmured.

Everyone laughed, but they understood completely. Pastor Paul had spoken the plain truth, and there was nothing political, divisive or exclusive about it. They all got the message!

CHAPTER 64

ALL HAIL THE NEW KING!

Ike finished his last set of bench presses with a loud clang as 275 pounds came down hard on the bench. He sat up, grabbed his towel, wiped the sweat from his forehead, and looked around. Much to his chagrin, no one seemed to be paying any attention to his display of physical prowess. "Fuck these clowns in their asses!" he cursed under his breath.

The situation only added to his ongoing sense of injustice over the fact that he still wasn't getting the recognition and the respect from the other prisoners that he felt he deserved. He'd been consistently ignored for the last three days, and he was feeling increasingly angry about it! With a final disgusted look around the weight pit, he rose from the bench and headed for the shower room.

On entering the shower room, he was again irritated to discover that he actually had to wait—all four showers were being used. "Who the fuck are these punks?" he wondered, "and why are they showering during my time?" He stood there, glowering, until one of the showers came open, then stripped down and stepped beneath a flow of hot, soothing water.

The water calmed his emotions, and his thoughts turned to Micky White. The Irishman still hadn't traded cells with Ike nor had he checked into protective custody. "Perhaps I misjudged the little leprechaun," Ike silently speculated. "Maybe he's the reason that I'm still not gettin' any respect around here!

"Is it possible that these fools actually believe that he's gonna win this little turf war?"

Ike finally had to admit to himself that this was most likely the case, and he shook his head in disbelief. "DUMB FUCKS!" he exclaimed out loud as he stepped out of the shower.

He grabbed his towel and ran it over his bald head, vaguely aware that the flow of water had ceased in one of the showers behind him. Mentally distracted with thoughts of Micky, Ike paid no attention to the approaching footsteps. He felt a bump from behind as the individual walked by.

"Hey, punk! Watch where you're fuckin' goin'!" he hollered at the retreating figure.

There was no answer—the prisoner simply kept walking.

Seconds later, Ike's knees began to feel strangely weak. He looked down, surprised to see a crimson river the length of right his leg, pooling on the floor beneath his feet. Staring in disbelief, he reached tentatively around with his right hand and felt one end of the shank protruding from the lower side of his kidney area. In shock, eyes focused on the growing pool, he failed to notice that the flow of water from the other two showers also ceased, and he didn't see or hear the pair of assailants approach.

The assailants separated as they neared, passing on each side. In doing so, the one on the left thrust a blade into Ike's abdomen, the other successfully targeted his throat. Gagging and choking, Ike collapsed onto the floor, facedown into the ever-widening pool of blood.

Ike knew that he was dying. Fearful of death and desperate for oxygen, he tried to pray. Fear quickly turned into terror, causing words to fail. In a shadowy world, within the dark heart of Abaddon, Ike Bisbane breathed his last.

Filled with satisfaction, Irish Micky White watched it all from the doorway. "That's what you get when you fuck with Mick!" he snarled before turning to leave in order to avoid being caught in the vicinity when the body was discovered.

It was the same kind of thinking and language that Ike had once used, and it was that same kind of thinking and language that the next king of the South Block would use. Somehow they never seemed to learn from the example of their predecessors. The only winner—the only winner there would ever be—was the Spirit Tree of Abaddon.

CHAPTER 65

FROM THIS DAY FORWARD

Pastor Paul had counseled many a potential bride and groom in his thirteen years at Abaddon. Most of the time those sessions had resulted in marriages; sometimes they did not. Most of the time he felt good about the potential couple; sometimes he did not. However, he never allowed his personal feelings to play a role in the outcome. His sole function as a premarriage counselor was to help the potential partners in matrimony to get to know each other in a deeper way in order to ensure that they appreciated the gravity of the step that they were about to take.

The chaplain had never felt better about a couple than he did as he prepared to marry Sylvester and Vivian. Their counseling sessions had revealed their maturity, their genuine love for each other, and their spiritual unity. So much so that today's ceremony almost seemed a formality—it appeared to the chaplain that God had long ago blessed the union of these two people, and he was proud to be part of the process by which they formalized and declared this union to the community.

Henry and Maggie Southerman were just as confident in their daughter's choice of a husband. Over the months that'd they'd traveled with Vivian back and forth to visit Sylvester, they'd grown to believe that this relationship was, indeed, God's answer to their prayers.

The two of them had long since come to terms with the whole prison thing. So much so that, on the way out to the prison, Henry actually joked, "If St. Paul had been of a mind to, he could easily have been married under the same conditions!"

Maggie scolded the joke, "I love him too, but he's no St. Paul!"

Henry laughed while patting her on the knee. "I know that. I'm just saying that there's nothing here to be ashamed of. This is a good thing that's happening today!"

He truly meant every word of it!

Steve, Ray, and Sylvester were dressed in their best casual clothes. Steve had the ring, and as he'd promised, Ray remained clean and sober—at least for the day.

Ray glanced at Sylvester. "You never did tell me how it is that you and Vivian met or how the two of you got to know each other. I'd like to hear about it someday!"

Sylvester began to laugh; it was a laugh greatly amplified by nervousness. Several seconds elapsed before he finally gained enough control to speak. "You know, Ray, you're the one person who'd probably believe me if I told you, and I promise you, someday I will . . . but not today."

Unsure just how to interpret those words, Ray simply shrugged his shoulders, declaring, "I'll look forward to it, my friend!"

Nancy, Vivian's maid of honor, remained seated in the corner, semifrozen in a mild state of fright—she'd never been anywhere near a prison in her life. Now she was surrounded by criminals. However, she'd grown up with Vivian. They'd remained friends through many experiences, some of which Nancy chose not to remember. She was here for Vivian, no matter what!

Vivian flitted around the room like a hummingbird. She could barely contain her excitement and joy. She sat down and put her arm around Nancy's shoulder. "Thank you for being here for me. I know how hard this must be for you . . ."

"It's not that hard," Nancy lied in a shaky voice. "It's no worse than grad night, when I asked you to come to that beach party with me . . ."

"Oh no!" Vivian laughed. "Let's not think about that today!"

They hugged.

"If you're happy, then I'm happy for you," Nancy insisted, and this time she told the truth.

The ceremony was honest and simple; they'd partially written their own vows—to love and honor, from this day forward. There was laughter, smiles, and cheers as well as tears from Maggie when all was sealed with a kiss; and then it was over. Two people had managed to create some space for themselves, connect with like-minded brothers and sisters, and bring some light into a very dark place. There was no better way in which to honor their god, their community, and each other.

CHAPTER 66

THE BOOK

The private family visiting house was small, yet clean and functional—a one-bedroom unit containing the usual technology, a stove, fridge, washing machine, dryer, and television set. The living room was carpeted. There was a small couch and sofa chair, and the bedroom contained a double-sized bed. It wasn't Lucky's World, by any stretch of the imagination, but was adequate. Not that Mr. and Mrs. Alexander felt inclined to critique the facilities. Vivian and Sylvester had waited six months for their first conjugal visit, and they were both thrilled that the day had finally arrived!

Vivian checked the linen closet while Sylvester put away their seventy-two-hour supply of groceries. The sheets and bedding appeared to be fresh and clean, so she quickly made up the bed and returned to the kitchen to assist her husband.

Sylvester happily held up a three-pound piece of roast beef. "Look at this," he exclaimed as she entered. "I'm gonna cook it for you!"

"You're going to cook?" Vivian asked, politely attempting to conceal her doubt.

"You bet! I'm your husband, and I'm gonna do my share of the cooking. You and Ma took good care of me while we were in Lucky's World, and now I'm gonna take care of you!"

"Do you have any idea how to prepare and cook a pot roast?" she hesitantly inquired.

He looked at Vivian suspiciously, as though she were asking some sort of trick question. Then he answered with a question of his own. "It's a pot roast . . . you put it in a pot and cook it . . . how hard can that be?"

A gentle voice seemed to say, "It's the thought that counts."

Vivian nodded, albeit not all that enthusiastically. "It'll be delicious," she assured Sylvester while silently speculating as to how she might mitigate the pending culinary disaster.

"Fortunately I'm a nurse," she joked to herself, "and I know what to do in the event of an emergency!"

With the last of the groceries put away, they turned to each other in order to satisfy a different hunger.

Three hours later, Sylvester set the dining table, feeling every bit the king of the world. "Why don't you allow me do that?" Vivian suggested. "You go and carve the roast."

"Well, thank you, love," he responded appreciatively while turning his attention to the large portion of beef which remained cooling on the countertop.

"Damn!" he cursed a few seconds later. "These knives aren't very sharp." His breathing intensified as he continued to saw vigorously at something that would more appropriately be described as a dry piece of leather.

Vivian tried desperately to control her laughter. "Are you going to make any gravy to go with that?" she asked innocently.

"A nice piece of beef like this ought not to need any gravy," he insisted through clenched teeth, slightly out of breath from the effort of carving.

Vivian silently accepted her fate, seating herself and smiling sweetly when Sylvester planted the plate of beef in the center of the table. "Mmm, that looks delicious!" she lied.

Sylvester made a second trip for mashed potatoes and steamed brussels sprouts before proudly seating himself opposite her.

Vivian said grace. "Thank you, Lord, for all that you provide, and may we always be grateful." Then they began to eat.

Vivian was the first to take a bite of roast beef, watching with interest while Sylvester did the same. She noted the particular way in which the meat seemed to absorb all of the saliva in her mouth, creating the sensation of sawdust upon her tongue, and she watched in fascination as Sylvester's lips appeared to pucker like an overdried prune.

He seemed to chew for an extraordinarily long period of time. After two failed attempts at swallowing, he finally washed it down with a large gulp of water. "You might have been right about the gravy," he admitted with a fearful glance as the remainder of the roast beef on his plate.

"Mmmm." Vivian nodded in agreement, still chewing on her own mouthful and reaching for water.

Sylvester was about to spear a second bite when he thought better of it, placing his fork on the table. "It simply isn't edible," he sadly declared. "I don't know what we're gonna have for dinner, but we can't eat this!"

"Don't feel bad," Vivian consoled. "Pot roast is actually one of the most difficult things to cook, and it won't go to waste. I see several crows in and around the yard . . . I'm certain that they'd love the opportunity for such a meal.

"We'll feed it to them, and I'll fry a couple of pork chops for us. How do you feel about that?"

Sylvester brightened. "Sounds good to me, love!"

They lay awake, late into the night, not wanting to miss out on a single minute of their time together. There was so much to talk about and so relatively little time.

Sleep threatened, and Sylvester rubbed his eyes in an attempt to stave it off. "I sure am sorry about dinner," he mumbled. "I wanted to do something nice to celebrate our wedding . . . a kind of a present, I guess.

"Maybe I can give you something else? Is there anything that you'd particularly like for a wedding present?"

For a second time that day, a gentle voice seemed to speak to Vivian, this time urging, "Ask him to write a book!"

Vivian obeyed. "Have you ever thought about writing a book?" she inquired.

"What kind of book?"

"I don't know . . . maybe a book about you, me, Lucky's World, the things that we've learned and the things that we're learning. It would make a heck of a story!"

"No one would believe it!" Sylvester argued. "What would be the point?"

"It's like the experience itself," Vivian explained. "You write, people read it, and either they learn from it or they don't. Either way, the responsibility rests with them. What's important is that you make the effort."

"I dropped out of high school before graduation," he complained. "I don't know how to write a book."

"You don't know what you know or what you can really do until you try!" she countered. "Won't you even try?"

Sylvester thought carefully for a few minutes. He knew that by agreeing to her request, he'd be setting himself up for a huge job and potentially a huge failure. Then he remembered something else. "You know what's really strange about this?" he asked, and then continued, without waiting for an answer, "It's not the first time that this has been suggested."

"Someone else wants you to write a book!" Vivian asked in surprise.

"Not exactly—it was way back when you first came to me in the cave. I'd been wondering if there was something that I might do to help the other prisoners back at Abaddon . . . if there was anything that I could do. I'd forgotten about it until now. However, at the time, I seemed to hear a voice say, 'Why don't you write a book?'

"It was just before you arrived. And after you left, I could think of nothing except how sad I was that you were gone, but I remember now . . ."

"That's very interesting," Vivian admitted. "A similar thing happened to me just a few moments ago, when you asked if I wanted a present. I thought I heard a voice say, 'Ask him to write a book!'" She paused for a moment and then added, "To be honest, I really would like to see you write one!"

Sylvester relented. "I haven't got a clue how to do it, but I'll give it a try," he promised. "I'll do it for the voice that guides us, and I'll do it for you."

EPILOGUE

The elderly black woman sat on the park bench, feeding the tree squirrels. She came here often. She was many years retired from the hospital where she'd worked most of her life. Her husband had long ago died in prison. Alone in the world and with little to occupy her days, feeding the squirrels was both a self-designated job and a privilege—it brought her great joy!

There was a big gray one that she particularly liked. He somehow reminded her of a little ground squirrel in a dream that she'd once had. Oh sure, she knew the difference between a tree squirrel and a ground squirrel. Still, there was something strangely familiar about the big gray one—he carried himself with a certain energy. She leaned forward and tossed a few unsalted sunflower seeds in his direction. As she did so, she felt a sharp pain in her left shoulder.

The old woman knew what the pain meant—the nurse in her instantly recognized it. She didn't panic. She felt no fear. She was old, she was tired, she was lonely, and she was ready.

Ignoring the pain, she deliberately and calmly tossed a few more seeds in the direction of the big gray squirrel. The pain intensified. She leaned back against the bench, clasped her hand to her shoulder, and gasped for breath. Silently, she began to pray. "Please, God, it hurts so much . . . bring it to an end!"

The squirrel glanced in her direction, and it seemed to recognize her distress. Ignoring the seeds, it scampered over to where she was sitting, scurried up her body, and came to rest atop her heaving bosom. She looked directly into its large luminous eyes and recognized him for certain.

"Don't be afraid, Vivian," soothed the soft, familiar voice. "You're not alone. This isn't the end—it's only the beginning. We've long awaited this day, and it's time to come home."

As her consciousness slipped beneath a blanket of death, she surfaced in the pond, under the rainbow.

CPSIA information can be obtained at www.ICGtesting.com
Printed in the USA
LVOW13s1930111113

360844LV00001B/10/P